Have You Heard

BY THE SAME AUTHOR:

Home for the Day

Where She Was

HAVE YOU HEARD

A NOVEL

ANDERSON FERRELL

BLOOMSBURY

Copyright © 2004 by Anderson Ferrell

Excerpt from "Little Gidding" on page 152 from *Four Quartets*, copyright 1942 by T.S. Eliot and renewed 1970 by Esme Valerie Eliot, reprinted by permission of Harcourt, Inc.

Published by Bloomsbury Publishing, New York and London
Distributed to the trade by Holtzbrinck Publishers

All papers used by Bloomsbury Publishing are natural, recyclable products made from wood grown in well-managed forests. The manufacturing processes conform to the environmental regulations of the country of origin.

The Library of Congress has cataloged the hardcover edition as follows:

Ferrell, Anderson.
Have you heard : a novel / Anderson Ferrell.—1st U.S. ed.
p. cm.
ISBN 1-58234-189-3
1. Legislators—Crimes against—Fiction. 2. Attempted assassination—Fiction. 3. City and town life—Fiction. 4. North Carolina—Fiction. 5. Transvestites—Fiction. 1. Title.

PS3556.E7257H38 2004
813'.54—dc22
2003019574

First published in the United States by Bloomsbury Publishing in 2004
This paperback edition published in 2005

Paperback ISBN 1-58234-556-2
ISBN-13 9781582345567

1 3 5 7 9 10 8 6 4 2

Typeset by Palimpsest Book Production Ltd, Polmont, Stirlingshire, Scotland
Printed in the United States of America by Quebecor World Fairfield

For Dirk Lumbard

Listen what was on the news.

Muff Martin, reporting live from Branch Creek, North Carolina. Until a few days ago the talk of this small eastern North Carolina town had been the cotton combine parked on the front porch of the home of town eccentric Ed Oscar Ballance, and the tornado, so strong it ripped tombstones out of the ground in the cemetery of a nearby village. It is a place where people can tell you how many cars are on the freight train that passes through town each morning. A quiet, sleepy Southern backwater like so many others where nothing that happens would interest the rest of the world.

But all that changed this past Saturday when local florist and decorator Jerry Chiffon, a lifetime resident of this area, pulled a pistol from a fake Chanel purse and fired a round of shots at North Carolina's U.S. Senator Henry Hampton. Mr. Chiffon was wearing a red wool-crepe lady's suit. One eyewitness described the suit as the kind favored by Nancy Reagan. The witness went on to detail Mr. Chiffon's disguise as consisting, in addition to the purse, of navy-and-white spectator pumps, a corsage of white carnations tied with red, white and blue ribbon, a silk scarf printed with small American flags and fastened at the neck with a bald-

eagle pin, which is the insignia of the conservative women's group, the Lady Patriots. The witness also said that Mr. Chiffon was carrying a placard printed with the rallying cry of Senator Hampton's supporters, "Let 'em have it, Henry." Mr. Chiffon was subdued by local police and highway patrolmen and immediately taken into custody. His motive is not known at this time. He is being held at the Wake County Courthouse and it is expected that he will be arraigned this evening on charges of attempted murder. It is unclear at this time whether the federal government will assert its jurisdiction in this case. Senator Hampton was unharmed and has continued with his schedule as planned.

That's what they are saying Jerry did. It has, unfortunately, put us on the map of this sad and sorry world. Now everybody knows where Branch Creek, North Carolina, is, and you can't even sit on your front porch without some extremely ill-mannered person marching up uninvited and sticking a moving-picture machine in your face and a microphone up to your mouth, wanting to know what did you *feel* when you found out what Jerry had done. They have these trucks parked all up and down Main Street from which they can broadcast from here out into the wide world, and which most of the time interfere with my reception so bad that I can't even get the local news and weather from the Greenville station. Yesterday Greenville broadcasted a tornado watch for all of Toisnot and Newsome Counties, and I was without a clue. Every bit of North Carolina east of Branch Creek could have broken loose and blown slam to Bermuda, and I'd be ignorant of it unless I'd gotten in the car and started in that direction.

The rudeness of these TV people is that of a gang of drunk gorillas. I can tell you they haven't put a thing I had to say to them on the TV. One of them, this woman, I know you've seen her, who's with that outfit in Atlanta that fills the airwaves twenty-four hours a day with the wretchedness of the world, came up in my face this morning. I was going into the post office to see if the sofa pillows I had ordered from the best place in Raleigh had come and she, without introducing herself, starts asking me questions. Did I know Jerry? Did I ever witness violent tendencies in him before this? Did I know if he had been involved in something called gay politics? Did I think he had acted alone? The next question tacked onto the one before it without a breath between them so I could answer. Assuming that I would have answered her, which is nonsense.

Muff Martin, that's her name. Sticks this foam rubber microphone up to my mouth so close, if I hadn't stepped back I'd have caught every contagion she and whatever idiot had talked to her before me suffered with. At first, I was speechless. Could hardly think what to say. Be gone witch, you have no powers here, occurred to me. But Muff Martin is not at all witchy-looking in spite of her manners, and she does have power. Proof of which is that I've got reception on thirty channels that is best described as what they used to call psychedelic. Then it came to me as it usually does not. You know how you always think of what you ought to have said long after the opportunity is past. Jerry says the French call it *l'esprit d'escalier*. Well, this time it came to me at the top of the stairs, so to speak. I backed up a step or two, looked her up and down and said, Why don't y'all get a life? I've heard Jerry say that many a time, and although I'd never said it before, I had always liked it when he said it. Things he says are that way. You remember them and wish you'd said them. You wait for the opportunity. I got mine.

Well, of course they didn't put me telling them to get a

life on the news. I watched. Didn't want to, but had to because theirs is the only station coming in clear. They broadcasted the meandering and outlandish theories of people who hardly know Jerry. They put on the Baptist preacher practically giving a sermon against what he called the abomination of haymersexyality. Mrs. Elsie Moye Beamon, they got coming out of the bank and she laid it off to two things. She blamed those few years Jerry spent in New York City, which was ironic since it was she who had helped to make it possible for him to go there in the first place, but she didn't mention that part, and she blamed Djibouti and extemporized at length upon her theory that it was part of a plot by the government of Djibouti that Jerry had been tricked into taking the lead part in. She believes they, the Djiboutians or whatever you'd call them, have had it in for the Senator ever since he showed, on the floor of the Senate, that he hadn't the faintest idea there was such a place in the world as Djibouti. Claimed there weren't any African democracies, which apparently Djibouti is one. Well, I didn't know that either, but I do think it is reasonable to expect your United States Senator to know it. I'm sorry to have to say that Washington, D.C., is not the only haven of the limp-minded. We have a representative sampling of them right here in Branch Creek and they showed every one of them today on national television, but they did not show Mrs. I. C. Lamm telling them to get a life.

Jerry Chiffon would tell you himself that, for the longest time, there hadn't been but one thing he had been really proud of. It was an apricot *peau de soie* evening dress. He would tell you how he made the frock himself in home economics class from a pattern he got out of a *Vogue* book of wedding gowns and bridesmaids' dresses—size 16. "Which was mine to a tee," he'd brag. He would describe for you the empire waist and puff-capped sleeves, and with his forefinger he might languidly draw a semicircle just below his collarbone to show you what he meant by a scooped neck. He would mention that he basted it up on Charlsie Hapgood, the center for the girls' basketball team. You would notice his pride and you might sense his envy when he told you about how Charlsie showed it off to oohs and ahs in the fashion show the girls in the home economics class put on for the PTA.

I tried it on right after I finished it, and it looked better on me than it did on Charlsie, he'd confess. And if you were to laugh at him or he saw you even trying to hide a smile, or if he had the slightest suspicion that you were thinking something such as he ought to be ashamed, he'd say, You got a problem with any of this, sweetheart? Then he'd just snap his fingers in your face and say, Be gone witch, you have no powers here.

You might want to know what a boy was doing in home economics class in those days in a farm town like Branch Creek, North Carolina. Here, where fathers won't let mothers ask sons to help wash dishes or bring the clothes in from the line or weed a flower bed. Or you might want to know what any boy anyplace at any time was doing in home economics class. But you'd know; you would not have to ask if you had been living here as long as I have. For if you had been living here, you would know what I would tell you. That home economics class was the most natural place in the world for Jerry Chiffon. It wouldn't worry you a bit to consider that cooking, sewing, canning, and such were the most sensible things a boy in his situation could study. You would know the circumstances, that when he was not but seven years old his mother had died having his brother. Complications. Baby's head was too big. Two days she suffered. She walked the floor, rolled on it, hung by her hands from the door frame, trying to push down and down through and out of her, slow and determined, she knew not what. On the third day it got stuck. She stopped pushing or just plain gave out more likely, and all she had to show for her suffering effort was a large shiny forehead that looked wedged in more than squeezed out, above a pair of silly-looking eyes that were described as dubious by the colored lady who was trying to help. Nose and mouth popped out once, she said, like a swamp otter coming up for air, and then, as though it had got itself a good lungful, actually went back in. That it would resurface seemed unlikely, so the colored lady told Mr. Chiffon he'd better go into town for Dr. Anderson. Off he went as expeditiously as his tractor would carry him, which if you've ever gotten stuck behind one on a narrow road you know is not very. After what must have seemed to Mrs. Chiffon like a careless delay, Dr. Anderson finally came driving up in his septic green Rambler. Had Maggie Labrette with him, about whom more later. Got out of the car and shuffled up to the front door of the Chiffon place toting some chrome tongs to pull the bigheaded thing out with. Which he was too late for. About which more later of that, too. But for now just know that the calamity killed the mother and caused Jerry's brother's face, big as it was, to have that permanently squeezed look that told the whole story of how he came from where he had been. Also left him with less than one-eighth of the sense a head that big ought to hold.

It was near about midnight before Mr. Chiffon made it all the way back from Toisnot. Left the tractor smack at the front steps. Didn't even take time to turn the motor off, the way I heard it, and flew into the house still full of hope, they say, but found instead of a fair babe his wife passed away and a son who he could tell right off would never be anything more than one dead expense after another. Expense started straight off. Dr. Anderson, it is known to all, expects—nay, requires—payment upon services rendered. Mr. Chiffon had nothing but what you could see lying around. No money, just a tobacco crop in the field months shy of harvest-ready. He begged Dr. Anderson to let him pay the bill in installments. Dr. Anderson of course refused. Demanded payment on the spot or suitable collateral against the debt.

Doc, I got nothing but what I might have, is what they said was Mr. Chiffon's reply. How old was that tractor at the front steps was what Dr. Anderson wanted to know. He was told, and quickly calculated in his head that the value of the machine would not quite cover, but certainly would defray, the cost of his services. He borrowed a chain from Mr. Chiffon, hooked the tractor up to his car and brought it home with him.

I live next door to Dr. and Mrs. Anderson, across the street and catty-corner to Lyman and Marguerite Labrette, so the racket woke me up. I got up and went to the front door to see what in the world. It was past one o'clock in the morning, but I stepped out on my porch to get a better look. The doctor had poor Elizabeth Anderson, his wife and a saint of patience, out there in the dark and damp in nothing but her nightgown and housecoat, helping him unhook the tractor. The clanging and cursing went on until after two o'clock.

For a week or two, Dr. Anderson tried to sell the machine by letting it be known to patients, neighbors and townsfolk in general that he had a tractor to sell for the amount of money it cost to deliver a malformed baby and pronounce the mother dead, which was generally believed to be a price below what such a tractor would normally bring. But potential buyers soon found out that the fee for a not quite right baby was substantially more than for a plain healthy one.

Some tried to prevail upon him to soften. Marguerite Labrette was chief among them. She actually got the sheriff to tell Dr. Anderson that what he was trying to do was not in every sense of the word legal. I had been informed of when the law was going to be revealed to Dr. Anderson, and I arranged to be out in my yard. I didn't hear exactly what the sheriff said, but I sure heard Dr. Anderson tell him off.

I quote—Shut your goddamn mouth and get the goddamn hell off my goddamn porch, you goddamn son of a bitch, a goddamn bitch!—end of quote.

That sheriff was not reelected the next time he ran for office. I knew better myself than to try to interfere with Parch Anderson, and would have told the sheriff if he had asked me. Maggie knew better, too. Dr. Parchman Anderson gets his way here. Both of them knew that. He is the only doctor in a ten-mile radius. If we cross him he has the means to send us all careening into the hereafter if by no way other than neglect, all the time swearing to God and anybody who will listen that he has done all that medical science is capable of doing. We all try not to cross him, and folks like the Chiffons are practically enslaved to him.

Several times, Mr. Chiffon came up with what he thought was enough cash to reclaim the tractor, but the whole business had gotten to be not so much a test of Dr. Anderson's will as a display of it. He had started adding a daily storage charge onto the already overpriced thing, so the old tractor, which had sat out in the elements for weeks and should have depreciated in value over time, was increasing in cost as rust gilded it.

Winter was almost upon him before Mr. Chiffon had made enough on his tobacco to get the tractor back. Dr. Anderson had moved it into his driveway and in his unreadable handwriting had scrawled something on a sign that looked like a prescription for penicillin but which we all assumed said For Sale. How Mr. Chiffon and little Jerry, without the tractor, had been able to get the crop in, take it to market and live through the ordeal is a miracle. But one Saturday morning I was on my front porch, trying to cope with some Jehovah's Witnesses, and I saw Mr. Chiffon standing in Dr. Anderson's front yard. Just standing still as a statue, facing the doctor's front door as though he'd wait forever until somebody came out of the house. Go round to the back door and knock, I told him. Dr. Anderson makes everybody, except the very few of us who won't, go to the back door for any business they might have with him. It wasn't too many minutes before I heard that old tractor crank up and saw Mr. Chiffon case it out into the street and head toward the country.

I ended up agreeing to buy *The Watchtower* for the first time in my life from that depressing Jehovah's Witness woman was how confounded I was by it all.

I may die regretting it on the way to a doctor in Toisnot, but I swore right then and there that I'd have to be so near dead already that I couldn't stop them before I'd let any of my kin put a dime on my behalf into Dr. Parch Anderson's dry, avaricious, antiseptic-smelling palm, and to this day I have I. C. drive me clean to Toisnot for medical attention.

Now, to look at that bigheaded boy was to see the whole excruciating three days of his birth. The colored lady who was there part of that night used to iron for me on Tuesday mornings.

Miz Lamm, won't nothing to feed that baby but his dead mama's milk. Dr. Anderson laid the child up on its mama's breast, but that head was so big it kept sliding off. Won't nothing life-giving flowing from her no way, was how she told it.

I have witnessed young women and even little girls of an

age old enough to imagine giving birth scrunch their legs together upon seeing that poor baby for the first time. When they were around Jerry's brother, men said they felt like they were choking, and boys who have ever seen anything being born, and nearly all of them around here have seen at least a kitten, would, without even realizing they were doing it, screw up their faces and stretch their necks like they were trying to keep their heads out of water. I don't know why, but it seems that since that child was born, in Branch Creek it has become particularly hard for wives, mothers and girl-friends to try to hold their husbands, sons and sweethearts to a promise or bridle them in at all. Women here don't outright insist on anything. They have learned to suggest and wheedle—to hint, and in the same way as they bury bulbs in the fall and wait, sometimes even forgetting what they have planted or where, they plant their desires and needs in the heads of their men and forget about them until whatever they hope for sprouts and blooms or doesn't. Young straps here won't let their mothers help them with a necktie. They learn how to do it themselves early on from their daddies.

Ever since the time that baby was among us, the town has diminished in population. Fellahs have started to marry girls from other places if they marry at all, and lots of the young go off and don't come back. And it seems like every-body in the whole world has cut down on the number of children they're willing to have. It makes you wonder.

But all that concerns the world and this town. It is Jerry Chiffon about whom you are by now expecting to hear.

After Jerry's mother died, a lot of the women of Branch Creek, including me, went to the Chiffon place to help out for a little while—a week or so—but we had Jerry into that kitchen with us right from the start. We put an apron on him, wrapped the strings around his waist about three times and tied it good and tight, and he did the things a woman would have done ever since. I mean as far as the house-work—cooking, cleaning, sewing, canning, nursing, keeping the garden. So not much notice was taken when he signed up for home economics in the ninth grade, which is when it starts at the high school. Or if we did notice, which now that I think of it we did, it made perfect sense to us all by then. There are those who say it would have happened anyway. Some say that he was prone to things like home economics even before his mother died. Some of those who live out there close to the Chiffon place say that even before Mrs. Chiffon was split open and killed by the baby, it wasn't anything to pass by the place and see Jerry on the front porch, facing into the setting sun as though it was a spot-light, doing a can-can dance with a fertilizer sack tied around him to represent a dress. Mrs. Elsie Moye Beamon said she passed by there one morning on her way to some of her land. Summer was fresh, and the snap beans were coming off. Said it was about seven o'clock, but the sun was up good, she said. Claims she saw Jerry walking down the side of the road in a pair of little ragged shorts and no shirt; dressed like every other little boy around here dresses from late April through the middle of October, she said. Said except that he did have a hairnet on his little burr-cut head and was pushing an old doll carriage with a little fice dog in it, was how she told it. Well, I don't know whether that proves anything or not—whether it says anything about how he is now. What I think is, How can you tell if a person will turn out to be a certain way until they do? And none of us really lingers on stuff like how he seemed to enjoy dressing up in his mother's aprons and hairnets or doing the can-can. And now you couldn't find anybody who didn't think home economics was where he belonged, and I'll not be the first, but I'll be loudest to say that for a while Jerry

Chiffon looked after his squeezed-headed brother like a mother, and cared for his daddy as good as an unmarried sister would have. NO WOMAN could have done better.

And we all came to rely on him for so many things. There has seldom been a wedding in this town that he didn't have a say in one way or the other—flowers, music, dresses. So many things. Like when you can't decide how long your curtains should be—to the windowsill or to the floor. He'll just know what's going to look right. Nine times out of ten, it's to the floor, if you're interested. Or like how you shouldn't have chrysanthemums on the dining-room table unless they came out of your own yard. He taught me to never display a candle that hadn't been lit. He thinks a bathroom ought to be white and telephones black. Oh, and Turkish corners. It was Jerry who told us about Turkish corners. They were among the earliest things he learned about in New York City. We've near about got so we judge people by whether or not they know about Turkish corners. So many things he's taught us. Things that once you know about them you always notice their absence. Ways of doing things that separate us from people who do otherwise. A general outlook that gives Branch Creek tone. Which is not to say that this is a snobbish place. There are plenty of people here who don't know about things like Turkish corners, alas. And those of us who do, still remember when we didn't. It keeps us from losing the common touch. But that is not to say that there prevails here a live-and-let-live attitude. No, sir. We never leave each other alone or to our own individual devices. I am glad to say I know everybody's business, and I am proud they know mine.

We never left Jerry alone, but were after him all the time for something or other. Everything, from new fabric for a chair to an unfortunately plump daughter's prom dress, was chosen after taking into serious account what Jerry felt about it. We've all known the reassurance of hearing him say, The very thing, when a thing is, and it wouldn't take more than for him to drawl, Weee'll see, to send us back to Bolts-For-Folks Fabrics.

He got himself on the cheerleading squad when he was in high school. He's the only boy ever in the history of this town who wanted to be a cheerleader, and it was Jerry and he alone who turned that squad into the pride of Branch Creek and the envy of the world outside it at the time. He would watch Ed Sullivan on Maggie Labrette's TV and study the dancers who appeared on it. He could do a dance he saw on the TV just from watching, and he would teach the girls on the squad as much as they could do of it. But it was never as much as he could do, and I wish you could have seen him. I bet you he could have gone on the television or into a Broadway musical show if he'd been of a mind to. Mrs. Elsie Moye Beamon offered to pay for him to go to the Governor's School and study dancing and acting and such as that. She felt under the circumstances that the stage was probably Jerry's best opportunity of ever finding anyplace outside of Branch Creek where he might fit in and flourish. The exchange between Jerry and Elsie Moye was rich.

Keep your money, Miss Beamon, drawls Jerry, for you don't know what you are talking about.

I beg your pardon, huffs Elsie Moye. Who is it in Branch Creek whose cousin's sister-in-law was a Roxy girl, and did that girl not have the privilege, no, honor, of once auditioning for the late, great Mr. Noel Coward? Elsie Moye brings that cousin's sister-in-law up so often you'd think it was a connection to the Queen of England.

Miss Beamon, darling, he goes on—when Jerry and Elsie Moye got into it you'd think you were listening to Bette Davis and Tallulah Bankhead fighting over the last cigarette in the pack. Says, If you knew the first thing about the professional musical theater, you'd know that an at least hopeful gift for singing is required. I cannot carry a tune in a galvanized bucket. Further, you need to be handsome or funny-looking. Says, I am sadly not the first and thankfully not the second.

Not true—he was and still is very nice-looking, although he'd cut out his tongue before he'd say so, and he may not be funny-looking, but he is funny when he wants to be. Why, I myself once laughed so hard at something he said that I broke wind.

Lastly, dear Miss Beamon, he says, as you know it is my plan to stay here in Branch Creek, get myself training in floral design—which he didn't need any more than I need training in talking—so as to gain sufficient authority on such matters as to try to convince you that your desire to contribute to Sunday services floral arrangements of your own devising is one best redirected.

How's that for a boy born in a house where you could see the ground through the floorboards? Who says you can't get a good free education in this country?

Thing about Elsie Moye is that she is a person who jumps in and tries to take over once everybody else has decided a cause is worthy or a thing needs doing on a public scale. I suppose every town has such a person, but the unique thing about all of us and Elsie Moye is that we let her go on with her busy interfering and let her continue to delude herself concerning her indispensability. Marguerite Labrette can always handle Elsie Moye if her delusions actually begin to interfere with getting something important done. And Elsie Moye, bless her heart, if she does not have the most money in this town is the one who is willing to part with the most for a cause. There are those who think she is just showing off, but what I think is, Take the money if it's needed, and the rest of it is between Elsie Moye and the Lord. And Jerry stayed right here longer than I thought he would, got a little training at the Tech over in Toisnot, went off to New York and after seven years came back. The rest is history. And that to me is just so admirable, when somebody like Jerry who could have done great things someplace else chooses not to.

That didn't come out right, but you know what I mean.

He is ours. We were proud of him, and if you want to know what irritated me then and still does, it is this: when people who don't know him, don't know us or anything about Branch Creek, make fun of him—ergo, us and the town. This happened. Is happening now, I imagine. We suffered numerous indignities at the hands of opposing teams during basketball games when Jerry was a cheerleader. The boys on the Branch Creek team had to usher him to and from the athletes' bus. But we always closed ranks, considered the source and took our tolerance of and loyalty to Jerry and ourselves as consolation. I think we are seen by people outside Branch Creek and its environs as a little bit rare, decadent even. The Toisnot County version of it, anyway. Those common folks outside of Branch Creek wouldn't call us that. They wouldn't know a word like *decadent* if it applied to them. I really don't mind being thought of as snobbish if you want to know the truth. And I know there are towns in the wider world, such as Wilmington, Fayetteville, or Raleigh even, where live people who would consider us in Branch Creek as backward and unenlightened as all outdoors. It's relative, isn't it?

Hear about Mrs. Lyman L. Labrette, who could, if she chose, tell you exactly what she knows of Jerry Chiffon and how she came to know it. She has lived in Branch Creek all her life in the house on Central Avenue where she was born. This fact has everything to do with why she knows what she does about Jerry and his family, for in Branch Creek, North Carolina, you can only know something about everybody if nearly all your friends and relations come from among the people who reside on that tree-lined street. It is in the velvet-curtained sitting rooms, on the silk-upholstered sofas and around the polished mahogany dinner tables that these people who know things about themselves and others exchange that knowledge. At the edges of the boundaries between them and their neighbors, over waist-high but sturdy fences, truth is decided upon. Through the green filter of privet hedges and in the false privacy the luminescence of white sheets hung out to dry provides, things are observed, stories are heard, secrets discovered, plots figured out. Whether or not it is true everywhere, it is a fact in Branch Creek that only those who reside on Central Avenue can know something about everyone. Much about those privileged to live on that street of high green and sure opinion is obvious and similar. Information which each tries to keep confined within the family, as is the case perhaps everywhere, is eventually shared with a trusted neighbor and then emanates out into general earshot. And what each is proudest of and makes sure everyone knows about always reveals a flaw to some other of their friends or relatives.

There are none in Branch Creek higher than Mrs. Labrette. She is the leader of a group of women who not so much run things in Branch Creek as tend to a way of doing things which has always run itself. If they were ever to have a desire to test themselves against a superior milieu socially, they would have to go outside of town to do so, assuming they could find and acknowledge that such a place existed. Nothing interests them less than hearing how things are done somewhere else. And it is curious, too, how they can know so much more about their inferiors than their inferiors can know about them.

Mrs. Lyman L. Labrette knows the most, it seems, and the strengths and shortcomings, the troubles and the welfare of the poor and unfortunate of Branch Creek and its environs are her special interest. She is a Christian woman but of the type which is, she believes, less and less frequently encountered these days: one for whom the emotional side of her faith is subjugated. Having been brought up in the Branch Creek Methodist Church, which her great-grandmother helped to found, she is suspicious of any who have come to faith any other way. The Road-to-Damascus type of conversion she finds especially questionable. Although she keeps it to herself, she is slightly irritated and properly embarrassed by the tears-and-remorse brand of religion practiced most often she has noticed by the converted. Ye must be born again is a charge which annoys her every time she hears it, and an indignant inner voice always answers, But you can be born the first time. To assert that she had a personal relationship with her maker would be the pinnacle of arrogance to her. Except to give thanks, she prays to God as a very last resort, much in the way when she was a little girl she asked for help from her earthly father who demanded that she exhaust herself thoroughly trying to solve her arithmetic problems before she came to him for assistance. Supplication in the form of prayer, to her, is an admission of a failure of effort. Instead, she favors and seeks out in others what she has required of herself: the practice of charity over enmity and a willful control over the human tendency to judge one's fellow man. Self-regulation is a condition of comfort for her, and comfort both inner and outer is nearly a virtue as far as she is concerned. The keeping of a well-appointed house, a pleasant, fruitful garden and a tidy, inviting yard are activities that, when performed by Mrs. Labrette, approach the sacramental devotion of one with a calling, and she offers up her talents and advice concerning these domesticities to anyone who needs them. She is president of the Woman's Society of Christian Service. It is she who maintains the Communion service for the Branch Creek Methodist Church. She polishes the silver trays and the chalice for the celebration of the Lord's Supper, washes each Communion glass herself before and after every service. She keeps the altar, takes the choir robes and the minister's vestments to the cleaners twice a year and pays the bill herself. Flowers for the chancel are her special obligation and joy. Her displays are always unobtrusively elegant and conducive to piety, whether she has arranged them herself or has stepped in to save the day when a less experienced lady's attempt has resulted in a bouquet in which some, and quite often all, blossoms rebelliously turn on their own toward the wall. To such floral emergencies she responds with Styrofoam, wire, frogs, florist's tape, and, most important, her genuine flair to put things right and give the credit to the less talented. "I just helped," is what she will say when she feels a compliment is mistakenly paid her. And when she has done the thing herself unaided from the start and praise comes her way, she neither swells with pride nor indulges herself in false modesty. All she says is, "Thank you, it means the world to me that you like them." And it does.

People come to her for help less often than you would think, not because her aid and comfort are rationed out grudgingly or accompanied by any interrogation as to why the supplicant got himself in a position to need her in the first place. But it is simply assumed by everyone who knows her that she is busy with good works more important than any they might require. As she kneels before God, so the needy come to her; in extremis, at the end, when all else has failed. So that in Branch Creek the care of the sick and the burial of the dead are as associated with Mrs. Labrette as they are with sorrow.

And yet, she can describe a funeral as though it were a farce, and in that about which the whole world would laugh, she will graze for the lamentable.

She knows about life in Branch Creek, and there is not a lot more to know than what she can tell. One of the reasons is that she lives across the street from Dr. Parchman Anderson, and he prevails upon her often to assist him. Many would say *imposes,* and they fail to understand why Mrs. Labrette never refuses to go with him at any time of the day or night to attend the sick and afflicted.

Parchman Anderson, as his father before him was, is the only doctor in Branch Creek. He is therefore overworked, extremely irritable and irreversibly rich. No matter how serious their situation, when they show up at his back door or call him on the phone to come, people say that he always makes them feel as if they have insulted him importantly. He will curse them lavishly and waste what the patient must feel is precious time with questions as to the exact nature of the affliction. Slowly he will find his medical bag, warm up his car and finally step across the street to get Mrs. Labrette. She would have to be too sick herself to raise her head from her pillow to say no to Dr. Anderson.

It was with Dr. Anderson that she first came to know the Chiffon family and their sad case. She had been all day Friday at the church setting up the Fellowship Hall for a wedding reception that was to take place there on Saturday. She had gotten home after sunset, made supper for herself and Lyman, talked on the phone for over an hour with the bride's nervous mother about the preparations. By ten o'clock she was in bed, and immediately she fell into her usual deep, refreshing sleep that her husband Lyman never ceased to envy and admire.

"Maggie," he called her, short for Marguerite, "I would give my left nut to sleep as well as you do."

"Lyman, please," she might say, for she regretted and tried to moderate the pleasure Lyman enjoyed in expressing himself with language she considered to reveal in him too strong a familiarity with the gutter. It was the one flaw she had been unable to correct in him, she thought, but she never gave up trying. Having reprimanded him in the gentle way that was her habit, she might go on to explain her secret.

"Lyman, there are two types of people who can sleep well. Those who have exhausted themselves doing work they love. The other type who sleeps like the dead is the hopelessly stupid. You, darling, are sadly not the first type and certainly not the second."

Lyman's occupation, which gave him only worry and aggravation, was that of gentleman farmer. His toil was accomplished in a black Cadillac which he replaced with another every ten years, always black and always looking as new as the day it rolled off the assembly line. In it he made the rounds of his farmlands every day—in summer sometimes twice a day, taking careful notice and taking it to heart of the general decline in the quality of tenant farmers, falling prices, plagues of insects, too much or not enough rain. He owned substantial acreage of tobacco land in several counties. Two groups of people he despised. There were those whom he considered to be above him—though he would never admit publicly that such a class existed. This group included politicians, bankers and an imagined class of rich people who lived in the north and controlled things. Then there were those below him, which was with the exception of anybody living on Central Avenue who was not in trade, everybody else. He lay awake many nights organizing the world in his mind. It would be a place in which taxes were low, maybe even nonexistent, labor was cheap and grateful to the employer, and the enemies of progress and self-government had been vanquished.

His luck in life had been marrying Maggie. He knew that. He had not been her first choice. But he'd got her. What people who knew the Labrettes well thought and often said when the two were seen pulling up to the town hall on election days was, "There go Lyman and Maggie to cancel out each other's vote."

It started with a tractor deeply clucking in Dr. Anderson's driveway across the street, which woke Mrs. Labrette up. She first thought it must be morning, and immediately a list of all the things she had to do before the wedding that afternoon began to scroll down before her still-closed eyelids into her mouth. She tasted purpose. She sat up ready to work, but through her blue silk curtains she did not see the cool predawn light in which she was always glad to awaken. It was still dark. She got out of bed to see what was going on at such a late hour, and how an idling tractor came to be in Dr. Anderson's driveway in the middle of a Friday night. She meant to find out what was wrong and to help if she could.

This will be one Parchman will come after me for, she thought as she opened her front door and looked across the avenue. She could see the doctor's shape outlined against the screen door by the hall light. Standing on the dark porch was a tall skinny man. She could not make out what he was saying, but both his hands were in his hair and he was stepping nervously in place, almost like a child who needs a bathroom. Mrs. Labrette went straight to her bedroom and turned on the ceiling light. Lyman was leaning up in bed on his elbows, waiting to hear the news.

"Maggie, what in hell?" he asked.

"Something very bad out in the country, I think," she said. "I don't know what yet."

As she was dressing, she heard the tractor leave Dr. Anderson's and head out of town. She hurriedly took off her nightgown, stepped into a clean cotton dress and put on some low-heeled shoes.

Dr. Anderson was already waiting when she got to the hall. In one hand he carried the medical bag. She was almost as familiar with that old battered black leather satchel and its contents as the doctor was. But the hair on her arms stood up when she saw chrome tongs dangling brightly by his leg.

Mrs. Labrette took a kerchief from the hall tree to cover her untidy hair and knotted it hastily under her chin.

"I'm ready, Parchman," she said.

"I doubt it," Dr. Anderson said coolly.

"What is it?" asked Mrs. Labrette. She had seen what she thought was every kind of medical calamity on her missions with Dr. Anderson. Limbs that had been chewed off by farm machinery—the part still left on the victim, pulsing blood uncontrollably; the severed part, twitching in the grass. Skin fried by unspeakable afflictions. That the poor usually waited until it was too late for any help beyond numbing, undoing the home remedy, cleaning up, tying off and the offering of a prayer that too often served as no more than an introduction to the hereafter was a hard fact that Mrs. Labrette had observed repeatedly. She had seen death and horrible disease, but her heart had not been hardened. She knew Dr. Anderson's methods, and they were nearly always cruel, brisk and abrupt. Turn over. Give me your arm. Hold still, damn you. It was Mrs. Labrette's soothing voice, a gentler interpretation of Dr. Anderson's irritable bark that most often either pulled the patient through or sent him to his grave a little less terrified. We're going to turn you over, darling. Can you hold your arm out? I know it hurts, honey. Try to hold on. Squeeze my hand. Holler if you want to.

There had been only a few times she was not able to keep looking. Moist bone, glistening white. Blood, red and flowing or caked black, she could always stare down, nor did she have to avoid the eyes of the suffering to do it. She thought she was prepared for any kind of misery, but Parchman's grave and unruffled warning this time had frightened her.

"Tell me what," she said, as the doctor backed his car out of her driveway.

"Man's name is Chiffon, and the best I could get out of the fool is there's a baby stuck in his wife," said Dr. Anderson. "Says she's been in labor for three days. Strictly speaking, a medical impossibility. They had a colored midwife, but Chiffon says she 'give up' and left this morning. I don't expect this Chiffon woman will live. She is probably dead already."

Mrs. Labrette had come to trust Dr. Anderson's expertise, and although she had never known God to overrule His own laws of nature, until it became clear she should not, she maintained solid faith in her hope that He might change

His ways, so she said a short but fervent silent prayer asking that what Dr. Anderson had predicted would not happen.

At the edge of town they overtook Mr. Chiffon on his tractor. Mrs. Labrette looked back but could not see him in the dark wake of Dr. Anderson's car. The rest of the trip to the Chiffon house took place in silence. The doctor calmly navigating the car through the countryside. The headlights turning night to the sides of the road like a sharp plow through black earth, and Mrs. Labrette in the seat beside him drawing in her mind a map of the way.

Leave them there then, both faces lit in the golden glow of the dashboard lights, poised forward toward whatever wondrous affliction awaits.

He tried all his hiding places. But even when Jerry climbed up to the top tier of the tobacco barn, his mother's cries of pain, trapped in the gables like a flock of frantic birds, were already beating the stifling air. Underneath the house where he hid up against one of the brick pilings, he breathed her suffering in with the dust. No matter how hard he tried to find a place where he could not hear, he still heard her begging his daddy to get it out of her. And when his daddy had gone into town for the doctor and in her delirium Jerry's mother had called to Jerry for help, he could not resist. He climbed down from the top of the barn, and like a mistreated but obedient dog crept to her bedside.

Jerry saw in between his mother's legs what had been living in her for so long. It was a turtle, bigger than any he had ever seen. Two closed eyelids and two nose holes, and a wet shiny forehead. It was that dirty turtle living up inside her that was making her so sick—clawing and snapping, opening and closing its hard-as-a-rock shell. It had come up for breath and got stuck.

Know that Jerry was horrified by what he saw, and know that he was dazzled by it, too. That a body could hold so large a thing in it, that an opening in the body could unfold such an immensity. It was an observation come too soon— one he could never cut from his memory. But wait for the final effect the event will have on the grown man. Hear more about the curiosity itself.

See him standing at his mother's bedside. Her arms flail, her hands paddle the bedclothes. She reaches out and grabs Jerry by the wrist with a grip so hungry for help that his hand goes numb. Think as he does that she is killing him piece by piece to stay alive herself. Observe her pain-ruined, red jelly eyes.

Hear what she says to him—Why won't God help me?—and how she says it pitifully, drawling out *me* like she believes God has thoughtlessly helped others who have suffered less than she suffers.

The room is changed from what Jerry has always known it to be, a tidy place with its faded but clean patchwork quilt on the bony iron bed. Look at the pine floor, usually smooth and washed clean, all littered now with bloody rags and puddled with spewed-up liquids that had been meant to help. Pain is the misshapen thing inside her. She has lost any other feeling. Pain has cornered her mind.

"Get it out!" she cries, still squeezing Jerry's wrist so tightly his fingers curl and throb. Then she lifts her head, releases Jerry's wrist and stretches her arms toward where the thing is in her. Watch her try to reach in between her legs to pull it out herself. Her fingers claw at the skin as though to dig through—to free herself from the biting snapping fury inside.

"Oh, God, get it out!" she cries again. "I'll kill you if you don't." She takes hold down there with both hands, and in her effort to rip herself open tears out the hair. Climb with Jerry onto the bed, lean close and watch him push his hands into her and feel for something to hold on to. On either side of the head of the thing he finds what feel like ears. He pulls. His mother screams, but the thing slips out a little farther. It does have ears so Jerry grabs them and leans back. There is a pop. Smell a breeze of steel-scented air that lightly lifts the hair hanging over Jerry's forehead. The thing slithers out riding a gush of blood that drops it between Jerry's knees and soaks the sheets red. Jerry can hear the blood dripping to the floor. The little swamp creature is still attached somewhere inside her by a skinny, slimy, blue sausage, and Jerry is afraid that it will use the nasty rope to climb back inside his mother if he does not cut it loose from her.

"Don't let it back in," he tells his mother, but when he looks up, he sees she has gone to sleep. He tries to wake her, but she cannot be stirred. She has stood so much, Jerry thinks that she can stand this. He goes to the kitchen and gets a knife. He comes back to the bed and cuts the sausage in two. The creature is blue and smeared in what looks like bloody lard to Jerry. It lies motionless on the wet, red sheets. He tries to pick it up, but it is too slippery. He looks around for something to pick it up with. He gets one of his daddy's shirts and spreads it out on the bed, then pushes the thing onto the shirt. His plan is to get rid of it. Ride his mind to the solution that is in a memory. He is five and he sees his daddy walking toward the hog pen with the shovel. In the blade of the shovel is a lamb born too soon to live. As his father approaches the hog pen, the big sow lifts herself from the mud, grunts, throws back her head and sniffs the air. The other hogs run after her as she waddles toward Jerry's daddy who pitches the dead lamb over the fence. It lands with a smack in the mud. Jerry's daddy turns and walks away. The hogs pinwheel around the dead lamb, stare for a second. The big sow takes a quick grunting sniff, then grabs it in her mouth. The other hogs swarm around her. Squealing angrily, the ones that can't get to the lamb are biting at the rumps of those nearer; they devour the dead lamb in less than a minute, then, calm and satisfied, go off and settle in the mire.

In the memory is Jerry's plan. He will throw this ugly little monster to the hogs. But when he picks it up, it moves and becomes light with life in his arms. The enormous face silently contorts, then reddens until Jerry thinks it will explode. It screams and when it opens its eyes, it fixes a confused, unfocused but wonder-filled gaze on Jerry, who looks back down at it and becomes brother and mother as naturally and ineluctably as if the baby had come from his own body.

The head must be supported by a hand. Always. In order to lay him on his back, the head must be wedged between two pillows. If the head is held erect, the legs kick like those of any robust infant. The arms float and flap and the fingers curl and open, but let the head drop over in any direction, and naturally the body goes limp conserving oxygen and time in seconds. The windpipe crimps. Air is cut off and a pale gray creeps over the face, then dusky blue and suffocation. Death comes as inevitably as if the infant had been hung by the neck from a rope. It is by perilous experience that Jerry learns how to care for his brother.

Nothing ends. What has happened keeps happening as long as there is someone to remember it. Yes, things befall in the absence of eyes to see, ears to hear, an intervening will or a heart to rejoice or lament. But without the tightly woven cloth of experience there is no history, no story nor event. There is just diaphanous imagination. Go back after the funeral to the country church aching with filtered violet light, the floor before the altar where the bier was placed, sparsely littered with crushed blossoms. It is and always will be a sadder place than it was when the body was laid out for viewing surrounded by floral tributes freshly courageous. Where there has been a violent death, the act which caused it stirs in the air like the last exhalation of the victim long after the room has been scrubbed and the case closed, leaving a decorous, lonesome, abandoned feeling. Standing by the oil-stained, blood-smeared road after a fatal collision of vehicles fills the mind with morbid sounds and carnassial visions not fresh but real. And following a happy occasion— a wedding for example, a light-footed version of the ceremony lingers, sometimes forever. The clutter and chaos of event amuses or distracts the mind and entertains the eye. And when an incident is over and the perfume of color lingers in the air and the shadow of occurrence falls over a place, the heart is more often broken than quieted. Emptiness is an illusion. Reality relocates. Facts fade. Truth takes up. Shapes change. Places move. Nothing ends.

Jerry stood leaning against the doorway, his thumb in his mouth and the forefinger of the same hand probing one nostril, in a room where things were changing places. He watched as the doctor and the town lady tried to rid the room of what had happened in it, but each action, every effort to clean a stain, upright a chair or straighten out some bedclothes fixed in his mind forever that the chair had been turned over and would remain so, the floor spattered with blood now and forever, the bed always a storm of dirty sheets.

He learned how to prepare the dead and care for the living. The doctor, after he had assembled a makeshift cot from two chairs butted up against each other, laid the baby on it and hovered, listening to its heart, running his finger in the baby's mouth, probing the ears and nose.

At the deathbed, Mrs. Labrette passed a hand over Mrs. Chiffon's eyes and wiped away the staring, hopeful expression from her face and then gently led Jerry up to the bedside to look at his mother. For a few minutes Mrs. Chiffon lay as if sleeping. Death settled into the body and the body into death. Then, as though astonished and insulted, the eyes popped open and the jaw dropped, and Jerry thought his mother was mad at him and was going to give him a whipping. Mrs. Labrette calmly reached over and closed the eyes again, then rolled up a dish towel and put it underneath the dead woman's chin so her mouth would stay closed. Then she pulled the bedclothes up around Mrs. Chiffon's body, forming a shroud of the bloody, sweat-stained sheets. Only the face showed, composed and serene, and Jerry calmed, too, and looked up at Mrs. Labrette not like she was his mother, but like he wished she was.

The men from the funeral home came to take away the body. The metal, velvet-draped gurney barely fit into the house, at every jog and turn scraping the door frames and banging and gouging the walls.

"Who prepared the body for removal?" one of the undertakers asked as he let down the wheels of the gurney.

"I did," said Mrs. Labrette.

"Are you a nurse?" asked the other undertaker.

"No. I've seen how you do it," said Mrs. Labrette.

"Wish they were all tidied up like this when we come to get them," said the undertaker.

The men lifted the swaddled body onto the stretcher. They gathered up the ends of the velvet drapery and zipped it up, enclosing Mrs. Chiffon in a purple sack embroidered with gold letters spelling the name of the funeral home where her face was. Jerry reached out a shaky hand and stroked the velvet sack as if it was a barely tame animal. He had never felt velvet before.

"You poor little thing," Mrs. Labrette uttered almost beneath hearing. And Jerry took his hand away from the rich purple cloth and looked up at Mrs. Labrette, not understanding why she would say such a thing about him. He had been a poor thing, but no more, for now he had touched velvet.

They rolled Mrs. Chiffon out of the house, clattering and bumping, and slid her body into the back of the hearse, which sailed away morbidly into the night with its sad cargo—a black vessel in a black sea.

Jerry watched. It did not occur to him that he was watching his mother leave the house or that he would never see her alive there again, for although she was gone, her absence was not, and that, the lack of her filled the house more than she herself ever had. What was left of what had gone was what he wished they could have tied up in a soft shiny bag and taken with them.

Above the mantel hung a picture of Jesus that Jerry had won at the county fair. For a dime, he had bought a chance to select a yellow plastic duckling from a bobbing flock that floated on a watery oval track. On the bottom of one duck was a lucky red dot, which meant that you won your choice of a group of prizes hanging in the very top of the booth— the best prizes. He picked the picture of Jesus for his mother, and did not discover until he held the picture in his hands that he had won two pictures in one frame; that depending on how you tilted it and later after it had been hung over the mantel where you stood in the room, it would change from a picture of a pretty Jesus to a Jesus, briars wrapped around his head, eyes lifted heavenward, tears and blood streaming down his face, dying. When he brought it home and presented it to his mother, he had been careful to hold it steady in front of her.

"I won it for you," he told his mother, and she kissed and hugged him. "Now look," he said, and he tilted the picture and knew from his mother's saddened expression that the picture had changed. Her eyes filled with tears and she kissed and hugged Jerry again, and he was proud that he had been so smart without trying.

"I got two pictures. I thought I was getting one," he said.

"That's the way it is with Jesus," said his mother. In time Jerry had learned the exact spot in the room where he would see the happy Jesus, and he learned exactly where to move to so the picture would change. Now Jerry could find no fixed spot from which the world could be guaranteed un-deviating. But there was Mrs. Labrette and velvet in the middle of the uncertainty.

Then he saw his daddy, in the front room sitting in an old chair covered in brown plastic. He was a ball of grief, slumped over, his forehead on his knees, arms wrapped around his shins—blind and deaf to obligation.

The doctor left the house. A place now where what he could do would not help. Mrs. Labrette said she would stay the night.

"Tell Lyman to come and get me in the morning," she told Dr. Anderson.

They brought Mrs. Chiffon back to the house in a cheap casket of gray flocking applied to look like it had been quilted. They set it up at one end of the front room, resting on the two chairs that had held Jerry's little bigheaded brother, who lay now in the bed in which he had been born, where he made no sound other than to cry when he was hungry. Having been fed, he would blink dumbly at the ceiling for a short time, then fall asleep until hunger woke him again.

Mr. Labrette came and got Mrs. Labrette as he had been instructed to do. She stayed home just long enough to bathe and change into a pretty but somber lavender dress and make the necessary telephone calls. Then she had Lyman take her back out to the Chiffon place.

And the ladies of the Branch Creek chapter of the Women's Society of Christian Service gathered, a high-intentioned, effi-cient, casserole-bearing, flower-scented army, mustered to the scene of sadness by Mrs. Labrette over the telephone in less than thirty minutes. The house was dusted and scrubbed, all signs of suffering scoured away. Breakfast was made and served, then lunch. An order it had never known, seemingly leaderless, discernible only from tidy result, was imposed upon the Chiffon place. The yard, which before the ladies arrived had been dusty and littered, but now swept clean and scored with a reed broom, was as serene as a Zen garden.

Even if Jerry had not had the apron tied around him that morning and had not been put to work stirring ingredients for corn bread, or sent in search of a pot or a rolling pin in his mother's kitchen when the ladies' instinct for where another of their own sex keeps things temporarily failed them, the intricate patterns of women at work, cooperating, needing no instruction, and the tender, sensible calm left over the house by their ministrations would have been irresistible to his mother-deprived, broken heart. He needed women too much now. Aproned and flour-dusted, he willingly switched tribes and was initiated.

After he had helped the ladies, Jerry got his daddy, arthritic with grief, from the chair by Mrs. Chiffon's casket and led him by the hand to the kitchen table. The women swarmed around him, pouring tea, plopping ladlefuls of food onto his plate, then stood back to watch as he dripped tears into what he was eating. Jerry stood before the table. He dreaded anyone eating at it. The ladies had brought a white tablecloth and a bowl of white chrysanthemums. At first he didn't believe that it was the same old table where he had always eaten his meals, but then he lifted one corner of the tablecloth and saw that it was the same underneath. They had made something so ordinary into something pretty in such a short time with so little trouble. And he had never seen this much food on this or any table before. It was all so beautiful and sad to him, and he hoped that if he could not have his mother back he could at least have the table and the house stay always as these sweet-smelling ladies had made it.

"Do we have to eat it?" he asked Mrs. Labrette. "It's so pretty."

"Aren't you hungry, darling? You must be starved," said Mrs. Labrette. Then all the other ladies fell in.

"Fix him a plate," said one.

"I bet he hasn't had a morsel in days," said another.

Mrs. Labrette got the plate that she had set for Jerry and, making her way around the table, took some of everything until the plate was full. She handed it to him. The ladies, some with arms folded in self-satisfied expectation, prepared to watch their charity be rewarded. They wanted to see Jerry eat, for then they could leave the place, contented with their good work. Others, assured that the grieving were properly served, lined up to help themselves to a little taste of everything there, less out of hunger than the desire to see whose cooking might have slipped or which of their friends had outdone another.

Jerry did not settle into the place they had set for him at the table. Slowly, carrying the plate of food in both hands, he walked out of the kitchen and into the front room. He went up to the casket where his mother lay, and put the plate on her chest.

"Here's some food for you, Ma," he said. Then he walked out onto the front porch and took a seat on the top step. He sat there for a long time, still and quiet, looking to those ladies who occasionally peeked through the front door to check on him as though he would never move until he was carried away. But in his mind lodged a riddle. He was happy and knew why, but did not know if it was right. The table, all white and ready and waiting, had forever altered his idea of what a table was for. It had been made beautiful just so they could eat off it and eating off it ruined it. And his mother, who had never had the will or the time or the money to have herself fixed up was beautiful now that she was dead. How, he wondered, could he be as happy as the table had made him, probably now stripped of everything they had placed on it, as he was made sad by the fact of his mother lying in her casket in a pale lavender silk shroud, her face rouged for the first time in her life and her hair finally set. She would remain that way forever. The table had died in a way and lost its beauty. His mother died and got hers.

But before he could figure it out or even decide if he wanted to keep trying, there were flowers. Two men, dressed in black suits and white shirts, unloaded the flowers from the back of the truck. Jerry, now hopeful that wonderful and beautiful things appeared in surprising ways without warning, went out into the yard to look closer at the truck and the men. One of the men, tall and blond, tanned and rich-looking, got out of the truck and scrambled Jerry's hair with a spice-scented hand.

"Hey, sport," he said, smiling at Jerry. He was yellow and white like the spray of blossoms he held and as bright and blinding as foil. Looking at him broke Jerry's little heart. The man was the most beautiful event of a day filled with them, and Jerry burst into tears as two words floated into his mind and lodged there. Going away. Going away. Before he knew he was going to, he blurted out to the beautiful man what he felt.

"Everything is going away," he said.

The man put the spray of flowers down and squatted beside Jerry and folded him into his arms. "Yes, yes, I know," he murmured into Jerry's ear as he stroked the hair on the back of Jerry's head. "Everything goes away."

"Miss Thing!" a voice hissed from behind Jerry, startling him and the beautiful man apart. The man with the snakey voice was dark-haired and had a soft face. His eyes were half-opened as if he were sleepy, and his lips were pressed together in a way that made him look as if everything in the world was boring and smelly to him. "That little chicken, I would have thought, is the one thing in pants about which even you would have known better." His nostrils flared, and he re-pressed his lips together more tightly, like a stubborn mare refusing the bit. He looked at Jerry as if he were something to be shooed away or trampled, then snapped his fingers loudly; the sound was like that of a thick dry stick breaking. "Be gone witch, you have no powers here," he said, stepping out of the back of the truck. He scooped up a pot in each hand and walked quickly toward the house. The beautiful man stood and picked up the spray of flowers and went to the back of the truck to get another, and the still, safe moment crying in the man's arms went away, too. But as the man left to take the flowers into the house, he turned his light-filled face back over his shoulder and smiled again.

"Sometimes, some things do come back," he said. But even then, dazzled as he was at such a young age, Jerry knew the man was wrong.

Then, more beauty. Flowers. Jerry blossomed. He was contented for now with what he felt like doing—engrossed in it. He watched the men put the flowers on the floor around his mother's casket. As soon as they left, Jerry got to work. Not speaking a word, he stood back and just looked for a few minutes. Then, hesitantly at first, he began to rearrange the potted mums and sprays of gladiolas. The flower men had lined the flowers up in an uncaring way on either side of the casket. Jerry, having seen the table so carefully set and decorated, had the idea lodged fresh for the first time in his mind that there were ways of doing simple things like eating at a table that were different from how he had always done them, and that eating could be turned into more than just filling your stomach. He could see that the flowers around his mother's casket had been put there just to get them out of the truck and into the house, so he set himself to arranging and rearranging them, learning in the process what looked best and how what looked best

36

made him feel better than what looked just fine. One way the flowers looked just fine was spread around the room. A potted mum on an old end table that would have been of more use as kindling now looked to Jerry a little more like what he had such a short time ago learned to hope he might have around him. He set a spray of gladiolas on top of the cold black heater. He put a pot of pink azaleas on each end of the top porch step. The ladies watched silently. Some marveled and appreciated. Ladies who were more strict about what was a boy's work and what was a girl's rolled their eyes in disapproval of Jerry's new enthusiasm or hid smirking smiles behind their hands. But Jerry was falling in love with something about himself and wouldn't have cared what they thought of him even if he had known. He spent over an hour moving the flowers around the house. When he had completed each configuration, he tried to fix in his mind the mood it created. Why did gladiolas, the long spiky ones, and azaleas, the rosy bubbly ones, look good together but not azaleas and mums? The fresh frothy pink of the azalea seemed to him if not unreal then not lasting—like spring, which never lasted long enough, while the mums' frosty, artificial hardness seemed as permanent as winter does. His mind craved fixed rules and definition—logic, if he had known what to call it. The play of opposites was not his taste for now, so that what seemed to go together naturally ruled his budding talent. And he came to see that to try to make a sooty black coal heater into a place to put flowers just made you think what would happen if a fire was lit, and that the girlishly pretty, full-of-themselves azaleas placed on the shoddy end table made the table look like it ought to be thrown out and the flowers look ridiculous, like a girl in a fancy dress sitting on a chamber pot.

He was standing in the middle of the room, holding the azaleas and figuring out what to do with them, when Mrs.

Elsie Moye Beamon came in and tried to take over.

"Let me do that, son," she said tersely. "You go outside."

"Elsie, let him alone," said Mrs. Labrette. "It's his mother lying in the casket." Mrs. Beamon started toward the kitchen, hurt and angry but not daring to defy Mrs. Labrette, for her word was law among the ladies.

"All right, Maggie," she said as she left, "but it's not a healthy thing for a boy to be doing." That day a battle, as irritating for them as it was amusing to some, between the two ladies over Jerry's nature was begun. And once it was established what his nature would be, another battle, more entertaining for them and all who witnessed it, was fought over who could best nurture Jerry's talents and propensities.

For now, Mrs. Labrette had won the skirmish for Jerry. And it was later thought by many that there was a kind of genius awakened in him that day because of Mrs. Labrette's gentle encouragement. When the story was told and retold by Jerry himself, it was just after the stiff exchange between Mrs. Labrette and Mrs. Elsie Moye Beamon that in a flash of inspiration there came to him the guiding principle of all he was later to do for the town and its ladies. The test of what separated that which looked just fine from that which looked best. What's a thing for. This was what came into his mind that day, he would say, that these flowers had been made for his mother, and with that he brought all the pots and sprays back into the front room and grouped them on the floor around the casket where they had been put in the first place, but placing them just a little more carefully with an eye toward shape and color and size with which the two indifferent funeral home men had not bothered, thereby creating what Mrs. Elsie Moye Beamon herself pronounced "a wonderfully deceptive illusion of abundance."

Where Jerry comes from, people will sit up all night if a corpse is in the house. Not just the bereaved, but neighbors and friends, indeed just about anybody with the slimmest connection to the deceased or the grieving. And whereas in other places this might be seen as a morbid intrusion into the private grief of the departed one's family, in Branch Creek this watch is expected and appreciated. Jerry and his daddy would no more have asked those gathered in their house to leave as bedtime approached than they would have gone off to bed themselves and left the assembled sitting there. Everyone stays and everyone stays up, and as the night progresses, the corpse becomes less and less regarded by the mourners as a reminder of mortality and putrefaction, but more as an amiable guest, silent and listening at a long talking party. Old stories often heard before are told again. Connections between people present are tightened and sometimes rejoined. Emotional expressions of grief occur early in the evening and are quickly dealt with, like something spilt or an out-of-place knickknack. These are not the drape-yourself-over-the-casket-and-weep type of people. They do not cry out in grief even in private. Tears fall silently here, and then a stoical expression is assumed that sometimes lasts for life.

Food is plentiful. A table is set at regular mealtimes, and in between the casseroles and roasted meats, fried chicken and cakes and pies are left out, for it is thought that nourishment makes grief bearable.

At each mealtime, Jerry watched in confused amazement as his daddy, a man who Jerry had never seen cry, salted his food with his own tears. He ate every bite that had been prepared for him, then pushed his plate aside and composed his face into a mask that belied all feeling and conscious thought, as though loss had made him stupid. Groggy with and cocooned in grief, Mr. Chiffon took his place at the foot of the casket, as a mute, leftover, somehow resented chaperon of the evening. When they noticed him, which by intention was not often, any lightheartedness was tempered. Raised voices softened. Light, frivolous conversation was halted or taken up outside the room.

It's a spotty business trying to piece what happened all
together. You get the news reports continually, but you don't
know a bit more about what really happened after you watch
them than you did before. Of course, they focus on the
outlandish aspects of the thing, which leaves you with more
questions than answers so that you won't change the chan-
nel or turn the TV off the next time they come on. String-
along reporting.

Everybody wants news about the news. My sister down
in South Carolina wrote me a letter wanting to know what
in the world. Here it is.

Dear Sis,
   What in the world? Sit down and write to me this
minute. I am dying to know.
   Love, Sis
   P.S. Maggie Labrette must be happy now that she
has another opportunity to show all y'all how's the
right way to behave. I bet she's sticking by that
hermaphrodite. She loves misery better than a fly loves
filth. Her problem is she can't tell the difference
between a pitiful situation and one that is just the
result of sorriness. That boy, or whatever he is, has
had Maggie fooled for years, and the rest of you put

together don't have sense enough to figure out that he belonged in the army or the crazy house, but you all indulged Maggie's misguided sense of the Lord's work. And what's Elsie Moye saying? After all it was she who paid for him to go live in New York City where he learned such behavior, I'll vow. You've all indulged yourselves in some grand fantasy of Branch Creek being this rarefied place where beauty and culture was invented by Jerry Chiffon and patented by y'all. Oh, how the mighty have fallen splat on your faces. Y'all will never learn. What will it be now? Bake sales? House tours to benefit the Jerry Chiffon Defense Fund?

Now that little missive is Sis all over. P.S. longer than the letter. Lord she can branch off the subject. But a defense fund for Jerry was a good idea, I thought. Bake sales were out. Maggie would never allow such a thing. Doesn't believe in bazaars and harvest festivals and such as that. Some, not any of us on Central Avenue but others who can't just fork over the cash, have tried to organize bazaars, chicken suppers and quilt auctions to make money for the church. Maggie always stops it, and cites that story in the Bible of how Jesus threw the money changers out of the temple. She's fixed it so we all pledge what we are able to at the beginning of the year and the church budgets itself accordingly. It has gotten to be a dreary routine—the minister, one Sunday at the beginning of every year, giving a sermon *about* giving. Then the next Sunday, a sermon about what are we going to do, the gifts are way short of what we need to run the church. Usually by the next Sunday, but not always, sometimes it takes a Sunday or two, we are treated to a joyously delivered reproof of all who doubted that the Lord would provide. That through miraculous circumstances, which he is not at liberty to reveal, for another year the budget will be met and then some, thanks be to God, praise Jesus, blah, blah. Whereupon I. C. says nearly loud enough to be heard, God nothing. Maggie called Parchman Anderson, and he wrote a check. Then I have to pinch I. C. to make him hush.

But the house tour, that was something we'd never done around here. All these news people in town and nothing to do but stand around waiting for something to happen. We could really make some money. I thought, I'm going over to Maggie's to see what she thinks, but I never got to Maggie's. Here's what happened.

On the way over to Maggie's I stopped in at the post office to see if my sofa pillows had come back from the upholsterer in Raleigh. We send everything to Raleigh because that is the nearest place to get the best work done. With sofa pillows it is der rigor. And yes, I know that is not how you pronounce it. It's a joke between Jerry and all of us to say it that way. For Raleigh is the closest place where you can find anybody who knows how to do Turkish corners. It is hard to arrange and expensive to mail fabric samples back and forth. Who would have thought sofa pillows weighed so much? Drives I. C. crazy. I've tried to impress upon him the difference between a well-made pillow with Turkish corners and a cheap one. Showed him how the regular kind we all used to have get dog-eared, and no matter how good a fabric they are done up in they end up making whatever you throw them on look cheap. Contrast that to the carelessly chic look, a look that says, We had these done correctly at considerable expense a right long time ago and won't see the need to get news ones for a good while. That's what you get when you spend the extra for good fabric and Turkish corners done in Raleigh. But it all just makes I. C. despise sofa pillows in general. A large part of my day is spent picking them up from where I. C. has flung and cursed them. I replump them and rearrange them on the sofa until the next time he has his little tantrum. And that's when I really appreciate the difference in quality and am so thankful to Jerry for showing us the way. Couple of pats and a chop on top and they look like they did the day they arrived, whereas the square-cornered kind you have to near about beat to death with a baseball bat to get them to even give an imitation of anything you'd want to have in your home. House, I mean to say. You live in a house. You are at home. Jerry pointed out this distinction to me. But I'm branching off.

In front of the bank there was Elsie Moye spelling her name for a reporter, then proceeding to put before him her outlandish Djboutian theory. She was giving the reporter an earful of her limp-mindedness, and was soon surrounded by six or seven of the rascals. Once one finds out you'll talk to them it's like hogs to the trough. I thought I never would get into the post office. They didn't pay a bit of mind to the fact that the post office is a public place with a public entrance and that some of us have more important things to do than blabber nonsense to them about what might or might not have happened. They all do this; make up theories or listen to anybody else's, no matter how ridiculous, and spread them around for something to do until the unadorned and usually boring truth comes out. They tried to get me to say something on the air. Something intentional.

Stop me if I've told you this before.

This one, this Muff Martin, sticks this rubber microphone up to my mouth and asks me how did I *feel* when I heard what Jerry had done. I backed right up away from that thing. I wasn't about to stick my mouth up to it and pollute the air with any more nonsensical talk about the whole sad mess. I just flounced right on by all of them intent on my own business. Then just as I got to the door of the post office it hit me what I would have to say to them if I did have something to say. That *l'esprit d'escalier.*

44

Why don't y'all get a life, I said, and turned and went in. Didn't faze a one of the reporters, but Elsie Moye was dampened, I think. She got this sheepish look on her face and quit talking to them immediately. She races up the post office steps and sidles up to me all pinched and prissy once we're both inside.

I declare, these news people just won't leave you alone! she says, barely containing her joy.

That so, I say.

Yes, she says. Haven't they tried to interview you?

They tried, I say. Who around here ever used such a word as *interview* before now? is what I thought. You could tell Elsie Moye thought being interviewed was what should have been happening to her all her life. Then I made my slipup. I don't know why I didn't have sense enough to keep my idea about the house tour to myself until I had talked to Maggie, but I thought I'd vomit if I had to listen to another second of Elsie Moye pretending to be put out with all the attention she was getting from the news people.

So I say, Listen, Elsie, just got a letter from my sister in South Carolina, and she had the most wonderful idea of how we might help Jerry out of this mess. You know how fond she is of him, how grateful she was to him when she was here for Papa's funeral a few years ago, and Jerry told her it was probably not the best idea in the world to wear so much jewelry to any funeral but that to put it on for your own daddy's burial looked celebratory. Pared her down, don't you know, to a single strand of pearls and her wedding ring.

Hateful Elsie Moye says this: I remember Jerry telling her she looked like a Christmas tree, and I remember her telling him he could kiss her *a-double-s*.

Elsie Moye will argue with a signpost, dig it up and argue with the hole. She goes on. And I remember it was I who took her off to the side and explained to her that here in

45

Branch Creek we didn't wear jewelry to funerals, and she would fit in a whole lot better if when in Rome she'd do as the Romans do, says Elsie, then takes out her compact. She puts enough powder on her face to be in a Kabuki show. What I, Mrs. I. C. Lamm, remember is my sister asking Elsie Moye which of the two of them had actually been to Rome. I, says my sister, then she says, And I did just like I do in Passiflora, South Carolina, the entire time I was there. But I didn't get into all that with Elsie Moye. Most of the time you have to let her have the last word, or eventually you'll just have to invent new ones. She can just wear you down that way.

At any rate, I say, My sister suggested we establish a defense fund for Jerry right away and kick the fund-raising off with a tour of our houses. All these news people in town and nothing for them to do but stand around most of the time. Plus everybody who never gets to come into our houses would be lined up to get a look. I think we could make some money for Jerry.

At first I couldn't believe my ears. Elsie says, Well, sure. Excellent idea.

It is not Elsie Moye's usual way to agree so quickly to something before she has convinced herself it was her idea to begin with.

Then she wanted to know if I'd spoken to Maggie yet.

I say, No, but I thought I'd go over later today.

I'll go tell her now, she says. Oh, hell, was what I thought. Maggie tends not to like ideas that come directly from Elsie Moye. That day was not the day I learned to keep my mouth shut.

Outside the post office the only activity was the clump of reporters standing around like bored teenagers, some smoking, others gnawing on something. It hadn't seemed to have dawned on them yet that this is a small town and you can find out whatever you need to know from whomever you need to know it in about a half an hour.

Oh, I wish there was some way out of here besides through them! says Elsie Moye, taking a pair of shade glasses out of her purse and slipping them onto her face. I thought I would laugh out loud.

So out we go. I couldn't see much but my feet. The sofa pillows had been shipped in a pasteboard box that a dwarf could have lived in comfortably.

Mrs. Beamon! Mrs. Beamon! they're all shouting at Elsie Moye. And she says, No comment, rushing along, and I think to myself, That's a first. Then one knocks into my box of pillows and I nearly go over, and I must have made some kind of sound because they all run over to me thinking I'm going to talk. The rest I can tell not because I could see what was going on at the time, but because I saw it later on the six o'clock news. On the TV I am a body with a big pasteboard box for a head. So if you don't know me, you can't tell who I am. I'm kicking a path through these TV people while Elsie Moye sails behind me like a swan. I can be heard using a word I've never before said out loud. I am not going to repeat it now.

I didn't go with Elsie Moye to Maggie's, which was a mistake, but I had sofa pillows uppermost on my mind. Plus being sick of her and the TV people. I came home and unpacked my pillows and placed them on the sofa, and they were so pretty and inviting that I just sat down in them.

They are gorgeous. What Jerry would call the very thing if he were here to see them and not locked up in the Wake County jail. My sofa is covered in chintz—red roses on a slightly off-white background. Big red roses, don't you know, fully opened and dewy with lots of green leaves and actual thorny stems and, if you look close enough, some little red ladybugs and some adorable blue and yellow butterflies and a red ant now and then in the pattern. But it is that little bit of yellow in the butterfly I picked up for the pillows. Had them made up in this buttery, jonquilly, lemon-sherbety silk shantung and trimmed with a brush fringe that is mainly blue silk, the same blue as in the butterfly which is the blue of a *dark* blue delphinium, but there is also red silk thread in the fringe, the red of the chintz red roses. It looks perfectly beautiful. And again I wish Jerry was here to see it. I took a whole roll of pictures of the sofa with the pillows. I am going to send some of them to Jerry in jail. That will really cheer him up, if I know my Jerry. Nothing makes him happier than a thing well done. It was being around Jerry that made it possible for me to pull this off. I have really got it right this time. Rakov, Ralston & Walston in Richmond couldn't have done better. I for one cannot wait for the house tours to begin.

I got so involved in admiring my handiwork that I just forgot to worry about Elsie Moye being at Maggie's, and thoroughly exhausted with pleasure, pride and wrangling with the press, sat down on my sofa, nestled myself into the new pillows and fell asleep.

I couldn't have been out long when the phone tore down to ringing. It is not my custom to sleep on my living room sofa in the middle of the afternoon, so when I woke up I didn't know where I was, what a phone was, that there were any such people as Maggie Labrette or Elsie Moye Beamon or Jerry Chiffon. It was as though I had never heard of a house tour or knew what the words *house* or *tour* even meant. I was in that moment before I had realized myself, when there is neither before nor after, up nor down and you don't even know what, let alone who, you are. I hate it when that happens and am so happy when everything I know reveals itself to me in an instant of recognition and *I* click back into place.

It took me a second to have sense enough to answer the phone. It was Maggie. Wanted to know if I was busy. Well, no, I said. May I come over? she asked. Said, I need to talk to you about something. Sure, I said.

The second I put the receiver back in the cradle the telephone rang again. It was Elsie Moye. She said, Listen, two things. One, next time you talk to Maggie, above all else be sure to tell her the house tour was my idea, and two, I'm coming over.

She hung up before I could sputter out, Don't.

I fluffed up the sofa pillows, took a quick look around the room to make sure everything looked nice, then went out onto the front porch to wait for Maggie's arrival and dread Elsie Moye's. In no time the big old Labrette Cadillac turned the corner, light sparking off the chrome bumpers and sliding along its black curves. Lyman, of course, was driving, and he stopped the car in front of my house, got out and went around to the passenger side to open the door for Maggie. I'll have to say this for Lyman. He either is, or has been taught to impersonate well, a gentleman. A sight you can see all over town is him opening doors for Maggie, carrying her parcels for her, putting out a hand to help her out of the car or up from a chair. When they are walking together, he offers his arm, and she takes it. I'm always touched by it. I don't think gentlemanly behavior is something he grew up knowing much about. The Labrette men have always been pretty gamy in general, and the women they marry just put up with it. The fomentation of scandal and mayhem by Lyman's father, Mr. Ball Labrette, is well known around here. They tell about the time he was downtown just standing around in front of the bank with some of the other townsmen and Elsie Moye, who was then a teenager, walked up to him, poked his big old belly with her finger and said, trying to tease him, Mr. Ball you look like you're about to have a baby. That stomach of yours looks like it belongs on a woman. Elsie Moye was simply a younger version of what she is now in the sense of thinking she was cute as pie and clever and that everybody adored her. Mr. Ball looks down at his rotundity real serious and says, Does it now, little Elsie Moye? Well, it ain't been long just got off one.

Now there is wit for you even if it isn't fit to hear. Then commenced the thigh slapping and whooping and hollering by the men. Elsie Moye turned red as fire, burst into tears, threw up and ran home is what they say.

I didn't mean to go off on another tangent. I am always having to apologize for branching off. Some think I lose track of what I'm talking about. But I don't, you see. It's just that everything that happens in Branch Creek is so dependent on what has happened or will happen or never happened that your stories can get long. Lyman's chivalrous ways aren't much of a marvel unless you know the kind of people he was brought up by. There are a lot of so-called well-brought-up men who won't open a door for a lady or stand up when one enters the room. Lyman does. It is one of the reasons, I suppose, why he can say exactly what he pleases, no matter how abrupt or offensive, and not be despised for it. And people say there were some disappointed and envious girls left in this town when Lyman Labrette married Marguerite Bonner.

Anyway, after Lyman opened the door for Maggie, he went back around the car to the driver's side, got in, tuned the radio to something not music and just waited for Maggie.

I said, Come in, Lyman, won't you? I had to raise my voice.

He said, No, thank you, in a way that made you know that even if he wasn't exactly sure of what was about to take place, he did know that he wouldn't get involved in it for anything in this world. Which was too bad, for I thought there might be less unpleasantness when Elsie Moye showed up if Lyman was in the room. He tipped his hat to me, and got back in the driver's seat, stared straight ahead and just waited like waiting was a calling.

Maggie coming toward me was inspiring. So much so that for a little while I was able to put out of my mind the turmoil I feared was beginning. How do I describe her demeanor? It was clear from the look on her face that this was not a social call. Certainly, her usual warm smile was absent. Yet she wore no trace of discomfort. No look of rue that would be natural if you knew you were going to have to say things that might cause hurt feelings or, worse, outright anger. No fear that perhaps controversy might ensue when it has been long established that you conduct yourself in such a way as to avoid, deny and float above all contention. No embarrassment.

The fact that Elsie Moye was also about to descend seemed impossible, and all I could do besides admire Maggie was fear her in a way that took the form of wondering if everything inside my house was presentable. It is always that way with her. You just want to be perfect, and you want to do the one thing she has always wanted done for her if you can just divine what that is. But what you get the minute you start to think like that about her is the profound feeling that she wants nothing. She seems to be without desire, so that even when she takes actions that appear to be designed to make things come out her way, which always turns out to be the best way, you don't feel any imposition of her will. You end up thinking she doesn't want to control anybody or anything. She is nothing but ministration and usefulness. That is what it is in her that calls up those contradictory feelings you get of wishing you could help her, knowing all the time that it would be like giving feathers to a bird and that, if she were to ask you for some little thing, it would be because she sensed you needed her to want it from you.

As admirable as it sounds, this can be wearing. And still,

as always I felt honored and grateful that she was walking up to my door.

I greeted Maggie and invited her into the house, all the time watching for that big old some-kind-of-Buick that Elsie Moye drives herself around in. We went straight to the living room. I let her go in first so she could get an unobstructed view of my new upholstery and sofa pillows.

All she said was how pretty everything looked. Then she sat down and removed one of the pillows from behind her back.

Maggie, can I get you a Coca-Cola or something? I asked.

No, dear, she said. Said, I can't stay long.

If she knew there had been a change in my decoration, she did not comment on it. I guess I wasn't surprised. She is as peculiar about that sort of thing as the English earl Jerry told me about. He says this earl never invited a guest back to his house, who, quote, had the cheek to compliment my chairs, unquote. The idea being, I guess, that if you compliment somebody on something, you are implying an improvement. It's like you can consider yourself flattered if she doesn't comment on your decoration or cooking or flower arranging. But really a compliment from somebody as kind and polite as Maggie Labrette is not something you can cherish anyway, for you know if she didn't like something about you or your house, she would never come right out and say so. There is a lesson in that. Don't say anything too good, and you won't have to say anything too bad. Now Jerry, he would tell me right away if I had gotten things right or not.

Maggie started in with, Poor Elsie Moye has just been to my house.

Really, said I. You have to be cagey in these situations or you will nail your flag to the wrong mast before you know it. How is Elsie Moye? I asked.

Fine, I think. In the physical sense, Maggie said.

I said, Oh, is something wrong with her mind? Keep steady, I thought. Only go on what has been given to you.

Maggie smiled, it looked like, in spite of herself—nearly laughed, I think, and said, No, there is nothing wrong with her mind. Said, But you must know how she is. She said she had just seen you before she came to me.

Whoops, I thought. She's on to both of us. Best to just tell her exactly what happened.

I admitted she had, and I asked Maggie, Is this visit about the house tour? I thought I'd head her off at the pass, take the wind out from under her, but her expression did not change from what it had been the entire time, which was as always kind, concerned, a little bored and completely devoid of any indication of what she ultimately hoped to achieve by coming to see me.

With this faraway look on her face as though she was remembering something long past and trying to recall the minutest and most obscure detail, Maggie said, Mainly yes. Said, Elsie Moye said it was her idea. Asked, Was it?

Right then and there, for the first time in my life, I had to question how we live life in Branch Creek. Of course, with Maggie sitting there in front of me, the situation became one through which I felt I must navigate carefully. Suddenly, all the ways a harmless little house tour could turn into something regrettable surged up in my mind. And look how the off-hand joke my sister made had become a major upheaval. And how quickly it had become such. It all just made me contrary. So I decided then and there to straighten the whole thing out if I could. The truth would come out, and I would be the source of it, and if it ruffled feathers, fine!

Brazen as brass, I said, Maggie, the house tour was my idea. Said, I am the one who thought it would be a good thing to do. Said, I told Elsie Moye about it.

I confessed the truth to Maggie in an effort to save face for Elsie Moye, for I was thinking then that Maggie thought it was a bad idea, and I didn't want it attached to Elsie Moye, although now I couldn't say why I would want to spare Elsie Moye and why I thought telling Maggie what I did would do anything of the kind. She can just get you all bumbled up that way.

Ah, I see, said Maggie. I was sure she thought the house tour was the pinnacle of tackiness. It wasn't anything she had said, and you certainly could not have read disapproval on her face. But if I had thought that this admission on my part, right to her face, would cause her to feel the least bit uncomfortable or worry that she might have insulted me or hurt my feelings, I saw immediately that I was wrong. And I maybe should have felt ashamed, but I didn't.

I ought to have known, Maggie said, patting my hand. Elsie Moye, she kind of murmured, bless her heart, she can certainly complicate things. Said, I am sure it's just because she wants to help out.

I started to feel right irritable. All this fuss about who thought up what.

What I said was, Maggie, I already know Elsie Moye told you the house tour was her idea. I know you have come here to ask me to help you try and stop what you think is an ill-advised and inappropriate enterprise. And probably we should. More than half of the reason I brought it up to Elsie Moye was so I wouldn't have to hear her talk about TV people and reporters and her ridiculous theories.

What Maggie said next floored me.

I think it is the best idea anyone has had ever. She said, It is the perfect thing to do for Jerry—tasteful and appropriate. He has done so much in so little time to help promote culture and beauty in this town. It is the perfect way to both honor him and help him out—and so on and so forth. That

Maggie Labrette could turn a mud-wrestling match into a high-minded charity.

But what, Maggie wanted to know, will we do about poor Elsie Moye?

Did you find her out before you came over here? I asked, and she said she was pretty sure the idea hadn't really been Elsie's. Said, Something in the way she told me. I mean coming over to let me know rather than calling, and then how she looked right at me after she told me, with a kind of innocence that in her is nearly always the sign of a lie.

But, I said, you let Elsie think you were just coming over here to tell me what she had come up with. I paused to look for signs in Maggie that she and I were coming to the same conclusions about what to do. She smiled sadly, tilted her head slightly to the side and lowered her chin once slowly in a gesture that made me know that the plan of how to deal with Elsie Moye that I had thought I was hatching up on the spot was the thoughtful, kind solution Maggie had come to the instant she had gotten the slightest whiff of what was happening. She had simply come over to let me know, in the quietest way possible, what our plan was. I was awed.

We can't let her be in charge of this, said Maggie just as sweet.

I said, No, we really couldn't. Remember the Pet Parade she organized for the Methodist Youth Fellowship? Said how my grandson still hadn't found his cat, and all three of Tiny Mager's prize dominicker chickens got eaten by that German shepherd.

It would be a circus, she said.

And I said, Three rings.

We could never let her know that we know she has told us an untruth, said Maggie.

And I said, Never.

Leave it to me. I will guide it toward you, Maggie said. Said, She'll get tired of it anyway when she sees how much work is involved.

Then from outside was the unmistakable sound of Elsie Moye's Buick rear-ending Lyman's Cadillac.

I had been wondering what was taking her so long, and said so to Maggie. We both hurried outside.

Two good things about Elsie Moye rear-ending Lyman: One, for the time being, trying to hide the fact that we knew Elsie Moye had lied to Maggie was easier. Two, hearing the exchange between Lyman and Elsie Moye was worth the whole controversy. When we got to the scene, Lyman and Elsie Moye both were still just sitting in their cars, waiting as if to see what the other one would do—Lyman looking up into his rearview mirror and Elsie Moye looking forward. Aside from the weak plume of steam lazily escaping from somewhere under the hood of Elsie Moye's car and the red taillight glass scattered like rose petals on the pavement, you would not have thought there had been an accident of any kind. Lyman and Elsie Moye seemed so calm.

When Maggie asked Lyman if he was all right, his answer was to get out of the car. We could see that he had all his parts and could ambulate. Elsie Moye looked at herself in her rearview mirror—patted her hair, smoothed down the collar of her dress. With her thumb and middle finger she rubbed off lipstick that had strayed from the corners of her mouth, and, turning and tilting her head back and forth, up and down, took a last appraising, and, I thought, approving look at herself. Then she emerged and immediately started apologizing in what seemed a rehearsed stream of self-blame. I couldn't help thinking she had, in the last split second as she rounded the corner and saw Lyman's car parked there in front of the house, cooked the whole thing up as a diversion. Had decided that ramming Lyman's car would get her sympathy for a while. She'd do the same thing when we were in school—plan some little disaster for herself when there was a test. One time, when she stayed out of school for two days, she came back claiming the reason for her absence had been that a favorite aunt had died. What had really happened was that she had been spreading some very odd gossip about a girl from out in the country named Toughie who, when the stories and who had told them got back to her, had threatened to pull Elsie Moye's hair out of her head and strangle her with it.

Lyman had his tactics, too, we were to discover.

Oh, Lyman, pealed Elsie Moye, I'm so sorry.

Lyman said, Nonsense. Said, I am entirely to blame.

Lyman, don't be silly. I ran right into you. I never will forgive myself, she said.

Stop that right now, Elsie Moye. This is my fault and mine alone. Don't you worry about it one bit, he said.

I thought Lyman had been hit in the head. Even Maggie had a look of confused amazement on her face.

Elsie Moye said, Lyman you are talking crazy. Said, I'll pay for every bit of the damage to your car. Are you all right?

He said he was fine, then started a walk around both cars, assessing the damage that he kept insisting was his doing.

Elsie Moye followed, spewing apologies. She clawed through her purse and found her checkbook and a pen.

By this time the neighbors had come out of their houses; people who had happened along in their cars stopped and got out to see what was going on.

Elsie told him she was going to write a blank check. Said, Have the man fill it in for whatever the cost of the repairs.

Elsie Moye, put your checkbook away, darling. For the last time, I'm telling you this is my fault. None of your own.

Lyman, how can you say such a ridiculous thing, dear? she said.

And Lyman, that rascal, smiled big as sunshine and tipped his hat to Elsie Moye.

Saw you take your car out of the garage this morning, and knew you were abroad in it, he said. Said, This would not have happened if I had stayed home as I should have done and given you the roads to yourself today.

By the next day the tale had spread all over town and the extraordinary Labrette wit and drollery had been reconfirmed by those who heard the story as well as those who told it.

I take it you are both all right, said Maggie.

Better than ever, darling, said Lyman.

You could see he was enjoying himself mightily.

I don't *think* I'm hurt, Elsie Moye said, whimpering. Said, No bodily harm, anyway. She gave Lyman a look that would peel paint off a wall.

Maggie told Lyman to take her home, please. Said, Elsie Moye, honey, maybe you ought to let Parchman look you over, just to be safe.

Both cars more or less worked, so off they all went, leaving me alone on my front porch, facing the gathered onlookers.

I told them it was all over and to go on about their business. I went inside myself and thought for too long of the ironies that had snapped into place in that short amount of time between when Maggie arrived and when she left, and could not for the life of me figure out who had won, who had lost or who was ahead. No one, I supposed.

Except Jerry. And just maybe the town, because the first ever Branch Creek House Tour was about to take place for his benefit and in his honor.

It was April. Around the Old Capitol building, sun-gilded pollen powdered the air between the new-green lawn and the light-sifting, high green of the ancient trees. For over a century, slaves, convicts, ladies' clubs and lately degreed horticulturists had gardened these grounds, and their efforts were paying off again. The sun shining through sprays of white dogwood tatted lacy patterns on the ground. Brazen azaleas bloomed against the blushy-gray stone of the primly grand Old Capitol. Under crab-apple trees blew little storms of pink snow. Ornamental pear and plum blossoms had come and gone, and the weeping cherry had shed its last petal. But all around the noble old building, monumental horse-chestnut trees plumed full-flowered atop their barky columns like white summer clouds, beautiful to the point of impertinence. Below this arboreal splendor lay a fresh green lawn stenciled with beds of red tulips in simple but formal patterns, which were themselves edged, as if embroidered, with blue and white hyacinths.

A scene of spectacular beauty that even he could be proud of, Jerry thought, marred by, but in the end overwhelming, the effects of the garish, coarse crowd that had gathered in front of the Capitol steps to hear what North Carolina's United States Senator Henry Hampton had to say.

Jerry had chosen his outfit carefully. He had dressed himself, made up his face, fixed and put on the right wig and assembled the perfect accessories, hopeful that he would give the impression of being a very well-off supporter of the Senator and what he stood for. When he was finished, he took a long look at himself in the mirror and was confident he had achieved the desired effect, and now that he was among the crowd gathered on the grounds of the Old Capitol, he saw that only Mrs. Hampton herself, standing just behind her husband on the Capitol steps, was dressed as well as he. He knew he could not only fool the riffraff that showed up whenever Senator Hampton spoke, but could have walked into a ladies' club or a church or strolled around in any department store in Raleigh without causing a head to turn except in admiration.

If he had been wearing men's clothes, Jerry would not have gone to the rally, for it was the type of crowd he knew he would stick out in, a firecracker kind of crowd, men mostly. There were some girls in jeans and a small number of women in pants. There were a few old farmers' wives in their best dresses saved for just such a time of coming into town or going to church, but none of these were the kind of women Jerry could expect to revel in his company. And the men were men who could tell right off by looking into your face that they didn't like you—that you were not like them. Had he shown up as himself they would have known immediately that he was not there to support the Senator, that he did not believe in their causes, that he was not one of them. They, Senator Hampton's supporters, had a sense, subtle and sure as a dog's, of who was an enemy. You could dress like him, drive the same kind of vehicle, live in the same kind of house, but you couldn't fool the Hampton man into thinking you were the same as he if you weren't. Jerry had come to think that it was something about the lack of suspicion in your eyes that this kind of man would not trust. Maybe he would notice how your curiosity flew lightly and freely and lighted onto whatever drew it, and he wouldn't like that. There might be a softly lucent delight in and around your eyes that made him sick. When he smiled, it was seldom in agreement or approvingly, but sardonically, accompanied by a snort of scorn and mindful of what he hated. He distrusted all politicians except Henry Hampton. Ambivalence filled him with rage. If he was a religious man, riches and worldly things were of no importance in his holy war against all the people and ideas he was sure God despised. If he was not particularly God-fearing and he lacked money and possessions, that would be proof for him of something gone wrong with the country that only Senator Hampton could fix. He wanted only what he worked for and hated charity. The way he thought of it was like this: Everybody except himself was undeserving, and he wanted no help.

Jerry knew he knew these people—understood their inborn suspicion—how they were each one held by the Senator's power to ensure that they continued to fear what they feared and hate whom they hated. Senator Hampton's ranting did not bring the crowd together. He had no interest or use in making them feel they were kindred spirits. His talent was an ability to give each man's sense of isolation his wholehearted approval. When the crowd cheered the Senator it seemed a collection of lone shouts and individual whoops rather than the affirmation of a group stirred by and united in a cause. Each was mad and dangerous in his own way. The Senator honored and encouraged division, reaction, opposition. Above all else he excelled in infusing each person's rage with a myth of independent power. These were feelings, although aroused in him by what he thought of as good causes and encouraged by people who were, to his way of thinking, righteous, that Jerry had known himself.

Hampton's followers were often goaded into violent actions, but they were nearly always secretive, individual acts of revenge and retribution. Of course the Senator always denied that he was responsible for any of his followers' behavior, and he believed his denial with all his heart. Some of his most avid supporters were Klansmen and others of that sort. They understood that he could not publicly support them. They attended his speeches and rallies, but they never wore their robes and masks.

But that fine morning Jerry passed among the Senator's supporters unmolested. Wherever he walked, the crowd parted for him. Women smiled deferentially as they would have to a lady of quality and means who they believed to be on their side politically if not socially. They made way for him. He was able to stroll right up to the front of the crowd. It was as though people thought he were someone important to the Senator and a special place had been reserved for him.

Hampton was running for a third term. This time he was being challenged by a black man, a lawyer of high education and accomplishment, who, it appeared, had a good chance of taking the seat that the Senator had held for so long. But for the last few weeks the Senator's campaign had started to run an advertisement on television. In it a black woman of enormous girth, wearing dangly gold earrings and tacky expensive clothes, was in the checkout line at the grocery store. The advertisement showed a close-up of the cash register and the total amount of the bill, over two hundred dollars. Then the camera cut to another close-up of the woman's brown hand—carefully although garishly manicured, a ring on every finger, paying for her groceries with food stamps. All during this transaction, an irate voice told the viewer how hard he and others like him worked, what a difficult time it was making ends meet. A white grocery boy pushing an overflowing shopping cart followed the woman out to her brand-new car where he loaded her purchases into the trunk, then as she drove away, he stood shaking his head in disbelief. Over the picture a voice, snide and insinuating, pronounced, *Your tax money at work*, then with sympathetic assurance commanded, *Vote for Henry Hampton.*

The ad had infuriated the black population of the state, and an unexpected number of important and influential white citizens had criticized Senator Hampton in every public forum available. He had been denounced from the pulpits of nearly all the name-brand churches. Across the state the prevailing wonder seemed to be how could even Henry Hampton sink this low—then the wonder became the realization that not only had he, but that it was working. Dating from when the ad was first aired statewide, stealthily, shamefully, underneath the scorn and outrage, the Senator's standing in every poll taken had reversed from a steady, downward slide to graph-spiking highs. North Carolina was mocked and berated by people of integrity in every other state in the union, but here and there across the country, some politicians had started watching Senator Hampton's campaign carefully. They studied it and learned.

It was not this ad that had compelled Jerry to come to the rally on the Old Capitol grounds. As much as he disliked what the ad had to say and rued how effective it had been, Jerry had his own reasons for coming. And it was not welfare cheats and liberal government programs that the Senator had on his mind this morning. He had come to rally his supporters and assuredly win new ones by talking about something vital to his salvation, for he was a Believer and therefore was sure that when he met his Maker he would be asked what he had done to rid the world of evil and turn those who sinned to the right way. He knew he would be held personally responsible, and although he might not be able to change the world, he knew God required him to try—to fight the good fight with all his heart and soul. His mission was to do everything in his power to make people like Jerry change themselves or vanish from this earth. The rally had been advertised as one at which the Senator would make a major speech concerning his views on the menace that he saw and what he intended to do about it. It was not the first time he had spoken out about this kind of thing. He had been trying the speech out other places. Jerry had heard it the day before on the radio. But this was the day Senator Hampton really meant to throw down the challenge.

Jerry did not hate the Senator, as many of his friends did, nor was Henry Hampton someone he feared. By this time in his life he believed he had learned to eliminate fear from the emotions he felt. It had taken a long time and had been accomplished at a great price, but after having harbored—as well as having been the brunt of—more hate and fear than most would call normal, unexpectedly but incontrovertibly he had found he afforded fear no room in his heart. It seemed to him that he had simply exhausted those emotions and in their place slipped a calm self-recognition—knowledge of who he was and how he was made up and that in his heart and soul if not his body he was a different kind of man than any he knew about and had what he believed was a woman's way of thinking about things like fear and hate. Or rather, more simply, maybe he had been graced with the ability—bestowed, perhaps, by a Benevolence the nature of which he was dubious about—to summon in himself courage so majestic that it seemed foolhardy, but without which he simply could not have survived. In short, possibly there was a God and He had given Jerry what he needed to get by in this world, being what he was. It was long, long in coming, this courage, and a sensible explanation of its acquisition or effects still eluded him, but when it finally had come, it left no room in him to love or hate. Or maybe, he sometimes thought, that's what love and hate are really, two varieties of courage, equal in intensity and, in the end, perhaps capable of equal destruction. He liked to think this way—about the contradictions in life and the play of opposites in the world. He was thinking like that when he took the gun out of his purse. As he aimed his first shot, he was in a reverie of wonderment over the incongruity between the stately Old Capitol with its tended, pampered grounds and the hateful rantings of the Senator. The tacky clothes the people were wearing and their vulgar faces among the elegant flowers and trees registered in his mind as he fired again. Even the gunshots snapping the flower-scented air seemed to Jerry to praise a savage, unattainable, contradictory perfection, fathomable to only the finest and most subtle mind, which situated the day in the province of mere beauty as well as transported it into the more truthful realm of the sublime, like the symmetry broken when the intentional flaw is woven into a Turkish rug. For an instant, all possibilities were present, and Jerry, although he knew as he felt it that the feeling would not last, had a momentary sense that his purpose and place had been revealed to him and that his purpose was to fix things, create harmonious surroundings, do away with what was not beautiful or logical as he had in Branch Creek, and that his place was here and everywhere—that when something was not quite right, did not go, was out of place in some way, he had to replace it with what was right, and if merely taking away the offense would do, to eliminate it.

He knew immediately that his shot had missed the Senator. Trying to manage the purse, the placard and the gun had been too much. He saw blossoms falling from a branch high up in a chestnut tree, and he saw the Senator standing dumbstruck on the Old Capitol steps, his wife looking stupidly up into the sky.

He watched what he was in. Nothing seemed quick or chaotic, but time and events deliberately unfolded in the most logical and understandable way, as if he had planned the aftermath of his actions as carefully as the weddings he oversaw, the flowers he arranged, the rooms he decorated. The crowd, accustomed to and appreciative of explosions large or small, had laughed and cheered at first, but when some near him saw the pistol in his gloved hand, sick grins abruptly took the place of laughter. Then around Jerry widened a circle of green grass edged by frightened people, pushing and trying to get behind each other. He saw a woman holding a small child up in front of her face. He saw the officials on the Old Capitol steps crouch, and he saw them disappear into a swarm of uniformed men. Then, suddenly a hand was holding his wrist, and Jerry let go of the gun. Two state patrolmen appeared and gently but quickly ushered Jerry through the crowd. They had almost reached the patrol car when a woman, red-faced and screaming, came out of the crowd and in a voice filled with anger sprayed Jerry with unintelligible words that had the cadence of Bible verses. She rushed at Jerry and tried to pull his hair, and the wig came off in her hands, revealing his real hair matted with sweat and plastered to his skull. At the sight of a man in woman's clothes, the mood of the crowd changed almost instantly from rage and hate to hilarity. Jerry heard familiar whoops of laughter, wheedling, insinuating jeers and wolf whistles.

The Senator resumed his speech. The officers walked Jerry to a waiting patrol car and locked him into the backseat, where he calmly removed the silk scarf that was pinned around his neck and tied it on his wigless head, as the car, its blue lights whipping the air and its siren clearing the road, sped away.

His arrest had been more like a chivalrous escort out of

an unpleasant situation than the seizure of a criminal. But Jerry was not surprised to have been treated well by the lawmen. A friend he had known in Raleigh had said that there was always less trouble with the police when one was dressed as a woman.

"Oh, they'll smirk at times," Jerry's friend had said, "but very seldom have I felt menaced." The friend said he'd been stopped and asked to produce his driver's license, often while he was in women's clothes, on the way to a party or just out for a hoot, and even when an officer was confronted with proof of his gender, the worst that had ever happened was a long stare from the policeman and a contemptuous snort as he handed the license back.

"Not a few have treated me with outright chivalry— 'ma'am' this and 'lady' that, and 'I'm letting you go this time,'" the friend had said. And more than once he had been asked for his phone number. And this was after they had seen his license and knew he was a man. Sometimes he had given it. An older trooper, graying and overweight, had written his phone number on a speeding ticket, the deep blue words *Call me* desperately pressed into the copy he handed back. Faced with the situation he presented to them, and absent of any physical threat, Jerry's friend had told him that the lawmen responded professionally, sometimes courteously, and at best, flatteringly.

"They seemed unable to bring themselves to harm anything in a dress," said the friend. "Even on the occasions when I sense that they might wish to, they don't. It's the uniform."

Jerry had shaken his head in wondrous disbelief at his friend's experience with law enforcement.

"These officers are Southerners first," he had explained. "It is the dress and stockings and such that is respected, not me particularly."

The ride to the jail was, if quick, also enjoyable and gave Jerry an unexpected feeling of complete safety. With these reliable, vigilant men, Jerry was able to delight mightily in the banks of giant azaleas full-blooming on impeccably mowed lawns for the people of the fine old homes situated in downtown Raleigh. When he looked away from the scenery for a moment, he saw in the rearview mirror that the officer who was driving the car had been watching him admire the spring flowers. There was a kind smile on the officer's face and a look in his eyes of what Jerry thought might be shared appreciation.

"The azaleas are as beautiful as I've ever seen them this year," said the officer.

"Aren't they?" said Jerry. "Every kind of pink there is."

Jerry wished that they could just go on like this, the three of them, driving forever from town to town to see what each place had to offer that was spectacular or odd or beautiful. An endless meander through America, witnessing countless displays of civic pride—Peach Festival, Rattlesnake Roundup, Hollerin' Contest, Daffodil Days, Collard Carnival, Chitlin Jubilee—on and on, from one event to another, they would make their way in wide-eyed awe. It would end like this. One day, distracted by and staring slack-jawed at some road-side oddity, they would run head-on into another vehicle. It would be a sensational collision, fiery and huge. They would all die in a state of amazement.

"Well, here we are," said the driver. "Looks like you got some fans, already."

Writhing outside the entrance to the courthouse jail in a confusion of wires, cameras and bright lights, was a crowd of reporters waiting to get a look at Jerry. Microphones on poles fished the air for anything he might say. The officer drove through the crowd of reporters, which parted then closed in around the car. Flashes of camera light went off in Jerry's eyes, so bright his brain shook, as if he were being hit in the head, but he did not turn away. He sat erect in the backseat of the patrol car and stared straight at the photographers and camera operators, arranging his face as near as possible to look like a grand old lady he had been introduced to when he was in New York. She was a leader of New York Society—a woman on whom people had to make a good impression if they wanted to climb the social ladder. It was the way she had looked him straight in the eye, stupidly almost, blinking in a way that was both innocent and impatient—this he was trying to duplicate, because the effect of her stare was that it made him feel he was of no interest whatever to her or anyone who mattered to her. He had thought at the time, She is looking at me the way I would look at God if I met Him.

The photographers snapped away, oblivious to his attempt at an annihilating stare. His eyes started to hurt from looking unflinchingly into the cameras.

"Like flies to filth," said the patrolman who wasn't driving the car.

"Yeah," said the driver, but Jerry noticed how he let the remark pass without laughing or adding to the insult.

They got out of the car and helped Jerry out, but when they shut the car door it caught the end of the scarf he had over his head and pulled it off revealing his sweat-soaked hair. The flashes from the cameras went off like the end of a fireworks show, and the clicking from the lens shutters sounded like tap dancing. The nice patrolman opened the car door and freed the scarf. He put it back on Jerry's head and tied the ends in a loose knot around his neck. The scarf had greasy black stains from being slammed in the car door.

"I swear," said Jerry, giving the patrolmen a mock-irritable frown, "a girl can't wear anything nice to this place."

Mrs. Labrette turned off the television set—they were telling what Jerry had done. She did not believe most of what she was seeing and hearing, and she did not wish to see and hear more. She preferred, instead, to think about when Jerry and his little brother had been hers to care for. What she remembered above all was not anything she had done, but Jerry and the dutiful, effective and unsentimental way he tended to his little brother. She had never been a very affectionate woman in the sense of hugging and pawing over people, and certainly she didn't gush with "honey" this and "darling" that like some women. But she had always told herself and hoped God in Heaven agreed that efficient care was as good a demonstration of love as any other. Her heart rejoiced to see evidenced in a child what she had hoped in herself was enough and right. It screwed a little tighter the faith she tried to keep in her own desire to be good, an aspiration that she had acquired long ago when, as a young lady in love, she looked into herself and found that, although she hadn't the courage for passion, what she had to offer was capability and effectiveness, and finding in her heart or mind nothing better, had prayed for those qualities to be consecrated. That efficient love could inhabit even this child was proof for her that God valued it. She thought of how getting to know Jerry and watching him care for his little brother had been a reminder to her of the difference between people who would do what they should and those who would not. And the lesson of Jerry made her think that you became one or the other early on by either facing up to what life's circumstances required of you or not. You can come to love what you have to do. This was the wisdom she formulated watching little Jerry on those Saturdays, and it was knowing him then and now that prevented her from believing that what she had just seen on the television about him was the whole story, if it was a story at all.

It seemed so long ago when they had started having their Saturdays together at her house. It was the first of those daylong visits that started the real friendship between them. From that time on, Mrs. Labrette always looked forward to being with Jerry. He could have been a burden and ought to have been, she would explain to people who asked what she saw in him. But he was even then a delightful child and an interesting person. She recalled Jerry's shy curiosity about her house and the things in it. How nothing seemed to escape his notice—his sense of subtle differences. How he could unaccountably distinguish the best from the good and above all how he understood and appreciated that you were taking time with him.

It was in those days Mr. Chiffon's custom to come into town every Saturday. And the second Saturday after she helped to bury Mrs. Chiffon, Maggie heard the tractor coming and ran to the street to flag it down. She told Mr. Chiffon to drop Jerry and the baby off at her house the following Saturday. She pointed out how convenient it would be for him to pick Jerry and the baby up on his way home, since the last thing in his day would be his usual meeting with Dr. Anderson right across the street from her. She waited patiently on the sidewalk in front of her house while Mr. Chiffon told her that he didn't want to be any trouble to her, and that Jerry and the baby would do fine by themselves for the time he was in town. She insisted that it certainly would not be any trouble.

"And I don't think it is a wise idea to leave them alone in the house way out there in the country for a full day," she added tactfully.

"They're there at the house by theirselves most of the time," Mr. Chiffon said. "Hit's hard to move that baby from place to place."

"But possible, Mr. Chiffon," she replied firmly.

Then, the day before the children were to come for the first time, she went to Lyman. He was on the porch after supper, sitting in the green wicker rocking chair that had been her father's. She liked seeing Lyman in that chair because it reared back on its own even at rest and gave to both him and his absence an air of authority and grandeur. It had always been a man's chair. Now it was Lyman's. Maggie sat down on the glider by her husband.

"Lyman, I'm going to take the little Chiffon boy in hand and see if I can help him," she said.

"What's wrong with him you can't help, honey," said Lyman.

"Still," she said, in a deferential but certain tone of voice that was as near to insistent as she ever got with him. Lyman offered no more comment on her plan, and Maggie knew she could take that for consent.

So on that first visit she was ready, standing on her porch waiting when Mr. Chiffon stopped his tractor in front of her house. He didn't turn the motor off, and made no indication that he saw her, but stared straight ahead down the street, only stopping long enough for Jerry to hop from the wagon behind the tractor and quickly gather the things he'd brought for tending to his helpless brother. Then the tractor puttered off, and without looking back, Mr. Chiffon waved his hand in a gesture that seemed to indicate resigned surrender rather than good-bye.

She was impressed immediately by how well Jerry was already caring for the baby. How he gently lifted it from the nest of pillows he had wedged it in for the trip into town. In a week's time he had learned to hold the baby in the crook of one arm and use the same hand to support the baby's head, then with the other hand, slip the head deftly into a sling he had made which was tied around his own neck. When properly rigged up, the head was held still and erect, and Jerry could safely carry both the baby and the sack full of bottles, diapers, rags, ointments, all the things he needed to look after his little brother. He hurried up the walkway to the house, trying to make it inside before he lost his strength and dropped the baby and the sack.

"Let me help you," said Mrs. Labrette. She started down the steps. Jerry was walking toward her quickly and carefully, like someone trying to win a race without letting on that there was a race to win. He was up the steps before she could get down them. "Open the door, open the door," he said. She hurried inside and held open the door and then ran ahead of him and pointed to a room off her hall. When he got into the room he fell forward onto the bed with the baby in his arms. It took him a moment to catch his breath, but when he did he asked Mrs. Labrette if he could take the pillows from under the bedspread.

"Yes, yes," said Mrs. Labrette. She watched Jerry carefully, for she wanted to learn how to help him take care of his little brother. She saw how he wedged the baby securely between the fat high pillows. The child lay there like an odd little hot dog. She planned to have the pillows in place the next time Jerry and the baby came to her house. Together they got the baby situated into the Labrettes' high mahogany guest bed.

Jerry asked her if she would warm his brother's bottle,

so she did, and he gave it to the baby. He finished the bottle quickly and soon was pulling in awful wheezing, snorting breaths, which, except for when they would stop altogether, were regular. Then the little arms and legs would jerk, and the baby would heave and shudder, and just when you thought you'd better go for help he'd start breathing again.

"Is that what he is supposed to sound like?" she asked Jerry.

"What?" he asked.

"That breathing. It's his normal way of breathing?" she said.

"Yes," said Jerry.

"Is it always that loud?" she asked, thinking, That awful.

"Yes," said Jerry.

"It must be hard to listen to all the time," said Mrs. Labrette.

"I just hear when it stops," he said.

In time she learned what he meant, and when Elsie Moye told her once that she wouldn't be able to stand it if it was she who had to look after that baby, and Maggie replied, "You get used to it," she realized that she had.

They waited there by the bed, the two of them side by side until Jerry seemed to see the signs he needed to see to satisfy himself that the baby was going to rest easy.

"He'll sleep like that for a while now," said Jerry.

"I'm going to get you something to eat, child," said Mrs. Labrette.

She led him down the hall to her kitchen. She uncovered a cake stand on her counter, lifting the lid and looking at Jerry with an expectant smile. He stared back at her without a glimmer of desire or appreciation for the cake. She cut a large slice for him and poured a glass of chocolate milk and set it on her kitchen table. He lowered his head and wouldn't look at her, and he cut his eyes off to one side. He looked up and over into the high corner of the room, his lips tight with impatience. He did not move toward the table and the things she had put there for him. He seemed to want to say something, but she could not imagine what. He acted like he had been caught on a fishhook.

"What's wrong?" she asked softly, kindly.

Finally, he looked not directly at her but just over her head.

"Hain't you got a tablecloth?" he asked. "My daddy said y'all had privilege."

At first Mrs. Labrette felt vexed and affronted. Then a feeling of shame drew up her sense of charity like rainwater on silk, and she remembered how, just a few weeks before, the little boy had stood bright-eyed at the table she and the ladies had set for his mother's wake. She smiled politely at Jerry.

"Of course," she said. "How could I have forgotten?" She went straight to her linen drawer and pulled out a nice tablecloth appropriate for the kitchen table. It was white cotton printed with pink dogwood flowers and green foliage. She removed the cake and milk from the table and placed them on her counter, then holding the cloth by the corners, unfurled it over the table like a fisherman casting his net. She watched Jerry's face collapse with sleepy pleasure when he saw the fresh, crisp cloth settle onto the table exactly in place, and she saw him breathe in deeply when the scent of starch and lavender reached him. She put the food back on the cloth, set a silver dessert fork by the plate and placed a pale green napkin next to the fork. She pulled the chair back and gestured for Jerry to sit, and he did, but he made no move to eat the cake or drink the milk. He just looked carefully at the place set before him. She could see his eyes shift from the fork to the plate, back over to the napkin. Then he looked at the glass of milk above the plate on the opposite side from the napkin and fork, and from there all around the edge of the tablecloth with its garland of dogwood blossoms and green leaves, and she saw or, thought for sure she saw, regret overtake his face like the look any other child would have watching rude and thoughtless children play with toys he has never imagined existed, in a yard he knows he will never be invited to step into. And there followed a sad dawning, a revelation, as if he had discovered where something had been that he had always wanted but until now had been unable to find.

"Surely you'd like to have some cake," said Mrs. Labrette gently. She picked up the napkin, and Jerry's head snapped toward her, and his face was a mix of panic and hurt.

"Are you taking that away?" he asked.

"No, dear," said Mrs. Labrette. "But it goes in your lap, like this," she said, unfolding the napkin and holding it at her waist to show him.

"Can't I leave it where it was?" he mumbled into his chest.

"Well, yes. Certainly. Why not?" said Mrs. Labrette. She carefully refolded the napkin and put it back on the table in its proper place.

"Then I'll have me some cake," said Jerry, almost grandly. He began eating the cake, taking little morsels with the fingers of one hand and putting them carefully into his mouth. From time to time he would stop eating and look up into her eyes and smile at her with the sweetest expression she thought she had ever seen on any living thing. Then he would eat a few more pinched off pieces of the cake and take a sip of the milk, each time replacing the glass exactly back where she had set it when she set the table. He pinched and sipped until the cake and milk were gone.

Each Saturday after the first one, Mrs. Labrette had the table set with a fresh cloth before Jerry arrived for his daylong visit. And each Saturday she was able to impart to him a little more of her knowledge of how to do. It was a slow but enjoyable process for her. The Saturday immediately following the first, she was able to get him to pick up the fork and use it, and he did not balk or seem disappointed when she stopped him from putting it back on the tablecloth in its place between the napkin and the plate after every bite.

"If you want to put it down between bites before you have completely finished," she explained, "lay it curved side down about half on and half off your plate. That way the server will know that you are not finished and will not take your food away." She watched Jerry's face light up with pleasure at the thought of such an experience as being served. "Shall we practice it?" she asked. And so several times they went through the routine until he had learned exactly the right way, for her test was strict and she removed the plate if he did not put the fork in the correct position. He learned quickly and so well that once when she started to remove the plate to test him even though he had done things properly, he stopped her dead in her tracks.

"Wait! I'm ain't finished," he said desperately.

"Very good!" she said, returning his cake plate to him. "But it's 'I'm not finished,' and remember to speak calmly and pleasantly to the help." He laughed so hard at her calling herself the help that he almost fell off his chair.

The only interruption they ever had during these lessons was Jerry's little brother. He had to be checked on at what seemed the most inconvenient times, and Mrs. Labrette could see that Jerry was beginning to resent the distraction. She devised a way for them to have the baby with them at all times instead of constantly having to run back and forth, to and from the bedroom. Unaccountably, she had kept a child's rocking chair, which in a hopeful state of mind she had bought early in her marriage but had never had a use for. She got it out and determined that it could be rigged up for Jerry's little brother.

"No! No!" Jerry had shouted when she first showed him the chair and suggested they put his little brother in it. "He can't sit up in that thing by hisself."

"Himself," corrected Mrs. Labrette. She showed Jerry how it would work. She tore two long strips from a towel. She put one piece around the baby's waist and a narrower one around his forehead and ran them through the back slats of the chair and tied the baby into the rocker. It was a simple, secure solution, she told Jerry. "Like a papoose, only it rocks. Much better than one of those high chairs that you buy."

Satisfied that the chair would be safe for his little brother, Jerry consented, and by the next Saturday, Maggie had bought a pint of bright red paint and some decals of adorable little ducks and bunnies and cows and such to decorate the chair with. It was a blazing, vivid day, and there on the bright lawn of her back garden among the dusty pastels of her old-fashioned flowers, she watched as Jerry painted the chair so tidily that not a drop of red was on the newspaper underneath when he had finished. She let him decide where the decals would go. When the paint had dried and the decals were in place, Mrs. Labrette found some yellow paint.

"Now let's paint his name on the back of the chair," she said, and as she said it she realized she had never heard the child's name called. "What is his name?" she asked.

"Pa's never called him anything but 'the baby,'" said Jerry. "Pa ain't give him a name."

"Hasn't given. And that is nonsense, Jerry. Of course somebody gave him a name. Everybody gets a name," Mrs. Labrette insisted, although the unpleasant possibility that Jerry was right tapped insistently on her mind.

"Pa said we won't going to name him because it was more than a good chance the baby would never live to know its name, so why take up a name just to have to bury it with the baby before anybody's had any good reason to use it on him, was what Pa said," said Jerry flatly.

Maggie stood speechless before the pathetic baby in the red rocker. She tried her best not to show how shocked she was by Mr. Chiffon's callousness concerning his deformed child. But this would not do. This would not stay this way.

"Jerry, a name isn't like a piece of cake or a toy or even a person. It does not get worn out with use," said Mrs. Labrette impatiently.

"I know that," Jerry replied irritably. "I never said I didn't want him to have a name. It is Pa who won't give him a name. Pa don't name nothing. Not the hogs or cows. We got a dog hangs around the house with no name at all, but it'll come when Pa makes a certain noise, and it runs off under the house and shakes when Pa makes a different kind of noise."

"Anything, dear. Doesn't name anything." Then a startled, worried expression came over Mrs. Labrette's face. "Does your father call you by your name?" she asked.

"Well, sure, it was Ma who named me, I think," said Jerry. "She would have named the baby, too."

The logic impressed Maggie.

"Jerry, we are going to name your brother," she said bluntly. "Have you any preferences?"

She watched Jerry's face brighten, then dim as doubt overtook him.

"Its all right, sweetheart, anything you want. Then we'll have something to paint on the chair," she said.

"Labrette," whispered Jerry into his chest.

"What, dear? Darling, lift your head and tell me what name you want, loud and clear," Maggie said.

"Labrette," Jerry chirped. "Labrette Chiffon is what I think he ought to be called."

Maggie's hand flew to her mouth, and when after some time she tried to speak, nothing would come out for another long time. It was a beautiful name, she thought, lovely to hear on its own and nearly unbearably so when she also considered that Jerry, young as he was, had simply in a name managed to honor her and his pitiful little brother and to treat himself with something he would love to say.

"It is a beautiful name, Jerry," she said.

"I know," Jerry replied, in what Maggie thought was an almost impudent tone, which jolted her a little. It made her begin to wonder and worry over what was about to take place. Could this be right? Was it, after all, appropriate, as sweet and flattering as it was, to allow Jerry to name the baby Labrette? Did she really want that little helpless and hopeless idiot with her name? She imagined hearing him called Labrette outside of her house, uptown on Main Street, for example. What confusion might ensue? What kinship mistakenly assumed? She thought it would not sound so good out in the open. And what would Lyman say? After all, it was Lyman's name Jerry had taken for his little brother when it came right down to it. She was not sure she even had the authority to allow the name to be used, and with that thought she began to consider all the reasons not to name the baby Labrette, and a feeling of panic, as if she had broken a law, came over her. Could some of Lyman's people sue her? It was complicated. And she certainly didn't want a stranger or someone who might be new in Branch Creek to ever for one minute think that the child was actually related to her.

Jerry had already opened the yellow paint and was stirring it with the small brush she had given him. She watched him lift the brush from the paint, holding it over the can as a yellow thread fell from its bristles, coiling on then disappearing into the surface of the paint. He dabbed the brush on the rim of the can, and when he had unloaded enough of the paint from the brush, he moved it toward the top slat of the chair.

"Just a minute," Maggie said. "We better give the red a day to dry."

The red paint cured hard as enamel. The yellow, she closed up and put on a high shelf of her garden shed where it sat until it dried out and was discarded. No name was ever painted on the chair and although she had a strong suspicion that in Jerry's mind the baby's name was and would ever be Labrette, he continued to be called "the baby" by anybody who had a reason to call him anything. The little rocker, which everyone involved quickly regarded as indispensable for looking after the baby, was most often referred to as "the baby's chair," but sometimes in the hurry and urgency that the child's needs could often cause, it was called simply "the chair."

When the baby got fussy, she or Jerry would absent-mindedly set the little chair to rocking with a foot and go on with whatever they were doing, and soon Jerry was taking the chair with him from her house to his and back every Saturday.

Mrs. Labrette admitted to herself, and would have to anyone else if they had asked, that she suspected she enjoyed Jerry's visits more than he did. Lyman called Jerry her little playmate.

"Your little playmate's here," he'd call to her if she was not at the front door when Jerry arrived. Then he'd leave, very accommodatingly, she thought, to view again his farmland and to attend to his many commissions.

She would feed Jerry and get the baby settled and fed, then she would begin. "Now suppose we were dining in the

Governor's Mansion," she might say, and they could make a day's worth of fun and instruction out of that.

She simply did not believe that the little boy who had so readily learned good manners and right ideals from her, the young man she could take some credit for rearing, nor the grown man she admired and respected and who had overcome so much could be who they were talking about on the television. There was, of course, some mistake, some big mistake at the core of all this. She would find it out, and fix it. She had some influence beyond the limits of Branch Creek. There were people in Raleigh of some importance who held her in high regard. She would tend to this mess without delay. She went to the hall and telephoned somebody she knew in the Governor's office and told him to make whatever arrangements would be necessary for her to see Jerry in the jail. Then she hung up and called to Lyman, who was on the porch.

"You've got to take me to Raleigh," she said.

"Jesus!" spurted Lyman. "Raleigh?"

She went to the screen door and stood but did not come out onto the porch.

"Yes, Lyman. Raleigh," Maggie insisted, "not the moon, Raleigh." And although she could hear him mumbling disagreeably the entire time, she waited patiently there just inside the hall until he had readied the Cadillac for the trip, backed it up from the garage to the front of the house and, as always, got out, went around the car, opened the door for her and stood waiting. Soon they were on their way to the capital city and in a little less than two hours from when they left Branch Creek they pulled up to the side entrance of the Wake County Courthouse.

As Lyman was helping her out of the car, Maggie remarked that this was the first time she had ever had cause to visit a jail.

"I don't know how I ought to behave," she said more to herself than to Lyman. Nothing had prepared her for such a visit, and she couldn't remember a single verse out of the Bible that had to do with prisons and how to be in one or that dealt with prisoners and how to treat them. That, of course, did not mean there was no such verse. So with the idea of Christ in general swirling in her mind as her guide and model, she entered the building, sure that her own good-will and her large purpose would be evident to any and all with whom she might have to deal.

Immediately upon entering the jail, she saw what looked like a boy dressed up in a police uniform sitting behind a metal desk.

"I'm Mrs. Lyman L. Labrette, and I'm here to see Mr. Jerry Chiffon, a prisoner in your jail," she said to him as matter-of-factly as she could, considering she had never uttered such a sentence in her life.

The boy policeman asked to look through her purse.

"Certainly not!" she replied.

There was no door beyond the boy, but there was an open hall, so she started toward where it was obvious the cells were. She could not believe the impertinence.

"I'll wait here for you," she heard Lyman say behind her. A grown policeman came out of an office off the hall, smiling and offering his hand.

"Mrs. Labrette, come right this way," he said. It was clear to her he had gotten a call from higher up.

She had not expected such bright light in the jail. Her idea of what a jail would be like included darkness and dampness, creeping black mold and scurrying rodents. But this was nothing like what she had imagined. Although barred, the windows where clean and uncovered. Over the aisle between the cells, barred skylights checkered the shiny gray floor with bright sunlight. You could have done medical things in such light, she thought, or grow roses. She made her way past the cells, accompanied now by the deferential officer who, to his credit, had figured out that she was a woman of astronomical reliability and everlasting quality whose purse was not to be questioned. Smiling kindly, holding doors, allowing her to pass first through any threshold, he treated her the way she was used to being treated. She would remember him, get his name if she could—discover some tie of kinship, birthplace or religion, if possible, and reward him in a way that would cause him to be kind to Jerry. She did not usually have to poke around too deeply into someone's past, present or future to establish some link, some commonality. However loose the tie, she could snug it up.

They passed through a door to more cells. Here, along with the natural light streaming in from outside, enormous electrical lights, brighter than any day, shone into every part of the jail. This light was malevolent and accusing, something used to control and punish rather than reveal truth. This was the light of suspicion, and its mercilessness inclined her to believe that every person in that jail was innocent. What a terrible place it was, she thought, even more awful for its cleanliness and luminosity.

Nearly every cell had a Negro man in it. Caged and wild for it, exhausted by rage, they looked up as she passed, and glared like trapped bobcats. The few white prisoners, slumped over in metal chairs, seemed drugged with boredom and resignation. Some, completely vanquished, lay motionless on their bunks, faces to the wall. It nearly broke her heart to see men like this. How little progress has been made, she thought as she walked loftily past the men. She could never understand how this could happen—why some people elicited, at best, neglect and, in the worst cases, bad luck and centuries of persecution.

She thought of when she was a little girl and could not be made to understand why her father required that tradesmen and Negroes conduct business with him at the back door. She had asked him about it and argued with his explanations, and he had changed because of her. Out of love for her and a wish not to see her unhappy in any way, he had changed a custom older than the house itself.

"Come 'round to the porch," he would say from then on to anyone who appeared at the back of the house with a hand out or a plea on his lips. And Maggie had almost lost the pity that had fueled the reform when she saw that all the supplicants honored so at her family's front door chose to remain on the sidewalk below her father or mother, who stood up above on the front porch as though they had descended from an even higher place. Some would not even look up, but made their entreaties to the ground. Why could they not hold their heads up, climb the front steps to the door and greet her father respectfully and be greeted hospitably? Holding her in his lap, her father had explained the way things were—an unraveling of the mysterious relations between black and white, well-off and poor in Branch Creek. With his mouth to her ear, he shared with her in a tender, humid whisper, a secret so intimately told that he made her believe he had kept it to himself before trusting her with it.

"You see, sweetheart, it is to spare them that the back door is used for such encounters," he said. And she immediately understood when he put it that way, for how could you ever rid the needy of their neediness or expect them to rid themselves of the shame that went with it? And hadn't she been almost cruel not to realize this? How could she have required that they display to the street, in full view of anyone who passed or lived nearby, their pitiable circumstances? The faces in the jail were so like the ones she had seen at the back door of her father's house all her life. How little things had changed, she thought.

"We seemed to be determined to imprison these people one way or the other," she muttered, and her heart filled up with the same mixture of pride and sadness that it always did when she understood the sour truths others seemed unable to grasp.

She followed the officer down the corridor. Some of the prisoners stood when she passed their cells. A few bowed at the waist. One smiled timidly and waved. She did not acknowledge the prisoners and their courtliness. It embarrassed her, and when she bored deeply into the matter, she had to admit that such deference irked her.

"Hey, Duchess." She turned her head to see a man exposing himself. Here, even shame had been taken away from some. But if the prisoner had intended to shock or embarrass or frighten her, he would not get what he wanted. She had seen nakedness and more with Parchman Anderson. She had stood by as Parchman prodded and poked people in every kind of undress. She had watched him lance and inject both men and women in places not to be mentioned. What that prisoner had done was just a display of petulance and boredom and an uninteresting sense of humor as well. She stared the man straight in the eye and nodded as though he had tipped his hat instead of opened his pants. With that, the prisoner in the opposite cell exposed himself, and down the line of cells as she passed, the next prisoner having seen the one before do it, displayed his genitals. What looked to her like a teenage boy, too young to be in such a jail, bent over and wedged one of the metal bars between his buttocks.

The officer banged on the bars of the nearest cell and shouted filthy threats to the prisoners that Maggie knew she would not repeat when she would have to tell Elsie Moye and her friends about this. Order was restored, and the officer apologized to Maggie for what she was having to see.

"I had expected such as this," Maggie said. "I'm not surprised."

Up ahead, she could see Jerry, sitting on the cot in his cell, and what she saw did surprise her. Even dressed in women's clothes, he did not look out of place. Much as she held Jerry in high esteem, even loved him, she couldn't help thinking that he must have done something to wind up in such a place. Her heart felt hard and broken at the same time. She walked toward him with tears in her eyes.

Jerry looked around the cell for some place to hide from Maggie Labrette, but there was none. He dreaded her unblinking acceptance of him worse than her disapproval, worse than if she had shown open disappointment by word or deed, gesture or expression. Above all, he did not want her to see him in a dress. But he could not avoid her, so he sat down on the edge of the cot and waited. He would have to brazen it out.

Unlike other affections he had sorted through and connections that had been eliminated, his ties to Maggie would not be broken easily. She would understand why he had done as he had, or pretend to. She would refuse to pass judgment. As always, her ears would not hear Jerry condemned by others—never had and never would—and he knew in the years since he had returned from New York there had been rumors that she had heard and refused to believe, most not true and, in the end, harmless. They had grown even closer, had come to be thought of as a pair, thought of themselves that way, exclusive and almost conspiratorial, like two people in on a joke that no one else gets. As hard as some might try to get one to betray the other, or spread a rumor or just to express in the sweetest way possible a flaw in the other, neither ever had, and now he'd have to hate her for all that—for trying to be so good and expecting it of him. He did not have the time or energy for such as she. Nor did he want her love. He had learned it was often easier to be loathed than loved, and he'd learned, too, that he'd rather be harshly judged than pitied. He had come to appreciate how beneficial it is to give up being even liked. He had left Branch Creek not so much to gain that weapon, but he had gotten it. He did not now look to Mrs. Lyman L. Labrette with her unbearable goodwill, her sense of Christian duty and noblesse oblige to remind him of a code of behavior that was unattainable. The simple fact that it had been held up as the ideal for as long as it had and that she was the only person he knew who even tried to live up to it was proof enough for him that it was an undesirable achievement. In the intervening few years between leaving his home town and returning, he had loved, been loved, lost love and all need to be loved. He had barbed his hide and sharpened his tongue and gorged on what resembled love. Now, like an expensive suit out of style but too good for the needy, he stored his ill-fitting feelings away in a dark dry place. He had lived in New York City where whether you were loved or not seemed to be neither an asset nor a comfort. It was certainly no liability. He had been born into a remote corner of the Kingdom of the Unloved and had moved to its capital and lived there long enough to learn its arcana, to put on its unbending and archly chic conventions. He had gotten along fine—flourished often.

Of course, here in a jail, not free to roam and with Maggie Labrette bearing down on him, it was amusing to form in his mind complicated and twisted explanations for how he had become so drop-dead he could flick love from his heart as though it were lint on cashmere. Droll, too, to think that she who had thought to make him good had only showed him that you could change yourself. How and to what purposes were more infinite than her mind could wrap itself around. He could indulge himself in emotions for which she who was coming to help him had not the adventurous heart—think in ways she was not smart enough to understand.

This discovery in his nature of what he had been told was irony and its imbuement into his thinking and outlook had at first seemed involuntary, unintentional and unfortunate, even lonely and morbid at times. It had happened in the North, a place full of Northerners who all seemed to aspire to that condition of junglelike common sense, which holds that there is nothing to gain from trying to love what you don't. It was a place where it was better to be feared than loved, as the saying goes. The realm in which self-involvement equals self-preservation—the North full of Northerners who don't pretend you are interesting if you aren't. Chilled and chilly people who have little time for that kind of courtesy, no time for languorous goodwill, yet who in their rush and shiver seem to have all the time in the world for themselves. They even age more slowly than people in slow places like Branch Creek. He'd known people whose self-indulgence and acquired unpleasantness had been their success in New York. He had even spoiled himself a little among the spoiled. He had found out firsthand and had it confirmed by observation of others that no one can be as spoiled as one who has had nothing—has come from nothing. What do you want? Everything you've never had. What do you deserve? Not what you deserve. These kinds of desires cannot be listed. They are ever-dividing cells, malignant and untreatable. He'd found that out, seen it in people and watched them happily let the cancer grow unchecked. It was the least serious of the many sins he'd witnessed and hosted.

True, he had often worried that he was being ignored rather than feared. His way to New York had been guided by a wish, then a will, for anonymity. Then when he got there and saw how easy it was to disappear, his conduct changed to life-sucking self-absorption fashioned by bits of faulty wisdom and easy aphorisms, which could be picked out of the sooty air of that unsophisticatedly suspicious city: "Rule in heaven rather than serve in hell"; "The squeaky wheel gets the oil"; "Revenge on a cold platter"—that sort of not-thinking. The steady stare, the silence meant to costume ignorance as wily intelligence. There, he'd learned a lot of easy but valuable lessons, which had proved useful elsewhere. There, he had hope taken away.

Would he keep all this to himself and use what he had learned on Maggie Labrette when she got to him, which would be in the next few seconds? He had to think quickly, and he did, because all thinking is quick. He'd said that once, among some very smart people in New York. It had hushed the room for about four seconds, which was long enough for what he had said to become what he believed.

He would tell her more this time, more than he had ever told her before, the whole story, not just the parts he had always limited himself to when they happily discussed his time in New York and how it had broadened his outlook and polished his tastes and manners, all the selected details that had always made sense to her and confirmed her faith and belief in him and had satisfied her need to see him as surmounting all the conditions of his birth and upbringing. It would be the truth this time, and he would do this not in an effort to be understood or forgiven or helped, but to be abandoned—to sever the ties to his old tribe, to find the limits of her love, to prove the faults of her philosophy.

She arrived at the door to his cell in as near a state of perfection as he had ever seen her. She wore an outfit she might have gone to church in on a Sunday of no particular importance. The dress was navy with short capped sleeves.

It whispered expense but screamed quality. Nice beige piping around the sleeves and collar, a flat bow at the waistline the same navy color, so discreet you might have thought you were seeing something that was not there, a ghost of a bow. Also just at the waist, the fabric had been gently gathered and sewn by hand, which gave a kind of lushness to the dress without causing the merest waver down the skirt to the hem. The effect was not one of vain and costly embellishment meant to impress, but one of pride in craft. She wore beige gloves with navy buttons, short enough to show her wrist bones, which had a youthening effect, Jerry thought, and her shoes were beige-and-navy spectators. Her hair had been done, but not so recently that it still had that fixed look; rather, its arrangement gave the impression that she was blessed with hair that she herself cared for in a simple and straightforward way, her concern being more for hygiene than beauty. It was self-presentation so decorous, so prudently chic that it wasn't a presentation at all but more of a symbolic representation of a lady. She could have gone anywhere and elicited quiet admiration from women, been the cause and object of men's pride, drawn rather than repelled children and yet produced not a wisp of envy in anyone. Jerry hated her right then. If he'd been done up like that, he could have blown the Senator from the Capitol steps and walked off free as air. That turn-out and better aim, he thought, and he wouldn't be here in this jail in fake Chanel half-drag.

He watched Maggie take in the fact that he was wearing a dress. Saw her unflinching, examining eyes sweep the entire length of him and everything he was wearing, and he was not surprised that a look of disapproval was absent from her face. What showed was that she saw there was a problem. Her solution was direct.

"Get him something else to wear right away," she said

to the guard, who seemed so eager to do as she instructed that if he had saluted her it would not have surprised Jerry. She turned and, with simple hauteur, consented to be led away to another place, confident that her wishes would be carried out. A uniform was brought. The officer told Jerry to change into it and gave him a big paper sack in which to put the clothes he had been wearing when he was arrested. Then he was taken to where Maggie was, and the officer gave her the paper sack. It reminded her of how at a funeral home they return the clothes the loved one died in to the next of kin after they've stripped and embalmed and dressed up the body. Maggie had a quiet conversation with the officer, which Jerry could not hear but which looked more as though she were giving instructions than making requests, and then the two of them, prisoner and lady, were taken to a room, lit from above like an aquarium, glassed in and furnished with a table and two green plastic chairs where they could talk and be observed, like fish.

"Did you do what they are saying?" Mrs. Labrette asked Jerry, and all the years since he was a little boy at her kitchen table seemed not to have happened. There could have been linen and flowers and silver and her best china laid out between them. She used the same inquisitory method she had always used when he was a child.

"No," he replied, "but I was trying to."

"Why, Jerry?" she asked, again in the way of an adult drawing reason from a child not yet familiar with it. There were a thousand answers to that question, but Jerry decided to give the simple one.

"I had to end some way," he said.

It began like this, with Jerry arriving in New York City for the first time by train, a journey of pure anticipation most rewarding just before the end, when a tantalizing, glamour-quenching view of Manhattan is finally offered to the traveler.

It was a floating cathedral more than an island, he thought, highest at the portal, as if when the money changers were thrown out the door the once-faithful had forsaken the old religion and followed them, building twin towers to glorify a new holy place over an altar built to celebrate a bigger and more believable church founded on dollars and success. Like any great cathedral, one tower was unfinished, and Jerry was enchanted for a moment with the idea that it would remain so for all of his life. That he would have to live and die, like so many medieval men had done, sustained by nothing more concrete than the idea that the never-completed edifice was meant to represent. In the middle of the cathedral city, the Empire State Building rose up, aspiring as a steeple. Then space in the air, then more buildings urging themselves toward the same heights as their betters, and the whole thing drifting against the current of the river he could see and the one he could not but knew was there from the maps he had stared down into like Narcissus at his pool. But the journey had been to a mirage, for in sight of his destination the train hid city, river and all behind the high, dull bluffs of New Jersey, then, as if to correct the belief that you can have your heart's desire, darted underground and took it all away. When finally the train brought him out of darkness, it was into the artificial light of the city's underside. It was as if they had pulled into the crypt of the cathedral, but it was a place more alive than the busiest street in any other town. This was his first and only city then, and he knew right away even before he had seen anything but a small portion of its insides that he could never love another as much—that all others would be facsimiles, approximations, manqués, pale imitations and absolute failures. All the others would be towns compared to New York. And he knew this before he had even come up into what was misleadingly called the Pennsylvania Station—before he had stepped onto the streets outside. If this was the working part deemed not fit to see, what stupefying marvels were above?

It was the year the country turned two hundred, when he took his first steps onto those reliably uncooperative streets. And after he had made his way off the platform and up the stairs, then up escalators moving so fast it took the skill of a log roller to step onto them, then into the round confusion of the station, up more moving stairs and into the sunlight, which, reflecting off chrome and steel and glass and limestone, was the eerie, stubborn light of a partial eclipse, the tough light that got through to shine on the tough, his first impression was of walking into a performance in full progress. It was a production about a bustling city street, well into the opening number, and like good actors, the participants were performing full out, indifferent to the fact that he had arrived late.

"You wanna go out?" he heard a buzz saw of a voice ask him. He turned and saw what was clearly a streetwalker standing by the revolving door of the station. "You got any money? You wanna go out?" It was everything he had hoped his first contact with a New Yorker would be—direct and assuming that he was, too. He felt so included. Like that, he was in the play.

"Oh, no," he replied, "but could you tell me how to get to Sheridan Square?"

"I sell pussy. I ain't a directory," she said.

He wished he wanted her. She looked him up and down as though it had been he who had asked if she had money and wanted to go out.

"Sheridan Square? I'm losing my touch," she said, her voice instantly changing from the high-pitched, streetwalker dumb-but-tough tone in which she had first spoken to him, to one that was well modulated and indicated intelligence. "Number 1, IRT, downtown." She turned to face the wall she had been leaning against, pulled up the front of her tight skirt, tucked the hem into the waistband and urinated against the building. Jerry was impressed. He had seen men trying to pass as women before and had always thought he could spot one a mile away. The too-prominent brow or the coarse hair at the nape of the neck never fooled him, however artful the makeup or hairdo. This was intentional, meant to display amusing incongruities and to shock, for she could have hidden her true gender, but had, for him, at least at that moment, chosen not to—and in a very direct way. He somehow felt welcomed by her nonchalant toilet habits, as much so as if a committee had appeared with banners and a wreath.

He was headed toward a place to live for which he had arranged without having seen it. He had gotten to know some actors in Raleigh who were appearing in a dinner theater out by the airport, where he had in no time at all advanced from waiter to costume designer. One of them had sort of fallen in love with him, he thought, and invited him to come up and live with him and his friend, a woman—a real one, he believed—who was a singer variously named Davina Inc, Invina Dink or Ulga Gustafsen.

"What name she goes by all depends on the vibes or the stars or something on a particular day, unless she is going back again to audition at a club where she didn't get the job," the actor had explained. "She keeps a record of what name she has auditioned where with." It had all come together, this love affair, and Mrs. Beamon's wish to help nurture his nature, which would most probably be accomplished best, everyone agreed, in a place like New York. It had all seemed to point to the hand of fate.

The drag queen's directions may as well have been given in a mathematical language. Jerry understood nothing of the string of letters and numbers meant to convey to him how to get where he was going. He'd seen the colorful streamers on the map of Manhattan that were the routes of the subway system, and they had seemed to imply that it was the easiest thing in the world, a child's game, to get where you wanted to go in the city. He had almost expected that the same bright lines would be painted on the sidewalk, but there was nothing underfoot to tell him where to begin. No sign outlined in electric lights flashing Subway, Subway, with lit arrows strobing down a hole in the sidewalk. He walked in one direction a few feet, turned, and retraced his steps and went a few feet in the opposite direction and then returned to the spot on which he had been standing when the drag queen tried to sell him a date.

"The best place to start is usually the beginning," he heard the drag queen say in a perfect imitation of Billie Burke as Glinda the Good. "Just follow the crack of my ass. I live in that part of town, and I'm going home! It's bullshit here today. Gay boys and grandmas. Is it Wednesday?"

"Yes," said Jerry.

"Matinee day! No wonder," said the drag queen. She turned her back to him, and flapping her hand by her head to indicate forward motion, she gestured for Jerry to follow.

"This is so nice of you," said Jerry as she started off ahead of him down the street He hurriedly picked up his suitcase and slung the shoulder bag across his chest. It was a struggle to keep up with her.

"How long are you staying?" she asked.

Jerry had not thought that far ahead when he had been lured there by the dark, curly-haired actor who knew what he was doing when it came to enticing country boys to the city. Jerry had not known that two boys could do the things they had done. Part of the reason he had decided to come was to see what else was possible. For although he had not been specific, the actor had said there was a lot he didn't do. And now with the city all around him in full swing, Jerry had a sense of having come for more than that even. It seemed the happiest place he could ever imagine—every car horn a fanfare celebrating his arrival.

"Forever," he said.

"Traveling light for such a long stay," she said. "It is chic to travel light, you know. In your case it implies natural style."

"Really?" said Jerry. She could not have said anything that he would have wanted to hear more than that. Here less than thirty minutes and declared stylish by a native. "How do you know?"

"Honey, no one is more acutely aware of what is stylish and what is not than a drag queen. We of all people must know exactly, in every detail, to what we aspire. To achieve what effect it is that we alter, nay, defy nature." She took a red rhinestone-encrusted compact and a wide-toothed comb out of her shoulder bag and, looking coldly at herself, without vanity, tended to her thick blond, very beautiful and, Jerry was pretty sure, real hair. "The tragedy of a drag queen is that she knows what a dismal waste feminine style is on a real woman. How much more advantage she could take of what God gives natural women. How easy to be fabulous and to what dazzling effects but for hormones and plumbing. Why were women banned from the stage in Shakespeare's theater and even today in the Kabuki? Modesty? Preservation of feminine purity? No! Bad acting, sweetie. A woman doesn't know how to play a woman."

She closed her compact with one hand and, even while holding the comb in the other, was able to snap her fingers to emphasize her point. "Don't you agree to that? Surely you must."

"No," Jerry replied. "It doesn't stand up to reason. By your logic, a man shouldn't be able to play a man—or a child, a child—or a dog, a dog."

"But you ignore one thing, my little disagreeable friend. Men and dogs and children are not generally reviled for what they are. Throughout history, women have been despised simply for being women. I suppose it is jealousy mostly. Something to do with having total control over whether we all go on as a species probably, but it is an undeniable fact! I have been much more despised as a woman than when I went around as just your garden-variety homosexual. Even regular queens don't like drags. I think it is like the prejudice light-skinned blacks have against dark-skinned ones. I'm an extreme version of what they are. I don't do this for a living, dear. It is a sociological study, an experiment in gender identification. Anyway, we are way off the subject, and the real skinny, dear, about traveling light being chic? I read it in a *Vogue* magazine I got out of the trash can. But I recognized the truth of it. You see, there is youthful insouciance in traveling unencumbered, although now that I take a second look, that suitcase is rather weighing you down, and the way that strap distorts the drape of your shirt suggests a kind of harried arrival and a complete lack of a sense of comme il faut. No, I was wrong, for you see one would have to *know* you were staying forever to think that you were traveling light. It is relative, like so much, alas."

There was something underneath the disguise, Jerry thought, which was much more sophisticated, more intelligent than what he would have expected. This person was slumming somehow, or experimenting with some unsuitable way of life—on some sort of spree. She chattered on like this as they descended into the subway and stood on the platform, hot as a curing barn, waiting for the train. She leaned out over the platform often, looking down the dark tunnel to see if the train was coming.

"Before it pulls into the station, darling, do step back away from the edge. Meanie Meanies will push you right onto the tracks for sport." Jerry was grateful but not surprised at being cared for by a stranger. He was as acquainted with instant and undeserved kindness as he was with unpredictable, unremitting cruelty. He'd lived on both, and he knew when he had a friend.

Jerry arrived in Greenwich Village at a time when the highest ambitions of most of its inhabitants were sexual. Although it was early afternoon when he and the drag queen climbed up out of the Christopher Street station into Sheridan Square, from there and radiating out in all directions, that whole part of town seemed as clearly to be displaying its main attraction, which was men and boys and sex, as had the Pennsylvania Station been a place of trains and arrivals and departures, or he imagined, the Theater District emanated bright lights and grease paint and the glamour of wit and intelligence. As they made their way down Christopher Street, Jerry stayed close to the side of his new friend, who claimed the street like a parade. Men lurked in doorways dressed head to toe in leather, which, to Jerry, in broad daylight looked as out of place as if they had been dressed in sequins. Through open doors he could see other men in dark bars, packed in as though those places were the last breath, morsel and swig of whatever was essential for life. The electronic throb of a beat underneath the forced laughter and low gurgle of the crowd implied lust more than music. And all of it as dark and exclusive as guilt—closed off to anyone who couldn't dare and then take the consequences. Would what went on among this apparently leisure class of deviants be what the actor who had almost made him faint with pleasure have been talking about as that which he didn't do? Jerry was thinking that he could never go into a place like that, fearful of unspeakable things happening to him, bloodletting and worse, torture involving knives and probably fire and all so sinful, so depraved and, of course, ultimately so addictive that it resulted finally in his destruction. Then there would be a futile search, the trail of which would be the sordid recollections of those who had come in contact with him before he had vanished. His body would not be found. At last, for everybody in Branch Creek would come embarrassing acknowledgment and forever, fevered whisperings of his unimaginably humiliating suffering and annihilation.

"Hold on a minute, darling," said the drag queen. "We need to duck in here for a moment."

Jerry saw a look of irritation on her face, which told him that she had read fear on his and had no patience with it.

"Please! It's just a bunch of Marys exchanging brownie recipes and tweaking each other's tits for 'not coming to my brunch last Sunday,'" she lisped. "I won't let anybody hurt you unless you want them to, precious." She gave him a look which shattered false prudery. But he was not being coy. He was afraid.

"I'll wait here," he said, putting his baggage down on the sidewalk.

"As you wish, dear," she said, and disappeared inside.

Jerry looked into the gloomy bar and saw the crowd both part for, yet flamboyantly ignore, his new friend as she made her way through the room. Her presence was unappreciated and did nothing to cause a lull in the morbid, naughty fun going on among the men.

She was in the bar for a long time, and Jerry waited outside, embarrassed by the amused smiles on the faces of the men who passed and saw his belongings at his feet. A trio of large muscular men dressed like construction workers passed by. In Branch Creek no one would have taken them for anything but normal. One of them, to entertain his friends more than acknowledge Jerry's existence, said, "Hey, sugar, don't you want to unpack first?"

When the drag queen came out, she had reapplied her makeup and had spent considerable time on her hair. She looked pretty.

"You wouldn't think so, but they have the nicest bathrooms in a place like that. They're so demanding when it comes to *les toilettes* unless they are going to do the dreaded deed in one, then the more revolting the better," she said.

"You look nice," Jerry said.

"How sweet. Now, we shall find your new quarters."

They walked to a street called Hudson and headed downtown for a few blocks. They passed a lovely old church that would not have been out of place in an English village. Across from the church was a school, and at the corner a line of what looked to be first-graders stood behind their teacher.

"Look out for the dog shit," said the teacher as she stepped off the curb into the street to cross. Each child passed her exact words back to the classmate next in line as they walked out into the intersection, confident as grown people. He was in a place where a lot of what he knew was of no use, where much of what he expected didn't happen and where what happened he didn't see coming—a town where only innocence and earnestness could shock, a city fogged in with irony, evidence of which was always at hand, those filthy-talking children in the shadow of that quaint church, for example, which in turn was at the center of what seemed to be a neighborhood of independently wealthy perverts. How good it is not to be the only odd one, he thought. But even odd people are wary of any oddities but their own, and Jerry didn't miss the suspicious glances in his direction, nor did he fail to notice outright disdain on the faces of many he walked among.

The drag queen led the way, tossing her deluge of hair or exclaiming loudly over something in a shop window or whenever she felt she was not being noticed enough—commenting acidly on something a real woman was wearing. And although people looked at Jerry, they did so without any threat, which he knew was an essential difference between this place and any other place he had been. To bore, to judge, to maintain unswerving notions seemed more likely to get you a bloody nose. Stay out of the way and be interesting was what was tersely implied by the hurry and purpose all around.

The drag queen had stopped in front of a yellow brick building that would have been condemned in Raleigh. There was a liquor store on the street level, dark and dingy inside with faded advertisements for liquid cheer and a poinsettia plant from a Christmas long past in need of repotting and a dose of fertilizer, its leaves pressed against the glass as though in the middle of trying to escape it had been smashed like an insect.

"*Merde* and shit as well, six floors, no elevator!" moaned the drag queen.

She rang the buzzer more than once before a voice that Jerry recognized as the actor's came over the intercom.

"Yes?"

The drag queen gestured to Jerry. "Speak, dear."

"I'm here," said Jerry happily.

"Who?"

"Jerry."

"Fuck! Wait there," said the voice.

"That's exactly what we'll be doing in a few minutes," said Jerry to the drag queen.

"I think you didn't catch his tone, dear," she said.

They waited together in front of the building. Through the glass doors they could hear the sound of the actor running down the six flights of stairs. Jerry clapped his eyes on the landing and did not take them off until he saw the actor appear with a rueful, apologetic smile on his face. He came out onto the street, looking flushed. His hair, a black hurricane, needed combing. He was altogether unkempt and caught off guard by Jerry's arrival.

"We got a problem," he said.

There followed excuses and explanations and whinings about the precipitous nature of love, and *Who thought you'd really show up? Besides I just met him last night* and *You were already on your way* and *How could it have worked out between us?* Then, the brush-off. *I mean you're really not New York City, are you?*

And next the outright cruelty of *You were just the best there was available at the time* and finally, *Look, I have to go now.*

"Had I seen him in advance, I could have predicted your disgrace, my dear," the drag queen drawled as they waited at the bus stop on the opposite corner from the building where Jerry would not be living. "Irresponsible heartbreaker. He may as well have it tattooed across his forehead. I know the type, have been more than acquainted with such as he myself. And of course, you fell for it. You really have had the most blatant and subduing kiss-off, have you not?"

Jerry did not answer, but looked up at each window and wondered behind which he would have been if he had just left Raleigh a day earlier. He wondered what was going on there now.

"We interrupted them, you know. I mean, he fairly reeked of it. We caught them in the middle of about the third go, I expect! And you, down on the street with your little belongings, so full of hope while your supposed beloved was probably halfway into your usurper when we rang the bell," said the drag queen, flipping her slender manicured hands into the air above her head.

The bus stopped, and she got on. Jerry followed, noisily dragging his suitcase up the steps.

"What humiliation for you. How foolish you must feel," she said, as though no one was on the bus but the two of them.

"Ah, jeez," said the bus driver, and Jerry went warm with worry and embarrassment.

"How wonderful is the accommodating nature of New York's public servants," the drag queen announced. Jerry wanted to climb into the suitcase and die there.

"Give me a break!" said the bus driver. He closed the door and, with a disgusted snort, pulled off before Jerry could sit. Jerry staggered loose from his suitcase, and it fell over against him and nearly knocked him down. No one tried to help. Everyone just looked annoyed or looked away.

"East, man, and no more from you," the drag queen ordered the bus driver. "To the east, away from the scene of this poor boy's mortification."

"Jeez," said the bus driver.

All the way across town the drag queen tells and retells what has happened to Jerry so far that day. When someone new gets on the bus, she does not start the story over. It is a running narrative that starts again as soon as it ends and can be enjoyed without knowing its beginning, like the plot of a soap opera, and each new passenger picks it up or pretends to because it appears to Jerry that they fear the drag queen or think she is crazy and therefore to be indulged for the time they are in her presence lest a worse display be provoked. All of New York knows apparently what just a few in North Carolina have learned the hard way—that drag queens have short fuses and you'd best not antagonize one if you can avoid it.

"Think of it! All the way from the land of snake-handling, clay-eating and cousin-marrying. All by himself on a train! The loneliest place on earth," she says to some cautious but clearly interested old lady, who tightens the grip on her tote bag, but lowers her chin and cocks her head in such a way that it is clear she is trapped in what she is hearing.

"His first trip away from *Le Sud*, I'd say, wouldn't you?" The drag queen pauses and presents the evidence with a gesture that begins at Jerry's head and sweeps down to include the cumbersome luggage. "Certainly his first train ride. Carrying all his pathetic little belongings," she said with a sad, stagily sympathetic smile. "Coming to a place he has never seen, has only read of, perhaps. A place he has longed for over pictures in a book. Leaving home and safety, lured away by an imagined invitation not really extended, only alluded to during or after some meaningless yet by all reports ornate sex." By then, the listeners are spellbound, those who have heard the tale watching the faces of those who have not for the same signs of wonder.

"I find him lost, wandering pathetically around Penn Station, this close from falling into the clutches of the sex merchants," she says, narrowing the distance between good and bad fortune with her thumb and forefinger.

Two handsome men in expensive suits get on the bus.

One is carrying a big folder tied with black silk ribbon, and the other, an enormous shopping bag running over with chintzes and silks and tassels. Jerry looks out the window to see where men like this might be found again. It seems to Jerry that he is the first thing the men notice when they get on the bus. But they do not look disapprovingly at him the way the other passengers have done. They smile purposefully and keep looking even after they sit. It is a welcoming smile as much in their eyes as on their lips, full of merry intimacy, as though a somewhat racy, difficult-to-get joke had been shared. It is oddly reassuring, familiar almost, and homey like the smell of leaves burning or the clink and clatter of a table being set for supper. The handsome smiling faces for Jerry, frightened and unsure, are signs that he belongs in New York. He looks back at the men, studies their clothes, their hair, the relaxed assurance with which they stare at him, and, as has been his making in life so far, clicks a mental picture he will have for reference if needed. An unaccountably calm feeling comes over him, and he asks himself why, and a thought with a voice speaks in his head.

The comforts of home, it says, and he wants to know if he is feeling what he has imagined others feel when they speak those words, and although he is not sure and cannot then and there describe the change, he wonders if, hopes, believes the day will come when he will know how, will know as surely as if the man he is to become has boarded the bus and sat down beside him and told him what he is finding out today—that a new face can be as welcoming as a cozy room, that a strange face can become a home.

"Decorators, dear," the drag queen whispers to Jerry. "Beware. They are always into the rough stuff, but if in spite of that fact you are still interested, they are more often found farther uptown."

With the moist spray of warning in his ear, Jerry turns to

look at the drag queen. If some faces are homes, hers is a house.

"We are nearly there," she says to him. "You are, of course, most certainly invited to stay, my dear."

"What choice do I have?" he replies.

"The choices, sweetie, are endless," she says. "The outcome, however, is determined."

The bus halts abruptly, as though it had almost missed the stop, and with lots of banging and bumping and complaints from the passengers who protest at the slightest brush from Jerry's belongings or his person, he and the drag queen move to the door. It is odd and a little irritating to Jerry that in a city so crowded, the slightest touch is an outrage. Some of the passengers applaud the drag queen who blows them kisses. She gets off the bus, and Jerry follows, red with shame.

The apartment was on the top floor of an old three-story building with no elevator, and although Jerry could not have known to appreciate it that first day, the street was a rarity in New York. The trees were taller than the buildings.

Jerry followed his new friend's swaying behind up the stairs. As they climbed, his friend's girly walk became less exaggerated until, by the last flight, exertion had worked off the illusion. On the landing outside the apartment, Jerry put down his suitcase while his friend unlocked the door.

"I don't even know your name," said Jerry.

"Like this, I've lots of names," said his friend, opening the apartment door, then with a sweeping gesture he removed the wig like a Cavalier taking off a plumed hat. "Hugh Coy, at your service," he said with a broad, lipstick smile.

Inside the apartment, light streamed in through uncovered windows, which looked out onto an assembly line of black and silver rooftops.

Undressed, with the makeup washed off, Hugh was lithe, with a slight yet definitely male body. That he managed, when in his tight, short skirt, to conceal as thoroughly as he had what a man he really was seemed a miracle of deception to Jerry. The woman's clothes must have had a calming effect on the conflicted and lonely men who probably made up the majority of his pickups and, Jerry imagined, gave them an illusion of normalcy. But when Hugh was undressed, Jerry didn't see how there could be any mistaking that what they were going to do they were going to do with a man. What he did to Jerry he did with gusto.

It was oddly quiet here, and an initial, delicious sense of stolen and undeserved leisure made what they did all the more thrilling to Jerry. The quiet and the unfamiliar light reminded him of pretending to be sick and staying home from school. Then the house and all the staleness of where he lived was seen in a light like this at a time of day when he was usually away, so that what had been taken for granted or had gone unnoticed—walls, a chair, a view from a window—seemed changed, not unrecognizable, but better, new and luxurious.

The walls were white and the sheets were white and their sins were played out on such a background as to make them seem pure and poetic. Although almost all of what they did was new to him, Jerry tried as much as possible to respond enthusiastically without showing his inexperience and shock. They went at it for the rest of the day, falling apart from time to time but only briefly before some tender stroke or an electrifying bite or a kiss in some unexpected place would arouse Jerry again. Free, in a city where he was sure thousands of others were doing what they were doing at that very moment, Jerry for the first time in his life wore his skin like an expensive, tailored suit—with confidence and, most proudly, nonchalant vanity.

Finally, late in the afternoon, with the sky now powdered

a mixture of rose and gray, and the possibilities still unexhausted, they slept in the eddied sheets, not to wake until morning.

When he woke up, the first thing Jerry heard was Hugh's voice coming from another room. He rose up in the bed and held his breath so that he could hear better.

"He's scrumptious in every way, dear," Jerry heard him say.

"Really, would I like him? Would Mother like him?" another voice asked, and although the two laughed, the questions had been asked in a way, which, at the same time that they were meant to be a joke, made Jerry think, He really does care whether his mother would like me. There was an aristocratic quality in the voice and in the questions, which made Jerry want to measure up to both the person speaking and his mother. The voice was like none he had ever heard. Its tone was soft but clear, the consonants clipped, but there was a broad, awkward honk to certain vowels. It was a voice that, although it seemed to have doubts, was sure about something, too. It was skeptical, cynical, tinged with impatience and suppressed irritation, bored and interested at the same time—the voice of one disillusioned, one who out of habit is faithful to the idea of hopeless standards unattained.

"Are those his things?" the voice asked.

"Yes," replied Hugh. "Aren't they dear?"

Jerry got out of bed and stood in the floor, naked, still—ashamed and expectant. He felt as if he were waiting to hear the sentence for a crime he alone knew he had not committed. A mirror, in which yesterday he had seen glimpses of himself and his new friend breaking Old Testament laws, hung on the wall opposite the foot of the bed, and he saw himself in it now, his hair tousled, his face weary from travel and excitement, but changed. The person looking back looked like him, was him, but seemed to know something he didn't.

He smoothed his hair. On the floor by the bed he found the wilted white shirt and seersucker pants he had worn from home. He dressed and went into the kitchen where the voice was coming from.

"We can keep him. Can we keep him?" Hugh said when Jerry came into the kitchen, but what he heard did not register as much as what he saw. The person connected to the voice he had been listening to from the bedroom was a dream, a wish—Jerry could not believe he was in the same room with such a person. He was icily good-looking surrounded by an aura of remoteness and studied nonchalance. Handsomeness and disappointment seemed almost to own him like a pair of jealous, snobby friends. He was an inaccessible cold spring of sweet but poisonous water, as unattainable as contentment. Look, touch, love even, but it will cost you in ways you never would have agreed to, was what Jerry saw in the arch, sideways, seductive gaze the person turned on him.

Lust and hunger and the chance for something you've never had are quicker than loyalty, and Jerry instantly felt boredom when he took his eyes off the new person for a glance at Hugh, who with the curiosity of one observing a situation for which he already knows what the outcome will be, watched the two take each other in.

"We can keep him," the voice said. Then without getting up from his chair, the voice's owner held out his hand to Jerry.

"Meet Handiford Pepper Crompton," said Hugh grandly.

"Call me Handy," he said. "You will stay, won't you?"

Jerry said yes, and again felt the delicious safety and exclusivity of being invited by people he did not deserve to know to stay in a place better than from where he had come.

I am as mad as all outdoors. The house tour was a total flop, and I look like a fool, and I don't know who to blame, so I'm blaming my sister in South Carolina. I've written to her to tell her I could kill her. I really could. As it is, I am trying to decide whether I should kill her or just never speak to her again. I try to lean toward the latter, but then I consider the trouble her offhand remark has made for me, and how she got me so angry with her letter that I had to try to prove her wrong, plus humiliate her by taking what she considered a joke and turning it around against her, and when I think about how she has always tried to get my goat and loved it when she did, and how she has always hated and resented me because I actually left South Carolina and made an elegant and tasteful life for myself in North Carolina among some very nice people, probably me not speaking to her ever again was what she was trying to bring about, so I am now, and have been for over a week, actually thinking up ways to kill her and not get caught.

I have been bamboozled by the Women's Society of Christian Service or somebody. I'm not sure who. Not a thin dime was made on that house tour, and what I do know is it is all my sister's fault. And Maggie's. It was she who put me in charge of the g.d. thing. There are about five hundred reasons, all of them unravelable, for why Maggie might have done this, but I can't, to save my soul, decide which one is the right one. I've thought of ten she might have had, both well-intentioned and devious, for putting me in charge of the house tour that was to help out Jerry, all the time knowing I was not the one to run such a thing. They are in no particular order.

One. She believed because it was my idea I wanted to be in charge of it, and it would hurt my feelings if she took the thing over.

Two. She believed because it was my idea I ought to be in charge of it. She did not want to have to do it herself.

Three. She knew it wasn't my idea. (How she knew this, I haven't yet figured out, unless my sister called her up and told her, which is not only possible, but the most likely thing to have happened, knowing my sister and how she hates us here, *and* the fact that how *could* Maggie have figured it out. All of which makes me again think that killing my sister is the thing that will make me most happy, therefore the way to go. The only reason I have my doubts about her calling and telling Maggie is that my sister would rather have her finger cut off than stick it in a telephone dial to make a long-distance call. She might have put it on a postcard to Maggie, but too many people, including me, could have seen it, so I'm still at a loss as to how Maggie might have known that the idea did not originate with me.) Anyway, could she have known it was just a joke made by my sister that I took hold of and tried to turn into something to simultaneously shut up Elsie Moye, show up my sister and put myself into the center of the thing for reasons I still don't fully understand? In other words, Maggie *somehow* knew the actual truth, and was letting my lie punish me.

Four. Maggie thought I was the best woman for the job. (This is unlikely, but among the many possibilities I came up with, so I include it, and I can hear my sister laughing from here, but she can laugh all she wants and better enjoy it now because I bet I. C. can get me in touch with somebody who hates her guts down there in South Carolina, where for centuries mistreatment of the household help and tenants has been a condition of citizenship. I imagine my dreams of revenge are nothing compared to theirs. I bet someone like that would just be itching to carve her up in her sleep.)

Five. Maggie and Elsie Moye were in it together out of jealousy. But what of? Elsie Moye of course might have been motivated by jealousy. She does not have the flair for decorating that I do, and she is Jerry's least favorite of us all. But Maggie jealous? Never!

Six. Maggie was trying to quell Elsie Moye by getting on her nerves, and knew that putting me in charge of it would do that. (But Maggie knows she and I already get on Elsie Moye's nerves.)

Seven. Elsie Moye, realizing it wouldn't work, told Maggie to give it to me.

Eight. Maggie thought it would tip Elsie Moye and me over from being mildly irritating to one another from time to time to becoming bitter and permanent enemies. (But what would that achieve since if we were to become sworn enemies there would be a good chance that Elsie Moye and I would never want to be in the same room together again, and that would cause one or the other of us to have to drop out of the Women's Society, change churches or possibly even move out of town altogether, in which case, if it were me who was going to do the moving, I'd move back to Passiflora, South Carolina, in order to more efficiently supervise my sister's violent and suspicious end. Plus, be there to enjoy it!) But Maggie wouldn't do that kind of thing to Branch Creek Methodist Church nor would she do it to Branch Creek at large nor to its environs nor the state of North Carolina, for that matter.

Nine. Maggie thought the whole thing was a bad idea but

let me go on with it because out of kindness she couldn't bring herself to tell me what she really thought. (Perhaps, but Maggie is especially able when it comes to saving you from doing something stupid without hurting your feelings in the process.)

Ten. Maggie thought it was a great idea, but since it had not originated with her, she did not want it to succeed and, knowing I had no talent for organization, let me run it and sat back happily and watched the whole undertaking fall apart. (This is about the most unlikely because what has Maggie Labrette to prove to *anybody*, but it is probably the one my sister would like the best, evil and deserving of a painful death at the hands of a close relative as she is, since it fits with her overall cynical feelings about good people doing good works.)

There are undoubtedly more reasons, but I can't think of them right now. All I know is it was a disaster, and I was never so glad of anything as I was when the last of the visitors, about which more later, stepped off our lot and went home. To begin with, mine was the only house that ended up being on the tour. Did you know that just because somebody tells you in gushing terms what a good idea you have come up with and what a success it ought to be, and they are certain everyone else will think it is as wonderful an event and as worthy a cause as you do, it does not necessarily mean that what they are giving you is a commitment to take part in the thing? You've got to get their name down on paper of some sort.

I made phone calls to the high, middle and low of this town and in some cases went to their houses and gave my little speech about what we were planning. Not once did I hear anything like, Don't count on me. True, I didn't hear, Count me in, either, in those exact words, but when, would someone tell me, did things in Branch Creek change to the extent that you have to be so specific? Ever since I've been here, it was just assumed, unless you had a death in the family or had to go out of town for some reason at the time a thing was planned, and if you did not actually say, I cannot do it, that you were taking part in whatever it was you had been told about and to which you had responded with enthusiasm.

No more.

I had made up some little signs that said Welcome, and had the picture of an open door on them that all who wanted their house on the tour were to put in their front yards. A suggested donation of twenty-five dollars a head was to be collected and you were to provide refreshments to the people who took the tour of your house. These could be as simple or as elaborate as you wanted. The beauty of the whole idea was how easy it all was. I mean, all you had to do was clean your house, fling some flowers around, throw together something for people to gnaw on, and collect the donations.

I made up reminders. Passed them out along with the signs. I had it announced from the pulpit of every church in the county the Sunday before the Saturday of the house tour, and I had a notice printed in the newspaper as well. A few days before the thing was to take place, Maggie called to say that she would have to go back to Raleigh to meet with some important people she thought might be able to help Jerry out of this mess. Fine, I said to her. It was a disappointment, but of course Jerry was what the whole thing was about, and she could surely do him more good meeting with the influential than she could standing in her front hall passing out petit fours to the socially ambitious and explaining to them how the people in the portraits hanging high in her hall were related to her.

Turns out it was a fatal blow. Maggie's is not the most decorated house in town, but it is the one that people who don't get invited there want to be able to say they've been to. Many would have been lined up and pushing to get the opportunity to see the place so that later they might be able to pass a remark in general conversation that would, without coming right out and saying so, let the person they were trying to impress know that they had been inside the Labrette house. So and so and so, like in Maggie Labrette's dining room. That sort of thing.

Not that I was hoping to attract only the socially ambitious. Plain old gawkers were free to come, too. I had expected all kinds and had prepared myself. You know what I mean? After all this time working for me, my girl knows who gets to linger and who doesn't. And I thought it'd more or less be over by noon, and we'd all get a chance to go look at each other's houses—if there was a lull, don't you know, or it seemed that everybody who was going to come had. There were only a few who I really wanted to see my new upholstery anyway.

To make a long story more irritating, when Maggie dropped out of the thing, so did all the others. They assumed if she wasn't doing it then it wasn't taking place. I didn't know that is what had happened, because, as I said before, I was too trusting or stupid to pin down exactly which houses would be on the tour and which would not. Of course I've learned too late that would have been step one for somebody who knew what she was doing.

Now, when yours is the only house on a tour, even a low turnout can seem like a stampede. There was all morning a steady straggle of runny-nosed children and their poor mothers. It was Saturday, so all the tenant farmers and laborers were in town, and somebody up there—Elsie Moye, I'll wager—let the word out that there was free food at the Lamm house on Central Avenue. It is just a short walk from uptown to here, so while their menfolk were getting good and drunk and tending to what they call their business, the wives and offspring took in the house tour. You cannot, in your wildest dreams, imagine it. Barefoot women traipsing through this house and the dirtiest, most pathetic little children running up and down my stairs, getting into everything. The things that usually happen with such people around did. The bathroom was a particularly popular attraction. My refreshments, being more rich than any of them were used to, impelled instantaneous diarrhea in some cases and in others fountainous vomiting. Imagine, women holding their spewing children over my front porch railing. My azaleas are still not speaking to me. The changing of diapers on top of my grand piano, breast-feeding on the front porch steps, spanking and bawling any and everywhere were the order of the day. Most often in plain view of the entire neighborhood.

Have I mentioned that what's left of those TV people showed up and that not a one of them paid to look at my house? Is this what the Founding Fathers meant by freedom of the press? Tried to "interview" me with the scraggling unwashed of this county as a backdrop. I told them to get off my porch and out of my yard or I wouldn't bother with calling the sheriff. Told them I knew they were all staying at a motel out by the highway, and I would summon up and let loose on them the lynching kind if there was any of that sort left around here. That exchange, as I am sure you have already surmised, made the evening broadcast.

You can call yourself a liberal-minded person, and you can think you have a Christian tolerance for the poor and downtrodden, but it is all theory until it is tested, and I have come to the conclusion that a healthy dose of snobbery is a trait to nurture in yourself, and I for one am never going to pretend that I feel otherwise. At the height of the chaos, it crossed my mind that there ought to be some way of coping with what was happening that would save face, save my house and save the feelings of those poor trashy women and their children. What would Maggie do in a situation like this? is what I asked myself, but I was so addled I couldn't think what a gnat would do, let alone Marguerite Labrette. It was Ellen, my girl, who came up with the answer. She's a preacher when she's not working for me, so I thought she might be able to help me get rid of these people in a Christian way. Her solution was to somehow move them all outdoors and turn the thing from a house tour into a garden party or a picnic or an al fresco reception or a food fight if it came to it. I didn't care what, as long as I could get them out of the house.

I got their attention more or less and announced in the nicest way possible that due to the overwhelming turnout, we were being forced to move the reception into the back garden. The advantages of this plan were immediately apparent. To name a few, the guests would be hidden from my neighbors, spillage would not matter so much and the old privy from the pre-plumbing era was at the back of the lot and, although not used in years, was more operational for the purposes that these people would need it for than my floors and rugs had been. I thought I had really pulled it off in a manner that Maggie would have been proud of. That I had not only kept from hurting the feelings of these people, but had actually made them think I was honoring them. But as they were filing through the kitchen, me smiling and nodding and gently indicating the door to the outside, this one woman, big as a boulder, stops and smiles at me. I thought she was going to thank me for a nice afternoon or comment on the refreshments or how beautiful my house looked. Mind you, not another one of them had spoken to me directly that day. This is not unusual. These types seldom carry on much of a conversation outside of letting you know what they want you to do for them. So I believed I had come across at least one in which an afternoon in my house had somehow brought out the slumbering best. Fool that I am, in the seconds before she opened her mostly toothless mouth to speak, in my mind I fashioned theories about the civilizing force of a well-appointed house and elegant refreshments. How wrong I was.

She looked me right in the eye, kind of snorted and said, You wasn't expecting what you got was you? Said, I said to my sister Katie Mae, when we first got here, that as soon as you could, you'd find somehow to get shed of us.

Now don't ever let anybody tell you that these people are not on to us.

Somehow the out-of-doors did not appeal to them in the way that my house had, and before too long they had all departed. Not a thank-you uttered from one, nor a word of leavetaking. You'd just turn around and a few more would be gone. What we found in evidence of their having attended was a snotty-nosed baby in dirty diapers way back up under the picnic table. I panicked and had visions of me having to take that child to raise like Maggie had practically raised Jerry, and I've seen what that got her and want no part of such an arrangement. I sent Ellen uptown with the child to try and find out who it belonged to, but before she got down the porch steps she met its mother sauntering back this way, seeming in no hurry to reclaim the thing. Ellen said she was just as calm as if she had left behind a handkerchief, but she also said she thought the stupid woman, and the adjective here is mine, not Ellen's, was more upset about a colored lady holding her baby than she was with having forgotten it.

And there, as they say, you have it! I will never, ever again have my judgment so impaired by my own overcharitable intentions coupled with my pride of place. Next time, whatever the cause, I will simply write a check and draw the curtains.

I'm hoping to make it down to South Carolina sometime soon for a visit with my sister before I take her life. She best put her affairs in order.

"I was twenty-five already and hadn't found a life, so I suppose one found me. When you don't really know what your situation is or ought to be, any will do to fall into, the life leading you can look like the life you are leading," said Jerry.

Maggie sat opposite him at the table, listening quietly, her hands folded in her lap, ankles crossed. She did not have to determine to remain calm, impassive, unshocked by what she was hearing. For some reason beyond her ability to reason, Jerry's story was not the cause of the least bit of discomfort or embarrassment for her. If he thought that it was—if Jerry was testing her, was trying to elicit outrage from her with these vivid details of a side of his life that up until now he had kept from her, then she wished she could supply some if he truly needed to see it, but she simply could not. She had always suspected there were episodes he spared her, and that he had told her only what he thought she wanted to hear. She never assumed that he didn't have another kind of life. It was clear he thought he was revealing something about himself and the world in which he had dwelt that would disgust her. But as she listened to him tell about his adventures then—at times offhand, other times full of earnest rue—she felt only pity and she wondered how, for all the sophistication he thought he had acquired, he could in so many ways still be so awestruck, as much so as when he first came to her. Otherwise he would have known that this insipid story did not depend on vivid detail and coarse language, but that a few simple, polite euphemisms would have done well to condense a story as old as it was boring. His, after all, was a situation that had been faced before. If he had gained any real worldliness off in New York, he would have known that to assume everyone else was as sophisticated as he would be the sign of it. Much can be implied among people like that. Even she knew that, simple as she was. But in the blasé manner with which he said what were finally not provocative but merely tasteless things, and the lewd, inelegant attempts at irony and drollery, she saw a gawking, awestruck bumpkin, as stunned by and disbelieving of his luck at having seen something of a way of life he had not even known how to wish for as he had been the day he stood staring slack-jawed and runny-nosed at the table she and the other ladies had laid for his mother's wake. Knowing his secrets, which so far seemed unremarkable, changed nothing for her.

He paused briefly in his story after uttering a sentence that ended with an argotic phrase peculiar to men who engage in sexual acts that, although he insisted on describing to her, she was not getting any clearer about. Then he stared petulantly into her eyes, like a defiant child.

"You are mistaken, if you think this is interesting in any way, Jerry," she said politely. "What makes it dull is that all have consented to whatever happens or is done to them, including you. Recklessness is mistaken for daring, rashness for courage, delusion for discernment. There is a difference between being exclusive and being odd. Your actions and those of the others in your story inspire neither pity nor respect."

"Oh, I know that," said Jerry flippantly. The bitter sneer that had been on his face while he told the story disappeared, and he now looked wide-eyed and innocent, as though what he had said up to that point had been a joke or, more worrisome, as if he did not remember saying it.

"I don't think you do, dear. You could not. Don't you think that all the depravity that exists in the world exists everywhere all the time in one form or another? These things were not invented by the people from whom you learned them. In and surrounding this very town I imagine the same things are going on. The question for me is whether a person loves his misery or wants to be delivered from it. I need to hear how what has happened to you was not of your doing, was done to you against your will—without your cooperation. I can only help the helpless."

A look of sleepy disdain came over Jerry's face.

"Then surely you can't expect to help me," he said.

"But I do," Maggie said.

Just what form her help would take, she was not sure. She knew he needed her now as much as he ever had. But not more. There had been trouble for him before, perhaps as bad as now. This was not the first time she had put herself between him and its consequences.

After Mrs. Chiffon's death, before too long, the Saturdays with Jerry and his little brother came too slowly for Maggie. What at first she had told herself was something she ought to do had become a rewarding pleasure. Often she could not wait for Mr. Chiffon to come to town with Jerry and would send Lyman out to get him and the baby and the chair and bring them to her house earlier. In the winter she always did so, for in the cold, Mr. Chiffon took the uncomfortable ride into town on his open tractor only for what could not be put off.

She liked to go out to the Chiffon place with Lyman. He would wait in the car while she went in and helped Jerry gather together the things he needed for his little brother—bottles and diapers, jars of mashed peas that he had cooked himself, always a newer or better sling that kept the baby's head from falling over.

In the Chiffon house she saw evidence of the lessons she gave Jerry. He was caring for his father and the house well. He cooked and cleaned and washed and mended clothes, and with what furniture he had, Jerry made it a different place than it had been when she had first seen it the night of his mother's death—most certainly pleasant, but also exhibiting the right kind of pride that she had always thought came not from trying to hide yourself and your surroundings or pretending you were other than what you were whether rich or poor, but was the result of poise gained from a realistic, self-assured assessment of your situation.

Some things he had asked for from her were what he had used to decorate the house. Linens she no longer used he took home, and starched to standing; ironed crisp as a cracker, they dressed the little kitchen table as if every day was Sunday. Leftover lengths of upholstery he had draped over an old dresser and an old wooden box, and some curtain material she had bought and then decided against, he tacked up over the windows in the front room of the house. He had gotten Mr. Chiffon to take the old sofa off into the woods, and had not replaced it with something a little better, a little less worn, or stained but in pretty good shape. "Good enough for them," as she had heard people say, some of her own friends even, as they assuaged their guilt by forcing a piece of furniture or some old clothes on the poor. He had left empty the place in front of the window where the broken-down sofa, one legless corner leveled up with old magazines, had sat. He had simply cleaned the glass to disappearing, hung the curtain material up and let the window, framing the field across the road and the woods beyond, serve for decorating the wall as wonderfully as a landscape painting. For seating, just the chairs they had always had, simple wooden rockers, and side chairs of honest handcrafting that were, as she discovered when she sat in one, more comfortable than the dilapidated sofa had been. Some mismatched transfer ware she had let him have was propped up on a shelf in the kitchen in between the blue tin plates that were Mrs. Chiffon's legacy to him. He had arranged them in such a way that there was not a tinge of hand-me-down humiliation in the display. Colored glass vases that had come with florist flowers she had received, long stuck far back under her sink, he pulled from the dark, took home and put in a sunny windowsill or wherever in the house they would catch the most light. The rooms had the aura and simple elegance of a Quaker playhouse in which there neither had been nor would be any play. The only lapse in his taste, she thought, was the two-way carnival picture of Jesus on the mantel, but even that seemed deliberate. She had shown Jerry once the flaws woven into her fine Turkish rugs. Intentional breaks in the pattern put in lest an arrogant Oriental god punish a presumptuous attempt at the perfection only He could manufacture, and as her eyes fell on the picture and then toured the rooms of the little farmhouse, she silently had the lesson given back to her. Only he had let God represent imperfection. Whether intentional or not, considering his life so far, and even knowing that it was sinful to think so, she felt Jerry might have been correct to do so.

"The things we had left over, Lyman. Just things I hadn't gotten around to throwing out. These are what he asks for," she said to her husband with tears in her eyes the first time she saw how nicely Jerry had decorated his house. "How little he needs and how much we have."

She wished that Lyman could share her guilty feelings. He had always had a little joke with her when throughout their life together she had from time to time, over an especially delicious meal or when he bought her a fur coat or a beautiful dress, would say how hard it was for her to justify and enjoy buying lovely things and eating good food when the poor were without those things.

"It's all right, darling. They don't wear those sorts of clothes. They don't eat this kind of food." But when he tried to cajole her out of her guilt about Jerry's situation, she snapped at him. She began to look too often at his protruding stomach and his thick eyebrows and to think about the money he wasted, and she couldn't stop herself from compiling an uncharitably long list of other annoying habits he possessed that, before she knew Jerry, she had been amused by and for which she had felt softhearted enough toward her husband to tell herself she did not notice them. And she started to be irritable with him if he asked for something troublesome and other than what she had planned for herself and Jerry for lunch. If he needed her to sign papers on Saturdays when Jerry was at their house, she did so impatiently.

She made her heart try to care that Lyman was always willing to take her out to the Chiffon place in the Cadillac and bring Jerry and the baby and all the things he needed back. But then she thought of how little she had ever really asked for over the years, and how truly contented she had made Lyman all their life together, and she resented his tiresome sigh when he raised himself out of his chair to go for the car and how he drove slowly and silently, looking right and left at farmland, barns, timberland and tenant houses, tallying all the time, she just knew, crop yields and rents, cordage and price per pound.

When he did speak on their way out to get Jerry, it would be to disapprove mildly and gently tease.

"I hope you're not spoiling that boy for what I'm afraid is the life that a boy like that is likely to have," he said to her one winter day. She replied to him in a manner as cold as the air.

"How giving that poor boy a few of the things that you who have so much don't even know he needs is spoiling him, Lyman . . ." She could not finish her sentence for fear of how it might end.

Her irritation and slowly gathering resentment of Lyman made her feel oddly invisible. Lyman's presence was as vivid as ever, couldn't miss him, and he seemed not to sense her discontent. For he was the same with her, not kinder, not less patient. The same. The way she felt about him, because he couldn't understand what she admitted she herself didn't know, unaccountably, unexpectedly and contrary to any other ill feeling she had ever had, made her seem to herself when she was with Lyman to be disappearing, like she was only what was inside her, with no surface from which light could reflect Maggie back to Lyman.

Slowly, like that, over time she guessed, was how she had come to require her Saturdays with Jerry more than probably he needed them. When Jerry was there, she materialized, for in his eyes she saw herself bloom, color and occupy space. It had meaning, the time they spent together and the things they did with it, she knew. Maybe not much, but enough.

An icy winter storm in the fifth year that she had been having Jerry and his little brother over had been the occasion for a day of particular luxury. There had been a sign, when what all day before had been a steady rain splattering in puddles and falling on the roof with a sound like polite, gloved applause, toward night slowed, and sliding thick as oil over the bare trees and pavement, started to harden, then froze, fusing a shiny glaze on the surface of everything it touched. She went to bed full of hope and determination that the weather would not stop her from having Jerry come the next day. In the night she woke to hear that the muffled drum of the cold rain on the roof had been replaced by the dry and brittle sound, frigid and soothing, of ice falling.

In the morning she got up and dressed and went out into the backyard. The sun shone out from the inside of things. And a bright clear blue sky was as an enormous skirt falling over her head, its hem embroidered on the inside with a pattern of entwining crisscrossing tree limbs done in silver thread. And the icy crazy lace of branches were as a map of shining tributaries and streamlets, a frozen river system drawn by a cold-weather cartographer. Each tree trunk charting the single way up a lone broad river then the branches and twigs breaking into an uncounted number of watery routes toward heaven's ocean.

She went inside and got Lyman up and quelled his protest by going out into the street herself and rubbing the pavement with her fingers to test for ice. The road was good, the morning sun having stoked the pavement's stored warmth and thawed the ice there.

She watched as the Cadillac slid out of the driveway onto the street, finding its grip, a cold plume of white exhaust trailing thick as the fog of a crop duster.

They'd cook today, certainly, cakes with icings and candies coated in granulated sugar and cookies dusted in powdered. A warm roast and crescent rolls. Fires in all the fireplaces, and they would have dinner in the dining room with candlelight and silver. She went to the kitchen and started pulling out the equipment they would need. She lined the worktables and counters with baking sheets and roasting pans and double boilers, and from the drawer where she had always kept it since it was new and undamaged, she pulled out her cookbook, a fat sheaf now more than a volume, held together with a wide rubber band. The cookbook was as thick as a three-layer cake, its pages frilly with use, the spine long broken and stripped off because ever since it had been given to her she'd made the covers hold more than what the printer had put between them. A wedding present from her mother, it was the only messy thing in her house.

She removed the rubber band and, as she always had done, turned the pages over from the pile that was a ruin of the book that had been, stacking them to the left, the orderly rhythm of page numbers broken and ragged with interspersed recipes clipped from a newspaper or written in the hand of a friend on personal stationery. There were instructions heard on the radio and scrawled quickly in pencil on a piece of brown paper torn from a sack. Box-top recipes for dishes full of whatever the box from which it had been taken had held, and index cards, with the ink fading and then changing colors altogether as a pen dried out and a new one was taken up, were between the pages of whole smaller cookbooks compiled by the Women's Society and garden clubs of other towns, sold to raise money for good works, which themselves were contained within the unbound sheaf of pages, like scenes within a play within a play. There were recipes written in her own mother's hand and her grandmother's and in two even older cursives, which began with vague instructions, expecting from the cook experience with and understanding of ingredients. "Take some flour," one read. "Kill and dress your fattest hen," commenced another. "Shoot some partridges," instructed one ancestor.

As a young girl, she'd been courted by one other than Lyman, so secrets were tucked among the recipes, private papers, safer than if locked in a vault, for who looked here but her? They had been hidden there not to be found if needed, not placed at a numbered page or near instructions for a dish that corresponded in any way to what the paper concerned or would have aided her memory in laying her hands on a certain letter or poem or pressed flower, but put there randomly and quickly to be refound at leisure, delightedly come upon, or ruefully, not on a day like today when much had to be done, but on a day when she was alone in the house and had plenty of time and felt the need to go back over her life a little and weigh the decisions she had made, the paths she had taken and the ones she had been guided down. Time was needed and solitude for going through her cookbook like that, for the outcome was not assured. She could be filled with joy along with being reminded of how to make a peach chiffon pie, or she might send herself off to bed for the day, having discovered nothing more than the ingredients for sadness and regret.

But it was not a day for looking at old letters and brittle keepsakes. It was a day for festivities of the sort shared with someone like Jerry. She had fires laid in the dining room and the living room and in the guest room, then waited until, looking out of the kitchen door, she saw the Cadillac return. It passed, black, cold and shiny, and in the door panels she saw her house reflected and herself standing at the window of the kitchen door. In the backseat of the car she saw two heads, one erect on a thin stalk of a neck, its pose suggesting all the eagerness she felt herself. Facing Jerry was his brother, the dome of his large head just above the sling. And up front in the driver's seat was Lyman who looked sweet to her now driving the vehicle, which, for the time it made its way up the driveway past her, caught the house and her in it, and with the passengers inside, held them trapped together. The reflection slid along the side of the car and was gone like passing scenery, and for a second Maggie was so disoriented by reflection and movement and watching herself in them that she felt as if she and the house were retreating purposely back to a time when outcomes were reversible and, decisions already made, alterable.

The unloading had become less frantic than it had been at Jerry's first visits, and as they brought everything into the house, Jerry chattered in his lively and, for his age, she thought, intelligent way. He was excited, she could see, more than usual, and he talked so fast that she was unable to correct his grammar as she usually did.

"Pa like not to let us come. Said it was too slippery and cold, and he conjectured that by nighttime the roads would freeze over again and we'd all wind up upside down in a ditch somewhere trying to get back home. But Mr. Lyman told him that if it did freeze up he knew you'd want us to stay the night, so I packed us something to sleep in and brought some clean clothes for tomorrow."

That alone, that Lyman had thought to tell Mr. Chiffon that Jerry and the baby could stay over if the weather worsened, made Maggie regretful for what she had been thinking about her husband.

"Do you think it will freeze up again? I bet it does. Don't you? Don't you bet it freezes up again, Mr. Lyman? I believe it might have already started freezing up again. I bet we won't get home this night, no sir and ma'am. Miss Maggie, what would you sleep in if you were going to spend the night in the Governor's Mansion? And would you bring your own toilet paper and towels and such, or would you use the Governor's? I did bring a rag to wash the baby with, but I didn't bring anything to wash myself with. Is that the way you do it when you go off to spend the night with somebody? It seemed like it would be to me. I tried to think it through. We were in a hurry, but it seemed to me like you wouldn't bring those things for yourself, but you would bring something to clean up the kind of messes a baby can make, especially little Labrette—I mean this one. Pa said I looked like I was about to worry myself into a fit of worrying. He said you'd have thought I was going to my doom. But I didn't think anything like I was going to my doom. I knew right where I was going, and when I heard Mr. Lyman say that about if the roads froze over again we'd probably stay here, I couldn't make out whether I wanted to or not, because if I was going to do it, I wanted to bring the things that you ought to bring, and I didn't know if I knew what they was, were, and I just kept saying over and over to myself, like we do, 'Now if you were going to spend the night in the Governor's Mansion, what would you bring with you?' So I put in this here sack, this sack here, some clothes to sleep in, and a clean shirt and pants to put on when I get up, and I put in the same for the baby. I put in that rag I told you about and some soap, and I put in my good shoes and I put in the baby's. I put in some extra socks and I put in a picture of Ma. And I brought another shirt, too, because you remember when you said that they dress for dinner at the Governor's, and remember how you laughed when I said I didn't know anybody that ate naked, but what you had meant, what you meant was changing from what you had been wearing all day into something nicer to eat dinner in, in what to eat dinner. You know, I never did ask you what's been on my mind since you told me that. Do you take off what you put on right after you eat, and if you do, what do you put on then? Do you put on what you had on before you changed your clothes for dinner? I bet there is a pile of washing at the Governor's, don't you? Is that ice on the steps already? Look out, Mr. Lyman, I think there is already ice on them, those steps. Oh! I forgot to tell you. I slipped some ham out of the house for you. Isn't that funny I said *slipped* when I was thinking about Mr. Lyman falling on the ice and trying to tell you about the ham at the same time. I don't want you to cook ham while me and the baby is here, are here, the baby and I. I want you and Mr. Lyman to have it for yourselves one night for your supper."

"Son, take a breath now and then," said Lyman, and Jerry laughed at himself, and Maggie smiled.

They at last got everything into the house. The baby, although now nearly four years old, was still as helpless as what they continued to call him implied. He still had to be securely tied in the red chair. His legs almost reached the floor now, and he had taught himself to rock. He would kick both feet out in a fit of excitement at something he'd seen or heard or smelled and fling both of his arms up to get the chair rocking. He would rock for as much as an hour at a time. In general, the rocking was a sign of happiness, glee even, and it made Maggie and Jerry laugh to see it. A good smell or a sight he had not seen before and liked, would set baby and chair to and fro, back and forth. The merrier he was, the faster he rocked. That was the extent to which his mind and body had grown.

The sights and smells in the kitchen this day seemed to especially delight him. He rocked himself to exhaustion, and he fell asleep from time to time, but would wake and smile like a drunkard and rock some more.

"He does look like a pure fool, don't he, Miss—doesn't he, I mean—Maggie?" said Jerry. Together, with no one to think them cruel, they laughed unashamedly at the baby with his drunken smile and vacant eyes—his huge head tied to the slats of the chair. And the more they laughed, the harder the baby rocked and the broader and more idiotically he smiled. Jerry got the hiccups and Maggie's eyes teared, and she held her side. At the height of the hilarity, they saw the Cadillac back out of the driveway. And that struck both of them as the funniest thing yet, because they knew that it was their raucous gaiety that had driven Mr. Labrette out of the house.

And the cadences in Maggie's kitchen were happy and innocent—primitive as a kindergarten rhythm band. The oscillations of the sifter being cranked, the quick rap of a knife on the wooden cutting board as Maggie chopped nuts. Eggs cracking, the mixer's high whine, the scrape of the grater, the silence, then the drone, then the silence of the refrigerator motor. And under it all the rick-rack, rick-rack, steady as a machine, of the little red rocker on the linoleum floor. They put the radio on, and Jerry fiddled with the dial to find a station, and the first thing that came in clear was a high nasal gospel quartet singing, "Rock of ages, cleft for me," and they both fell out all over again.

Maggie set a lunch for them that was informal but nice. One that she might make for much loved and respected help, and they ate in the manner of people called in to do a job that was highly appreciated. Not hurriedly, but with the purpose of nourishing themselves and getting back to more tasks than perhaps were possible in the time left to complete them. At the kitchen table they had canned tomato soup, which she knew Jerry not only loved the taste of but admired for being in a can—creamy, pinky-orange steaming in her cobalt blue bowls looking summery and cool, and the kitchen so warm that if they had not put it to their mouths they could have pretended that it was the soup that was cold and sending off icy white vapors into the humid air. They had chicken salad sandwiches, the bread toasted and the crusts cut off, and Maggie gave Jerry a little coffee with a lot of sugar and evaporated milk in it because she enjoyed how drinking coffee made him behave as though he was much older than he was. She adored how he dealt with the baby in a slightly impatient manner—all prissy efficiency, as though the coffee were a drug the effect of which was to sharpen and mature the taker, and she felt that she was seeing a little of the man he was to become. But she knew it was only a child's idea of being grown up, and a cookie or a dime was the antidote that restored the boy.

It was during lunch that Jerry came up with the idea that the dinner they were preparing should be shared. Maggie saw the fun of it right away. They would invite only those who could walk to the house and didn't need to drive, since the roads were sure to ice up again, Jerry thought.

"That lengthens the list Jerry, darling. Unless you are crippled, you can walk anywhere in Branch Creek without too much trouble," she told him. "Even on ice." She watched in him the discovery of exclusivity, as the idea that some would be invited and some would not passed over his face in waves of concern and finally delighted perception, which she thought was exactly what should accompany the understanding of such a thing. She had instantly seen on his face the desire that no feelings be hurt and yet full knowledge that what they were about to do was for the select. It would be a ladies' dinner, they decided, and as formal as things got in Branch Creek.

"Well, it ought to be people who have been here before, then," said Jerry with unaccountable understanding and, she thought, an adorable kind of claim on the house and its contents.

Maggie called down through the heat register to Callie below, "Would you come up and clear the lunch things, please?" Then she and Jerry sat down at the kitchen table with paper and pencil to draw up the guest list.

Callie, tall and impeccable, came into the kitchen, tying an apron around her waist. "Going to have a party on a day like this!" she said in a tone of mock mild astonishment that acknowledged that there would be no talking them out of the idea.

"It's a perfect day for a party, Callie," said Maggie buoyantly. "You'll wear your black-and-white uniform, and we'll clean and shine and polish everything, the silver and the crystal and the Limoge. Look out that window, Callie. That is our theme. We are going to prepare a dinner fit for the Governor himself." Knowing that it would amuse Callie and get her into the spirit of things, Maggie added, "And then we will not invite him." For Callie hated the Governor, who had been elected by making trouble and more ill feeling than already existed between black people and ignorant, hateful whites.

"I wouldn't serve dog food to that scoundrel, Mrs. Labrette, let alone get out the good silver," said Callie.

"Jerry, Callie thinks we need an inspiration for our party other than the Governor," said Maggie.

Her maid had an unfailing sense of who went with whom, that brushed the borders of sinful on which, since she could not allow such transgressions in herself, Maggie depended. "Callie wouldn't serve them" or "Callie thinks they are not quite fine people" had become Maggie's excuse for weeding out what she would never have called the wrong kind. What she told herself was that, although her maid was not very broad-minded about people, she supposed even if she overruled her and insisted, the people whom Callie would exclude would not have been comfortable anyway, especially with the cold way she knew Callie would treat them even as she waited on them.

"You can pretend all are equal in the sight of God if you want to, Mrs. Labrette, but I don't have to because I know it isn't so. The Bible is full of advice on who to avoid," Callie said once when Maggie had tried to get her to change her mind about some people. It was Callie as much as Lyman and Maggie who people on Central Avenue played up to. All but Elsie Moye, who thought a bit like the Governor and refused to defer in any way to a black person, come what may. What came then was out-and-out ridicule of Elsie Moye by Callie, and Maggie did not intervene. Callie was extravagant in her distaste and disdain for Elsie Moye Beamon. There were those who enjoyed watching it.

A discussion began over who then should be the ideal imagined guest so admired by them all that they would be motivated to put on a party as they had never before attempted. It was Callie who raised the stakes for the selection of the honorary guest.

"Quit off on thinking of just people from North Carolina," said Callie impatiently. "Let's look on the national scene, or maybe the worldwide stage."

"Jerry, you know there are people who say the butler is the biggest snob on the estate," said Maggie conspiratorially.

"I don't deny it!" exclaimed Callie, and they all laughed and luxuriated in condescension. They gave themselves permission just for the day. The Queen of England was out, for they were good Americans and had a high-hatted disapproval of monarchy. They thought Mrs. Khrushchev might do, for it would require noblesse oblige of the highest order to be properly deferential yet convey in one's demeanor some superiority to the wife of the leader of Communism. But they might have to forgo using the silver and china and other such symbols of privilege and class if Mrs. Khrushchev was the honoree, and of course, that would make the ice storm as an inspiration for the food and decor difficult to achieve. And also, would a Russian woman want to go to a dinner where the inspiration for the food and decor had been ice anyway? And they could not remember if it even was Mr. Khrushchev who was still the leader of the Soviets. Mrs. Gandhi was considered, and Jerry suggested that a woman from such a hot and humid place as India might revel in a party with ice as its theme, but Callie said she was sure they could not invite her, since it was a roast they were planning to cook. And Callie eliminated Eleanor Roosevelt.

"As much as I'd like to meet her, Mrs. Labrette, you know Mrs. Beamon wouldn't sit down at the same table with Mrs. Roosevelt," Callie said. "Let's be safe and make it our First Lady, a woman of high rank and a Southerner."

And so with none other than the First Lady of the land confirmed as their guest of honor, they began to draw up a list of invitees, which, compared to the time it took to settle in whose honor the dinner was to be given, went quickly.

"Now read them back," said Maggie.

They had agreed that they would strike any name from the list if one of them objected to that person being invited, so Jerry looked up at Callie first after each name, since she seemed to be the one whose standards were the highest.

"Mrs. I. C. Lamm, Mrs. U. H Beamon, Mrs. Parchman

Anderson, Mrs. Lyman L. Labrette, Mr. Jerry Chiffon," read Jerry.

Callie gave out a contemptuous grunt when Elsie Moye's name was read, but it was not considered an out-and-out rejection. When the list had been revealed in its entirety, Callie laughed out loud.

"Same old bunch," she said as she went to get the silver and china.

"Well, it is more or less the regular crowd, isn't it?" said Maggie. "There is poor Elizabeth Anderson, who isn't here very often, but I wouldn't call her a new face in the crowd. We really ought to invite someone a little unfamiliar to us all."

"But who?" asked Jerry. The requirement that the guest be in walking distance was not looking like such a good idea, for everybody they could think of who they would call a new person to them lived outside a comfortable range for walking over to the Labrette house. Nice people little known to them in some of the surrounding towns and villages were brought up, and although many seemed acceptable, even suitable, none lived close enough. So they widened it to people they knew who lived nearby, but had never been inside the Labrette house, and the selection from that group was even smaller. In fact it seemed not to exist for they could think of not one person who they were sure had never been there.

"Well, Callie, of course!" said Maggie finally, in a tone without the slightest suggestion that Callie had ever been thought of as unacceptable at all.

Callie came back into the kitchen with a stack of porcelain plates thin as leaves. She put them down on the kitchen table, then one by one lifted them up to the light, tilting and turning each one to test it for sparkle. She made a separate stack of the ones which she needed to wash before putting them on the table. "I don't want to be invited if

Mrs. Roosevelt isn't coming," she said, dismissing the invitation with a wave of her hand.

"Why can't we invite Mrs. Roosevelt?" asked Jerry.

"I can't leave out Elsie Moye. I'd have to if Mrs. Roosevelt were here. I have to live with Elsie Moye," said Maggie.

For a while the party planning had the dismal feel of failure to it, like planning a funeral almost, where no matter how nice you intend it to be it never changes the fact that what you are celebrating is deficiency, defeat, disease and loss. The one empty place on the guest list was as deflating to their spirits as a casket flung open with a loved one on view would have been.

It was Mrs. Lamm who saved the party, a thing so rare as to be marveled at by Callie and Mrs. Labrette when it happened. It had begun to look as though the baby would have to be propped up at the table to fill the empty place when a telephone call came in from Mrs. Lamm on a matter those assembled in Maggie's kitchen didn't care much about and couldn't remember when the call was over. But it was revealed in the course of the telephone conversation that Mrs. Lamm's sister from Charleston was in town, and when Maggie told Mrs. Lamm about the preparations in progress for a dinner party that night, and said how wonderful it was that the sister was in town, and that they had an unfilled place at the table, Mrs. Lamm accepted for her sister but replied, Maggie thought, rather dryly, "I'm sure she'll be thrilled."

Callie laughed triumphantly when she heard who was to come. "I like her. I surely do," she said. "Seat her across the table from Mrs. Beamon."

Maggie seemed to recall that there had been some kind of ugliness between Elsie Moye and Myrtle Lamm's sister, but she couldn't recall exactly what the problem had been. So she put the thought out of her mind, confident that even if there was lingering ill will between the two women in question, she would be able to dispel whatever slight unpleasantness might, in the course of the dinner, arise from it. It could even be the chance to give Jerry a lesson—to show him the diplomatic skills a good host must have.

They wrote out invitations by hand on Maggie's good stock in the proper manner and addressed them to each guest. Just below and to the right of the lucky guest's name was written, elegant and underlined, the words *By hand*. Then Maggie and Jerry bundled up in warm clothes, left the baby with Callie and delivered the invitations to the guests' houses. It took less than a half hour, since everyone to whom they extended an invitation, with the exception of Elsie Moye, lived right on the street, and her house was just off it.

As the day progressed, the preparations, polishing, baking, starching, ironing, the clatter of the silver happy as tap dancing, intensified. All accepted by phone, except Elsie Moye, who wrote a note stating that, although it was short notice, she accepted with pleasure the invitation to dinner this evening and had it hand-delivered by her maid who lived on the lot.

There were to be, as in any life, for brief and bright periods in Jerry's, golden, nearly unobtainable people, to whom he wished to impart every wonderful thing which had ever happened to him, to whom he wished to reveal his heart's desires and his most precious and secret thoughts. People by whom he wanted to be understood and appreciated as thoroughly as if he were a joke that only they got. There was to be a man he loved, and there would be times when he would have died for the man, or so he thought. This did not mean that Jerry did not have tests his special people would have to pass. He always described to them the table that day when it was finally set. The dinner remained in his mind, the most beautiful that anyone had ever given anywhere. And it was essential that he see delight in the eyes of those to whom he would describe it. When he told them about the icy day, the happiness that he looked for in his lovers and friends did not only have to indicate that they saw with complete clarity the table and the silver and the food. Nor did they, when he had made the pictures vivid in their minds, have to agree that none other of these things had ever been as fine and as beautiful anywhere else. The smiling and the twinkling eyes could as contentedly have been an indication of the warmth they felt toward him for thinking this evening so. It was enough for them to love him for loving all the things of that day.

Unlike nearly all impressions from childhood of size and color and height and depth, which in adulthood, upon revisiting the room or climbing the tree or swimming to the bottom, are proved to have been exaggerated, the table that day was never surpassed in beauty or warmth, nor did he find a place soon again to which he felt so assuredly he belonged than there in that house in that particular chair at one end of that table and Mrs. Labrette at the other. It gave him confidence, not because it would be the highest test of etiquette any situation might require of him. There were to come dinners and parties where to faint would be preferable to committing a blunder. But from that day forward he never saw formality and strict rules of behavior and presentation, nor anachronistic table manners, nor polite, encoded conversation meant to deny any similarity between you and anybody other than to whom the argot bound you, nor exclusive lists, nor tests of acceptance as anything but acts of love and respect for an idea or quality or reverence for a place or certain people or one person. So that even when he was not sure how he should behave in a certain situation, he was confident that should he be found out, it would not matter. There would be no shame in it for him because of that day when not knowing exactly what to do had put him at the center of a celebration, and he had been surrounded by a group of women who cared enough to show him how to behave well.

The table was an epic poem. Even Maggie Labrette, whose handiwork it was, and who would never have been so pretentious as to say that it was a poem, had to admit to herself even before she had placed the centerpiece on the table or had lit the candles for a moment then blown them out so that the wicks were burnt, that she did sometimes set a very pretty table. To Elsie Moye and Myrtle Lamm's sister from Charleston, the table was a source of envy. To Mrs. Lamm and Jerry and poor Elizabeth Anderson, it was another reason to appreciate Maggie to the point of awe.

The light-catching damask, white and ironed smooth as cream, was overlaid with an almost imperceptible fog of silver. The napkins lay to the left of the plates, each fold not a brutal crease but more a gentle reversal of direction, a metaphor for turning. And in the shadow of the folds a blue-gray hue shone like a cave in an iceberg. The plates she chose for the day were white porcelain with silver rims. The crystal goblets, hoarding light, flirted with the icy branches outside. Jerry had helped Callie polish the silver, and Maggie had thought they would rub and buff until it disappeared. It lay on the table in its proper ranks, so bright that there seemed to emanate from inside each knife, fork and spoon an illusive, precious white metal more valuable than the argentine veneer of which it was the soul.

At last, toward twilight, the table had been set with linen, china, crystal and silver. Between the two silver double candelabra in the center of the table was left a place for Mrs. Labrette's most prized possession. It was an object of such rarity and value that it had last been used for her wedding, then put away for the day the daughter she never had would marry. It was an oddity more beautiful for being so, brought back from France by a bachelor ancestor of Maggie's mother in the days when every young gentleman of good family and good money took the "Grand Tour." That the treasure had made it back over a rocking ocean, packed in a straw-filled pine crate, was a miracle in itself that seemed to have imbued the object with mysterious, conflicting attributes. It had acquired an aura of fragile indestructibility since the time it had been brought over, which edged it into a status reserved for the revered and legendary. At some time a special case had been built for it, and it was rumored in the town that in at least one turn of fortune in the Bonner family, it had been of sufficient value to have saved the farms and town properties of one of Maggie's more squandering relatives. Large loans had been guaranteed on the value of this object, it was said, and it was a known fact that it had sat for a number of years after the depression of the 1870s in a bank vault in Raleigh.

The special box containing the piece was stored on a bottom shelf of a locked cabinet in the galley between the kitchen and the dining room. When it was time to bring it out and assemble it, Callie and Mrs. Labrette carried it between them, careful not to bump into the doorjambs or trip on a rug. They were so slow and deliberate, stopping once to decide the best and safest route, that they seemed like men to Jerry.

They lowered the box to the floor between the table and the mahogany sideboard. Mrs. Labrette opened the lid, and she and Callie stood gazing down into the box with expressions of relief and contentment. Jerry came over and looked in and saw tucked among the deep blue velvet folds, as though sinking in rough dark water, what appeared to be the wreck of a frivolous ship and its elegant cargo. Parts of objects, flowers, elaborate scrollings and curlings were strewn about, and best of all arched necks, fine-boned legs and flying manes struggled to stay afloat in the stormy, fuzzy, paralyzed sea. Mrs. Labrette began lifting objects from the grip of the velvet. She took the pieces out one by one in what seemed an established order—correct, safe and unchanging. She handed each piece of the treasure to Callie, who placed it on the sideboard. They worked slowly and laid out, like archaeological remains, the parts of what was to be the centerpiece for the dinner. At last, from the bottom of the box, a large, footed, mirrored tray was revealed. Mrs. Labrette lifted it out and put it directly onto the table in the place between the silver candelabra.

The objects when assembled formed a white porcelain floating conveyance that seemed to be popping to the surface rather than sinking. It was a mode of transportation out of a myth yet to be written, both boat and chariot but neither. There was porcelain water pouring off it in floes and curling froth, flowing back into the depths from which it had come, giving the effect of a grand fountain, and it was festooned with garlands of flowers, roses, laurel and lilies piled on the decks from where water would have fallen and returned if it had been a real fountain. Among the flowers and rivulets were squirming china fish and sea horses riding the flow off the decks, and there were individual figurines of these sea creatures to place on the mirror, which had been fashioned by the artisan in a way that captured the contentment and relief at returning to the water and life. And there were half horses or less, made so as to appear partially submerged or emerging from deep water, and each one sat on the mirror as though frozen in the height of a frenzied struggle to lift itself from the tranquil water. There were six of them—three on each side of the flower-filled boat going off in opposite directions at cross-purposes in the panic of drowning. The flaring porcelain nostrils and the tenderly opening porcelain roses had been so exquisitely rendered by the maker that they seemed to hum with the tension of something high-strung—alive and dying at the same time. The way the flower- and fish-filled boat seemed to have popped out of the water and the horses around it struggling not to sink, it was as though each thing had an indwelling spirit that had been stilled by some magical process so that it could be observed at length and, although motionless and mute, still seemed to speak the one thing it most needed to say. I am horse, I am hoof, I am petal, leaf. Total rose. The lily. Here is what is fish, liquid. Stone, mirror, porcelain, clay, bone, glaze. White am I. Reprieve. Doom. To look upon it was to understand the words *a work of art,* or if you had never heard that phrase and had little poetry in your soul and could not know what it meant, when you saw this wonderful object, its beauty, and the play of opposites at work in it, the phrase was not a phrase but the idea coming into your head, which caused confusion and uneasiness, or if blessed, a click of recognition of the sort that must come to those who, never having seen themselves, look into a mirror for the first time. "We had," Jerry would say when he would describe the evening to those he wished to know about it, "just then when the assembling was completed, the table set and unused, before the guests had arrived and the dinner would move forward, stopped time, frozen it hard and brilliant as the sunny ice outside."

"I'm right where I want to be," said Jerry.

"So am I," said Mrs. Labrette.

"What if somehow, just for a little while, you could be in something so beautiful . . . ," said Callie, her voice trailing off as she gazed at the watery scene.

But time really only stops once and for one at a time. And though for the three of them, the table was a joy and nourishment, Jerry's brother's delight was the fires churning red, gold and blue in the fireplaces. When they lit the first blaze, he made the odd yodel that was the sign of his pleasure and approval, and he rocked in his chair almost violently, grinning as if drunk on fire. They dragged the chair with them as they lit each fire, and his glee and fascination had not diminished when the last one was crackling away.

"Well, we know what to do with him during the dinner," said Callie.

Night came, and a harder freeze. The porch lights were turned on, and from inside, the shaded lamps in the parlor emanated out onto the street a warm luster, demure as moonglow. The chandelier in the hallway sparkled so brightly from its many facets that the glass fanlights over the front door appeared shattered, and through the side lights Callie, in her black uniform with its white pique collar and cuffs and the white apron tied around her waist, elegant as only simplicity can be, flitted in and out of view like a beautiful, busy bird.

The first guest arrived early. It was Elizabeth Anderson, Dr. Parchman's wife from across the street.

"I could see you all day through the windows, and I couldn't wait," she said when Callie opened the door for her. She was climbing the porch steps, her face lifted up, full of the joy of one who has not much of it in life and who by little kindnesses, too small to be noticed by most people, is made delirious. "Is it true that you have gotten out the porcelain centerpiece? I'm sure I saw Maggie and you carrying the box this afternoon."

"Mrs. Anderson, look down at those steps, honey. You have all night to see what's inside," said Callie with so much promise that Mrs. Anderson looked still upward and leaned to see past Callie into the hall. She tripped on the last step and giggled as though she did not understand that she had almost hurt herself, or didn't care, like the courageous, or the foolhardy, for whom the risk is more important than the reward. Callie caught her effortlessly, having saved her from minor injuries many times before. Holding Callie's steady hand, she regained her footing and crossed the porch into the house.

Callie brought her over the threshold into the front hall, and as she was helping her off with her coat, Maggie rushed forward from the dining room with a faint, sympathetic smile on her face that, if Elizabeth could tell was pitying, she did not show as she walked out of her coat in the manner of a little girl who flings off her clothes and runs naked just so her embarrassed parents will chase her. She always seemed to have been let loose from a prison where the sentence was stillness and silence, Maggie thought. A smooth, gentle and genteel hysteria threatened to erupt at all times, which Maggie was the most adept at keeping suppressed, for she knew well its cause, though thankfully she was not affected by it. Living with Dr. Anderson had made Elizabeth the way she was. Living with unrelenting irritability, and ever-withheld approval for anything she did well, was the cause of this nervousness in Elizabeth. Maggie knew that well enough. The Anderson home was decorated throughout with Elizabeth's pastels and watercolors of mostly pastoral scenes, which had, if certainly not the skill of a genius, a generous amount of one's eccentricity. In green bountiful pastures through which flowed peaceful, clear brooks grazed cumulous but cross-eyed sheep. Still lifes of oddly incongruous assortments of things were another feature of her work. One, which hung disconcertingly on her kitchen wall, was of a flower vase holding a smaller vase, beside it a spool empty of thread and a cheese grater, all haphazardly arranged on the draining board. In her bedroom hung a charcoal drawing of her husband wearing two neckties. Most of the ladies, chief among them Elsie Moye, thought it was a deficiency of technique in concert with weak-mindedness that was the source of the weird paintings on Dr. Anderson's walls, but Maggie, although she never said so, believed Elizabeth painted the deformities and peculiarities intentionally and was expressing the ironic, droll truth of her life somehow and, in her way, trying to warn her husband that there were limits.

"She's an interesting person," was Maggie's way of cutting off unkind talk about Elizabeth.

Maggie got Elizabeth seated on the sofa by the fire and brought Jerry over to her.

"Your reputation precedes you!" exclaimed Elizabeth giddily, as though she were meeting a famous person of whom she had only heard. It was a little odd, Maggie thought, for Elizabeth had met Jerry before and she knew his story. But her enthusiastic greeting and the way she sat and lifted her hand limply for Jerry to shake did start the evening off with a flourish of the gala. Jerry took her hand lightly and bowed slightly at the waist, as Maggie had taught him to do when meeting a lady.

Mrs. Lamm was next, with her sister. Callie greeted them at the door, and she and Mrs. Lamm's sister smiled at one another and looked straight into one another's amused eyes, silently acknowledging the affinity felt by reasonable people when among the foolish.

Finally Elsie Moye arrived, not walking as the others had done, but in her car, which slid quite a distance down the street past the Labrette house when she applied the brakes. Callie had heard the car coming when she might otherwise have not, for it was a night when a car engine was an improbable sound. She went to the window to see the car glide gracefully past the house and finally come to a stop well down the street when its tires rubbed gently up against the side of the curb where ice had not formed. Enough friction had been created to stop the vehicle. Callie called Mrs. Lamm's sister over to the window to watch Elsie Moye get out of the car and make her way from several houses down the block to the Labrettes' walkway. Her feet moved forward not one in front of the other but almost parallel so as not to fall on the ice, with tiny, mincing steps that made her waddle.

"Now I understand why penguins walk the way they do," said Mrs. Lamm's sister.

On the Labrettes' walkway Elsie Moye regained her high-headed, self-important sashay, which caused Callie and Mrs. Lamm's sister to snap their heads toward each other with expressions of conspiratorial glee, then turn back to watch Elsie Moye's progress, which was all the more hilarious to them, having seen her awkward beginning. She displayed the comic dignity of a pompous, spoiled Persian cat who, due to some ignominious disease, has had the back half of its body shaved but doesn't know it. She rang the bell and was let in by Callie.

"I thought that car was just going to keep on sliding until the ice thawed," said Callie, shaking her head as she took Mrs. Beamon's coat.

"Elsie Moye!" exclaimed Mrs. Lamm's sister, coming into the hall with a big smile on her face as though the main reason she had come to the party was to see Elsie Moye. "Now, I *am* impressed. I said to Callie as I saw how expertly you negotiated that icy sidewalk that I now know why penguins walk the way they do."

Elsie Moye stared at her royally, and did not say a thing. In her hand she held a small package wrapped in paper printed with summer flowers and tied with hot-pink ribbon that stuck out like a scar in the serene room with its muted colors and peaceful lighting.

Jerry came into the hall.

"Is that for Maggie, Elsie Moye?" asked Mrs. Lamm's sister.

149

"Yes, it is," replied Elsie Moye, brittle as the branches outside.

"Ah, Jerry," said Mrs. Lamm's sister. "I'm glad you are here. Now this is a lesson for you in what not to do. You see that little present Mrs. Beamon has in her hand? Well, it is absolutely the wrong thing to do. You bring a gift if you are coming for the weekend. What a gift implies when brought to a dinner party is that you have no intention of reciprocating. Of course, if you don't intend to return the invitation—"

"It is not for the dinner," said Elsie Moye, cutting the woman off.

Mrs. Lamm's sister lifted her eyebrows and nodded down to Jerry, as if to say, All will be explained to us.

"It is a birthday present I never got around to giving her," said Elsie Moye petulantly.

"Another unfortunate lapse, Jerry," said Mrs. Lamm's sister. "You see, now the hostess, Mrs. Labrette in this case, will have to deal with this little birthday present on a day not even her birthday. Open it, exclaim over it, show it around and then put it away, and at a time when she, above all, needs to be seeing to her dinner and tending to her guests. How much more convenient for everyone if Mrs. Beamon had sent it over in the afternoon with a little note saying how much she was looking forward to this evening. Remember this, dear, and don't ever do what Mrs. Beamon has done."

"*I* would not have risked the life of my help in this awful weather like that," Elsie Moye said pointedly. "In South Carolina, Jerry, they abuse their servants in the most awful ways."

"You are always so responsible, Elsie Moye, and of course you are right," said Mrs. Lamm's sister. "Jerry, don't you think, then, in that case it might have been better to wait until another time to give Mrs. Labrette her belated birth-day present? After all, Maggie has waited some time for it. I'm certain she would have enjoyed one more day or two of suspense, aren't you?"

"She did send over somebody with a note this afternoon," said Jerry.

"You don't say," said Mrs. Lamm's sister, putting her palm between Jerry's shoulder blades and guiding him into the parlor. Mrs. Beamon was left standing in the hall, holding the garish little package.

"You will learn so much this evening, dear," Mrs. Lamm's sister said.

At exactly eight o'clock, Callie opened the doors to the dining room.

"Dinner is served," she intoned. The guests rose, and as he had been instructed by Mrs. Labrette to do, Jerry, beginning with Mrs. Labrette, took each lady by the arm, one by one, and escorted her to the table. He was to pick which lady was to represent the President's wife by escorting her in last.

After Mrs. Labrette he chose Mrs. Beamon, and seated her to Mrs. Labrette's left. Next to Mrs. Beamon he put Mrs. Lamm's sister. He was to be at the opposite end of the table from Mrs. Labrette. To his left he seated Mrs. Lamm, and finally he ushered in Mrs. Elizabeth Anderson to be seated to the right of the hostess, in the place of honor. When she saw the table set with the bright silver and crystal and the white linen and the magnificent porcelain centerpiece oiled in the candlelight, she stopped in the doorway and her eyes glistened as brightly as anything in the room. Then there bloomed on her face an expression of such intelligence that Jerry, looking up at her thought that the silly, frail, nervous lady he had felt sorry for had been a put-on of some kind, that here was the real Mrs. Anderson, and everything he knew about her, what he had seen across the street from Mrs. Labrette's of her pathetic situation seemed more cruel. He knew very well that it was better not to know that you were pitiful in some way. That had been first among his early perceptions. She had a sad look on her face, as though she had been reminded that long ago she had been told she could not have the thing she most wanted, and that she should have waited for something or someone she had not. The door into her heart was one with no lock and too many had pushed through it on their way to someplace else.

When she spoke, it seemed that she had planned what she would say, although she could not have known she would be selected to represent the guest of honor—would never have believed she would be chosen. But she plucked from her mind the perfect words, as easily as she might have picked a flower from a stalk as she walked along a garden fence, never breaking her stride and never looking down to see that she had absentmindedly selected the most perfectly formed blossom in the garden.

> "When the short day is brightest, with frost and fire,
> The brief sun flames the ice, on pond and ditches,
> In windless cold that is the heart's heat,
> Reflecting in a watery mirror
> A glare that is blindness in the early afternoon.
> And glow more intense than blaze of branch, or brazier,
> Stirs the dumb spirit: no wind, but pentecostal fire
> In the dark time of the year. Between melting and freezing
> The soul's sap quivers."

In silence Jerry escorted Elizabeth to her chair.

"Well, that will do for a prayer, don't you think?" said Mrs. Labrette quietly. "Please be seated."

The tone had been set by Mrs. Anderson's recitation, and a spirit of goodwill seemed to settle over the assembled guests. Mrs. Labrette watched Jerry's eyes shine in the candlelight as each dish was brought in and served by Callie. Mrs. Lamm, with each new delight, slowly shook her head in wonder at Maggie Labrette's quiet, refined, seamless way of doing things. Her sister had not a thing to say during the entire dinner, which Mrs. Lamm knew, if the others did not, was a sign of her heartiest approval. Even Elsie Moye was heard to murmur under her breath several times that evening, "Beautiful, beautiful."

Mrs. Anderson met and surpassed her responsibilities as the guest of honor. Uncharacteristically talkative, she regaled the ladies and Jerry with amusing tales about her childhood in Virginia, and toward the end of dinner she told of the day she married Dr. Anderson, of whom her father had not approved. How on the day of her marriage, with all the preparations going on in the house, her father had, until the last minute, refused to get some of the boys to lift the heater out of the parlor. It was a June wedding, and although the heater was usually lifted out in late April or early May when the chance of an unexpected cold snap had passed, he had left it there, knowing that the wedding was to take place in the parlor in which the most appropriate and central place for the minister, wedding party and guests to gather was before the prodigally carved-and-mirrored mantel that towered at that end of the room. Right where the heater stood.

"To provoke me, I can't help but think," she said with mild wonder. "Can you imagine, a wedding taking place around a cold heater?" Her delicate hand scurried up to her throat as though to choke the laughter that was very plainly about to overtake her. "Maggie was there. She saw it."

"It was a beautiful wedding, Elizabeth, in spite of everything," said Maggie indulgently.

"'Papa, do pray go and get some of the farm help to lift that heater out of the parlor,' I begged. 'Heigh-yo, we just had the heater put in,' Papa said. It was nearly new, don't you see, bought and installed in the spring when he could get it at the best price. Then Papa put on his hat and went out on the front porch and sat down in his chair that only he could sit in, because it reared back and fell over when anybody else sat in it. But it tilted him back just enough so that, whether you were on the porch with him or looking at him from the street, he looked like he was staring down his nose at the world. And the way he was tilted back in the chair and would cock his hat forward, all you could see was that nose, not the eyes staring down it. Mama, who had a different description of his visage, which she called 'presenting his chin to the world,' knowing that there was no dealing with Papa when he got that way, started rummaging around the house to find something to drape the heater in, but no matter what you wrapped or covered it with, there was no mistaking that it was a big, shiny, oil-burning heater you were trying to hide. Finally, Brother had had enough of Papa, and he simply walked onto the front porch and announced to Papa that he was going out to the farm and get some of the boys to come and lift that heater out of the parlor. And he did, and Mama and I took off the guard from the fireplace and cleaned it out and filled it with magnolias, which were the most plentiful and the biggest anybody had ever seen them that year. She pinned some to the organdy curtains and piled them on the mantel and on the steps leading up to the porch and, excepting Papa in his chair, on anything else that would sit still. I carried white garden roses that Mama had picked from where they grew along the fence at the back of our yard. She tied them together with this wide piece of white organdy ribbon she had saved from her mother's grave. The roses still had dew on them when I carried them. The windows to the parlor were open, and the smell of magnolias and roses was so thick that you couldn't tell if it was coming from inside the house or out, and the gauzy white curtains would lift with the breeze sometimes, as though sighing like little girls who can't wait for the day when it will be they standing before a minister all in white, a bouquet trembling in their hands. Papa remained on the porch, and when the minister asked, 'Who giveth this woman to this man?' everybody turned toward the window. 'I suppose I do,' Papa said without even looking around at us. Then we went into the dining room where Mother had made the most beautiful reception, with the table draped to the floor in white linen and the big silver punch bowl shiny and full of wedding punch and wreathed in English ivy from the yard. But you know, as soon as the vows were spoken, Dr. Anderson went out to the porch, too, and dragged a chair up beside Papa, and they sat talking low and close to each other the entire afternoon until I changed into my traveling clothes and came out onto the porch, ready to catch the train to Asheville. Everybody says to this day, in spite of Papa sitting on the front porch and not coming into the parlor and standing up with us and Dr. Anderson seeming more interested in Papa than in me that day, that it was the most beautiful wedding they have ever seen, including ones where you have professional florists to decorate the church and dresses made in Richmond."

And because she did not laugh, they all could, and did, until at the end of the story Maggie and Callie looked at each other and cried a little. And although Jerry was not quite sure what was so funny about nearly getting married around a heater, he laughed to see the ladies, who seldom did more than smile politely, lean back in their seats and rock forward and jiggle with glee, their giggles pinging off the crystal glasses on the table and tinkling in the chandelier above.

They had, during the evening, improvised every situation in which they might be able to teach Jerry manners—each lady coming up with little scenarios. The difficult yet entirely practical way to eat soup by moving the spoon away rather than toward you started a whole conversation among the women.

"Now I also have heard that it is just as correct to pick the bowl up and drink the soup," said Mrs. Lamm.

"Huh!" said Mrs. Beamon. Maggie turned and smiled at Elsie Moye in a way that squelched her better than a frown would have.

"There are certain situations when you would be absolutely correct in doing that," said Mrs. Labrette. She then directed her attention to Jerry, staying out from in between Elsie Moye and Myrtle Lamm.

Mrs. Labrette began to question Jerry.

"What might be a situation in which you would drink your soup?" she asked.

"If you didn't have a spoon?" said Jerry.

"Well, yes, but what if you had a spoon, can you think of another reason you might lift the bowl to your lips?" asked Mrs. Labrette.

"If someone with you who had never dined in the Governor's Mansion or something like that, picked up the bowl and drank his, then maybe you'd want to do it so they wouldn't think they had done something stupid," said Jerry.

Mrs. Labrette looked around the table at the ladies one by one, fixing each with a look as near to triumph as she ever got on her face.

"It is clear he has been spending a great deal of time with you, Maggie," said Mrs. Anderson softly.

"Well, I certainly wouldn't do such a thing!" said Elsie Moye indignantly. "I mean, really, this indulgence of the ignorant doesn't do a thing but lower the tone generally.

What if the person picked his nose? Are you going to do the same? Where does it end?"

"I wonder, Elsie, dear, if that is the best topic of conversation at dinner," said Mrs. Lamm's sister.

"Of course, Elsie, you are right, there are limits, but then isn't that really the thing about manners, well, about life for that matter, having a sense of what to overlook and what to try to change?" said Maggie.

It seemed to several at the table that Elsie Moye was in a very bad mood.

"She's angry with herself for not being able to find something wrong with all this," Mrs. Lamm said behind her napkin to Mrs. Anderson. "It would be a lot more pleasant if she was just mad with one of us instead of at herself."

"If the soup was in a cup, you could drink it," piped Jerry.

"You are getting very close. Callie, go and get one of the cream-soup bowls from the china cabinet." The other ladies were now as interested in what the answer would be as Jerry. Even Elsie Moye, although she stared off to one side, could not hide the fact that her look of indifference was studied. Mrs. Anderson knew the answer, but watched Jerry delightedly to see what he would do when he found out.

Callie came out with the cream-soup bowl on a silver tray, and Mrs. Labrette took it by the handles on either side.

"It looks like it has ears," said Jerry.

"Indeed it does, and they have a use. You will find that very little of what we think of as useless custom or frivolous ornamentation is that. Nearly all these things have a practical purpose or are the vestige of one. This is a cream-soup bowl, only used at luncheon. The handles are there for the sole purpose of lifting the cup to your lips and drinking the soup. Now, it has become customary to use a spoon until just one last bit of soup is left, but then it's bottoms up!" Holding the cup by its handles she moved it to her lips as if drinking from it.

"Well, I always wondered why those things had those little handles, and other soup bowls didn't," said Mrs. Lamm, not the least bit embarrassed or offended by being instructed on the proper way to eat soup by Maggie.

"But, why, I have always wondered," said Mrs. Anderson. "It makes complete sense to me to ask why the difference to begin with. Why is it all right to drink the soup at luncheon but not at dinner?"

"You know, I don't know," said Mrs. Labrette, perking up and blinking comically as if she had been a bird who was asked "Why do you fly?" And they all had another laugh together, as good common sense can often cause to happen.

"Well, I can tell Pa he could have lunch at the Governor's Mansion as long as all they served was soup. He always drinks his out of the bowl," said Jerry.

"Some people do have a natural sense of how to do," said Mrs. Labrette.

Elsie Moye rolled her eyes, and Maggie saw her.

"Elsie, why don't you instruct Jerry on when to rise in the presence of a lady," said Maggie.

"When a lady enters the room or gets up from the table, you get up and you don't sit until she does," said Elsie Moye dryly.

In the middle of dinner, Mrs. Lamm's sister, on Jerry's right, turned abruptly and started talking to Mrs. Beamon. On his left, Mrs. Lamm stared silently ahead until he turned to engage her in conversation.

"Well done!" exclaimed Mrs. Labrette, who saw the whole thing from her end of the table even though she had begun what appeared to be an absorbing conversation with Mrs. Anderson.

He learned to serve himself from the platter as Callie held

it between him and Mrs. Lamm. After the main course, there was placed before him a silver-rimmed clear bowl on a plate, with a fork on the left of the plate and a spoon on the right. The bowl was filled with water in which floated a slice of lemon thin as paper. The same was put at each lady's place.

"Now I never did know how you're supposed to do this," admitted Mrs. Lamm. Then Mrs. Labrette demonstrated, directing her instructions to Jerry. She showed him how to remove the finger bowl to the upper left of his place, and to put the fork on the table to the left and the spoon to the right. Then dessert was served, Callie's specialty, meringue in which nested ice cream and peaches. They taught Jerry to eat it properly with both the fork and the spoon. Finally it came time to use the finger bowl, and although Maggie continued to direct her attention to Jerry, Mrs. Lamm's sister was to say later that she thought Elsie Moye got very quiet and attentive during the demonstration.

"Just dip your fingertips in the water, and if you wish you can lightly brush your lips with your wet fingers, but don't drip! Then simply dry your fingers on your napkin," said Mrs. Labrette.

With that, the dinner was finished. Mrs. Labrette rang for Callie and thanked her in front of Jerry and the ladies, and they all applauded, even Mrs. Beamon.

"I, as the hostess, will rise, Jerry, and announce coffee in the living room, and then you are free to leave the table," said Maggie, and she did so. They moved to the living room, laughing and talking. The baby was brought out, and they put his chair in front of the fireplace and he gazed at the fire and rocked.

Elsie Moye was the first to go. She rose and said her good-night and how much she had enjoyed the evening. They all listened anxiously for the sound of the car to fade away. One by one, the ladies left. Mrs. Anderson was the last to go. Maggie and Callie stood on the porch until she had crossed the street. They watched her climb her own porch steps and try the door, which was locked. She rang the doorbell, and Dr. Anderson appeared, opened the door and turned back into the house. They could hear him cursing as Mrs. Anderson stepped inside the house and closed the front door behind her.

It was decided that of course Jerry and his little brother would stay the night, and Mrs. Labrette put them in the guest room at the front of the house, which she had prepared for them. Jerry bathed himself and his little brother, then tied him back in the chair, and he put him in front of the fireplace to enjoy the glowing coals for just a little while longer. Callie turned the covers back, and Jerry got into the bed.

"You sure had a big time tonight, didn't you, honey?" said Callie.

"I've never seen anything like it," he said. Callie left the room, and Mrs. Labrette came to say good night, and he fell asleep.

It had been the best night of his little life so far. An experience that he would remember always and draw on not for what it was but for what it became for him—a kind of innocent, blissful lost time between tragedies, for when he fell asleep, he did not wake up until morning when he found his brother, strapped in the little red rocking chair, facedown in the fireplace, burned beyond recognition.

He pulled the rocker from the dead coals. It popped upright like a toy that can't be knocked over. The chair teetered back and forth, as if being gently rocked. His little brother's face was burned away, and in its place was a mask of ash and embers embedded in charred flesh. He ran to get Mrs. Labrette, who when she saw the dead baby still strapped in the chair made an odd, surprised sound of the sort made when something vital, almost forgotten, has been suddenly remembered. Then she dropped to the floor, like a curtain falling, unconscious.

Callie ran across the street to get Dr. Anderson, but it was clear to all of them that there was nothing to be done. Dr. Anderson revived Mrs. Labrette and then sent Lyman out to get Jerry's daddy.

"Tell him on the way back what has happened," warned the doctor.

The body was removed to Dr. Anderson's house across the street. The fireplace was cleaned before Mr. Labrette and Mr. Chiffon got back. When Mr. Chiffon came into the room, the only thing left of what had happened was Jerry and the little rocker, blackened all around except for the place, still red and shiny with little lambs cavorting on the back slats, where the baby's body had shielded it from the fire.

When they led Mr. Chiffon into the guest bedroom where the baby had burned to death, Jerry was standing in front of the cold fireplace by the little chair, looking down at the spot, swept clean now, where the baby's face had been. Mr. Chiffon walked slowly toward Jerry. Mr. and Mrs. Labrette were in the doorway. Callie stood behind them. In the hallway Dr. Anderson was on the telephone.

"Maybe we ought to leave them alone," said Callie.

Then, before anyone could move to stop him, Mr. Chiffon raised his cupped hand high over his head and brought it down on the side of Jerry's head. When the hand struck Jerry, it made a sound like a wet paper bag popping. Jerry collapsed, but Mr. Chiffon lifted him up and slapped him across the face again.

"I told you you didn't have no business coming here," Mr. Chiffon said, and hit him in the face again and let him fall. Jerry started crawling across the floor, but Mr. Chiffon caught him by the waist of his pajamas and pulled him back and lifted him and raised his hand and brought it down again. The blows kept coming. Jerry could not look up and could not see them coming and never knew when the next one would hit. Mr. Chiffon did not hurry, but was coldly methodical. He never raised his voice.

"You killed him both" is what they all agreed later they'd heard Mr. Chiffon say, *him,* not *them.* In his rage he looked around as if trapped, then his eyes fell on the fire poker, and he grabbed it and lifted himself up onto his toes and raised his arm and lowered the other shoulder to deliver what would surely have been a death blow. Maggie ran toward him and threw herself onto Jerry, who was balled up on the floor. The poker was already streaking down like a hot falling star and it landed with a gorge-raising, sick, tight thud on her back. Mr. Chiffon raised the fire poker again. He seemed unaware that Mrs. Labrette had thrown herself between him and his son or didn't care. When his arm reached the highest point from which it would be brought down again, his body stiffened and he leaned back slightly as though he were trying to gather all his strength to deliver a killing hit. He froze for a moment, reared back and ready, then grunted and sneezed, spraying a thick mist of blood in the air in front of his face. When the next blow did not come, Maggie lifted her head to look up at him, then felt him collapse on top of her. She felt Jerry stir underneath her, then pain in her stomach as he punched and struggled to get out from under her. She was pinned down by the dead weight of Mr. Chiffon's body and being gouged by the frantic squirming boy trying to free himself. Then she felt the weight removed and she raised herself slightly and Jerry scrambled out like a trapped wild animal let loose. He got to his feet. Dr. Anderson and Mr. Labrette lifted Mrs. Labrette and helped her onto the bed. As soon as she was laid down, she reached for Jerry, who ran to her and pushed his face into her prostrate body as though he was trying to burrow into her. He started to scream, and her dress got wet where his face was. Dr. Anderson got his bag and knelt beside Mr. Chiffon's body. He listened for a heartbeat but heard none.

"This man's dead," he said. Then he took a hypodermic needle and gave Maggie and Jerry a dose that put them both to sleep for the rest of the day, laid out side by side on the bed. Mr. Chiffon's body was taken across the street to lie beside his child, who had been deformed worse in death than he had been in life.

Jerry and Mrs. Labrette slept on the bed while the sheriff came and went and took statements and asked questions and huddled with Dr. Anderson and Mr. Labrette, then pronounced what everybody already knew—that this was a terrible and tragic accident.

Maggie and Jerry slept while Callie cleaned up the mess. And they slept while the sympathetic and the curious, with food and comfort as a pretense, came up to the front door, hoping to be invited in for the chance to get a peek into the room, until tired of it, Mr. Labrette had Callie draw all the curtains. When night came they did not put on the porch light, and it was rightly assumed that they were not to be called upon anymore.

Callie and Mr. Labrette sat by the bed in the room, keeping watch, and early in the evening the two, lady and boy, stirred at the same time, then woke up. The boy began to repeat over and over, "I don't care, I don't care," and the lady raised herself from the bed, went to the mantel silently and knelt on the hearth. She stuck her head into the fireplace and peered up into the chimney, as if trying to see whether or not the flue was open. Then she started to lay a fire with the unused wood that had been brought in for the party. Dr. Anderson was sent for. He came immediately and dosed the two again, and they slept through the long night and into the next day.

After seven years in New York, Jerry returned to North Carolina. He went to Raleigh, and got a job at Rakov, Ralston & Walston Interiors, which had expanded its business beyond its Richmond-based establishment to Charlotte and Atlanta as well as Raleigh. He did well there, climbed fast and made friends, but nearly every weekend he returned to Branch Creek, dispensing his acquired good taste and advice to the ladies of the town.

One weekend, a few years after his return to North Carolina, he was helping to plan Mr. and Mrs. I. C. Lamm's thirty-fifth-wedding-anniversary party. He had helped Mrs. Lamm pick out a dress for the party, which was to be an afternoon tea at her home on Central Avenue. He had told her he would do the flowers and assured her that they would be beautiful.

"But what, in the name of God, about my hair?" she whined. "I mean Jeanette uptown is fine for church and when you're a corpse, but this is a day on which I need to look more than good."

"I've a friend from New York who comes down once a month to the best shop in Raleigh. It's where the Governor's wife has her hair done. I think he could do something for you," Jerry said.

As always, Mrs. Lamm thought, he has used an opportunity to help as a chance to criticize, too, but like all the ladies in Branch Creek, she took his advice and made the appointment with Mr. Coy of New York. And although she didn't say so, she looked forward to meeting one of Jerry's friends from his New York days. What she might learn of that mysterious time was as enticing as being fussed over by a New York hairdresser—and a man.

On the first visit to the salon, dressed in her best, she mustered as much confidence as she thought a lady ought to have in such a situation and approached the French Provincial reception desk. Behind the receptionist stood a young man with his back turned to her. His hair was the prettiest in the shop, long and blond and tied in a thick ponytail that flipped when he moved, as if swatting away any worry that might try to enter his head.

"I'm Mrs. I. C. Lamm from Branch Creek, and I have an appointment with Mr. Coy of New York," she said haughtily.

The young man turned quickly to face Mrs. Lamm. "You are from Branch Creek?" he asked. "Do you know Jerry Chiffon?"

"Indeed I do. It is he who has sent me," said Mrs. Lamm. "Are you Mr. Coy of New York?"

"Call me Hugh, dear, and step right this way," he said.

"How did you and Jerry meet?" she asked. "Were you in decorating school together?"

Mr. Coy stopped still and turned his head slowly around like an owl and looked at Mrs. Lamm as if she had insulted him.

"Decorating school? He never went to decorating school. I found him wandering around Penn Station," he said. He turned back and continued past the line of chairs and beauticians busy with scissors and rollers, past the row of ladies under the dryers, then to a private room at the back of the shop where he alone worked.

"Have a seat, dear," he said. He stood behind her and

held her head between his hands, molding her hair into approximations of hairdos that he carefully considered in the mirror. From a drawer he took out a card to which were pasted locks of hair that had been dyed in sample colors, and held it up to her face briefly then put the card back into the drawer.

"Relax here for a moment, dear, and I'll come back and begin to tell you what you obviously have not heard," he said, speaking to her in the mirror. "Auburnish red, I think. Yes. Fabulous!"

Mrs. Lamm watched him leave, then shared a delighted smile with her own reflection. And she couldn't help feeling that Jerry had known Mr. Coy of New York would tell all, that she had been selected to hear it.

Once a month, whether she needs it or not, Mrs. Lamm drives an hour and ten minutes to have her hair dyed and done. She loves to tell her sister about her visits to her hairdresser, always using his full title when she refers to him.

Sit with Mrs. I. C. Lamm and her sister from Passiflora, South Carolina, near Charleston, on the wide porch of the Lamm house. They are so happy finally to be able to enjoy the porch, unmolested. The news people have abandoned the town to cover a story in which someone has actually been killed and the motives for the crime are easier to explain. The lack of interest the wider world has in Branch Creek and the lack of interest its citizens have in the wider world has returned. In that sense things are back to normal.

The new crime that has drawn the news people, like flies to filth, involves a grandfather younger than a grandfather is expected to be who has murdered his twelve-year-old grandson with whom he has shared a bed since the boy was nine. Here is one the news people can pick up and really squeeze the juice out of, but it is one that the people of Branch Creek cannot really discuss on their porches or across their clotheslines. Men just simply do not speak of it, and ladies talk one to the other in low tones of the unimaginable crime and hush up when someone comes into the room.

Jerry's story still interests them above all else.

Listen as Mrs. Lamm, resting in the nice old canopied glider, discusses with her sister, seated in a wicker rocking chair thick with green paint, what she has seen and heard of Jerry's life from the day of the ice-themed dinner party until just last week when he shot at Senator Hampton.

"They buried the daddy and the baby in the same casket," says Mrs. Lamm. "Open! Arranged the baby facedown on top of the daddy, so you couldn't see at all that the child's face had been burned off. They posed one of Mr. Chiffon's hands in the small of the child's back and the other on the back of the child's head, and it just looked like the daddy had fallen asleep with the poor little thing in his arms."

Mrs. Lamm's sister is needlepointing tiny Christmas wreaths on linen cocktail napkins although it is June. She means to have two dozen by the holidays for an open house she plans to give.

"I had never heard of such bad taste when you told me this insane story the first time, and I have not since," she says. She looks over her reading glasses at her sister. "Now it strikes me as morbid to the point of hilarity." She lifts her head so that she can look through her glasses and returns her attention to her cocktail napkins.

"People came from over the Virginia line to see it," says Mrs. Lamm, jabbing her finger in her sister's direction. "And that was before twenty-four-hour news. It was simple word of mouth, and it traveled quicker than the train. Many, many got here in time to have a look before the burial. They had to move the funeral to the high-school auditorium, and still there were people standing in the doorways and outside under the windows, listening."

Mrs. Lamm's sister sighs deeply and impatiently at having to hear it all again, but Mrs. Lamm, as enthusiastic and fresh as a conscientious actress in a long run, goes on with the often-told tale.

"It was little Jerry who made all the decisions, with Maggie's help, of course, but the one thing she could not make him change was the open casket and the way the two were laid out. His natural talent for arranging things she could not overrule.

"It was the biggest thing ever to happen here. Excepting the latest, of course. Although, in a sense, the funeral was bigger because it attracted more actual people than Jerry's current troubles. Not just news people, don't you know. The paper ran a picture of the two of them in the casket, with the caption 'Branch Creek Mourns Double Tragedy.'"

"A name in the newspaper is the height of fame to you, isn't it?" says Mrs. Lamm's sister. She puts her needlework down on her lap and folds her arms across her waist impatiently. "In all of his pronouncements, did Jerry ever tell you people that it is considered not quite fine to get into the papers more than three times in your life?" asks Mrs. Lamm's sister coolly. She has read this somewhere. She looks off over to the peaceful, stately yard of Dr. Anderson's place, with its high oaks and black wrought-iron gate, and it seems that finally the quiet dignity that her sister has always assured her was the main thing about Branch Creek perhaps has returned.

"Well, I don't know that Mr. Chiffon had ever gotten his name in the paper before this, but I'm sure that bigheaded baby never had," says Mrs. Lamm on behalf of Mr. Chiffon and his son who could not defend themselves now. "And I do know that it is all right to have your name in the paper if you die."

"But Myrtle, honey—a picture of an opened casket.

Really," says Mrs. Lamm's sister. She shakes her head, picks up her handiwork and pulls the wisp of green silk thread from her needle.

"You were not always so up on what is and is not proper for the grief-stricken. The bangle bracelets at Daddy's funeral," says Mrs. Lamm, lowering her chin and looking up from under her eyebrows at her sister, who ignores the little cut by intently rethreading her needle with red silk for the tiny holly berries in the design. She changes the subject with the thread to an aspect of the story that interests her more.

"Tell me this," says Mrs. Lamm's sister. "What, if anything, do you know of that period in New York? Therein lies the key to his later actions, I would say. Therein lies the explanation or justification for what he has done, I would think. What the law calls a bar to prosecution or a defense that justifies. These are strictly legal terms, as I am sure you may or may not know."

Mrs. Lamm's sister is acquainted with some medium-fine points of the law, for her husband, Arthur Boyette, is a judge, and since he has always leaned slightly toward the libertarian side in his politics and decisions, it is thought, by Mrs. Lamm, that her sister knows more about getting away with a crime than she does about getting caught at one.

"I don't know about any justifications for crime or bars to prosecution, but I do know that there has to be some good reason he has done what they say. I don't know if New York is the key to it all or not," states Mrs. Lamm. "But I did notice that he came back different."

"How so?" asks Mrs. Lamm's sister.

"He just was not at all the excited, sweet, enthusiastic boy who we put on the Palmetto Express to New York City. That morning he left here with a pocketful of money from

Elsie Moye, he smiled and waved to us like it was a roller coaster he was getting on. As it turned out, I guess that is exactly what we put him on."

"In what sense did he come back a different Jerry Chiffon from the one you had sent away?" asks Mrs. Lamm's sister prosecutorially. She does not look up but remains focused on her needlepoint, as though she is not really very interested in what her sister has to tell her.

"Well, he went off and broadened himself for one thing in a big way. He hobnobbed with the finest people." Mrs. Lamm pauses, and studies her sister's face for signs that her sister's feigned indifference is becoming more difficult for her to maintain. She thinks she sees a twitch, a slight lifting of her sister's forehead, which might indicate that she has heard something that intrigues her.

"He had always had sweet manners," Mrs. Lamm continues, "but now they were so perfect that sometimes you thought he might be making fun of you. Came back here looking at everybody and at everything we did and how we did it in a way not disapproving, but kind of like he pitied us. Except Maggie, whom he became even more attached to and in awe of. And she became more attached to him.

"But there was something else. Something kind of held in and wary. He was older, and I don't mean looked. Seemed. Like he had a secret that would explain him and a great deal about you if he told it to you. He had this sad sophistication which, it turns out, was fury, I guess, and grief."

"You run over the most interesting parts to get to the dullest," says Mrs. Lamm's sister.

"Do I?" says Mrs. Lamm. "Seems like I don't. Seems like something in the tale hit you head-on." She is quiet now— looking off to Dr. Anderson's house to see if there are any signs of life coming from there that might interest her. She has her sister's attention and intends to enjoy it.

Her sister knows what Mrs. Lamm is doing. She puts the needlepoint into her sewing bag and goes into her purse for a compact. She opens it and studiously begins to powder her face in a manner that will convey to Mrs. Lamm that anything she might want to hear about now is just conversation and of secondary interest to primping.

"How do you know, for example, that he socialized with good people?" asks the sister in a tone of voice meant to communicate bored suspicion.

"Do you really want to know?" asks Mrs. Lamm primly.

"You want to tell me, it seems," says Mrs. Lamm's sister. She puts the compact back in her purse, looks directly at her sister and places her folded hands onto her lap, as though she is about to indulge a child who wants her attention.

"You know, I go to Raleigh to have my hair dyed by—" Mrs. Lamm begins.

"Mr. Coy of New York," her sister drones in mock boredom.

"Yes," says Mrs. Lamm, patiently cupping the hair on the back of her head with her hand. Her sister looks at her and then to heaven.

"It costs a fortune, but look at me," says Mrs. Lamm, "Mr. Coy of New York knows the whole story of that time in New York. Mr. Coy of New York was right there. I'll try to tell it to you as Mr. Coy of New York has told it to me. Although I'm sure I won't tell it nearly as well as he does. And your hair won't be red when I finish.

"Jerry, immediately upon arriving in New York, was picked up in the Pennsylvania Station by Mr. Coy of New York, although he was not at that time known as such. He was then a young man who hung around train stations, and, as we would say, they took up with one another, for that night at least. Mr. Coy of New York is about Jerry's age,

I'd say, and was and is downright pretty, so pretty in fact that he spent part of his time dressed as a girl and walked the streets more for a lark, I think, than a living."

She stops for an instant and smiles, surprised and pleased with herself for how she has described Mr. Coy of New York's dubious past. Her sister stares disapprovingly at her.

"I cannot believe you have such conversations as what you are describing with a skilled worker," she says. Mrs. Lamm ignores the reproach.

"Well, Mr. Coy of New York was living with a rich roommate who was also on some kind of a lark. You know, bored, slumming, rebelling like they do sometimes, and he was from one of the richest and most prominent families in the North. Mr. Coy of New York said, Myrtle, he said to me, these people were in the rowboat that was sent out to find a place for the *Mayflower* to pull up to. Said, they're married all up into the best families in the North and the South. Vice Presidents and United States Senators among them, and nearly every state in New England has had one of them for a Governor at some time or another. All of them peering down into their bottomless trusts with which they support their stratospheric high-mindedness, is how Mr. Coy of New York put it. He gets even grander when he talks about them, flipping that little paintbrush around and slinging hair dye everywhere. Piles of old money molding under the new it has earned, he says, and hoards of these people living off the interest on the interest."

"I've never heard of such a thing, and I don't know that I believe it entirely," says Mrs. Lamm's sister. "These boys like your hairdresser and his friend are prone to improving upon the manner in which they have been brought up. There is usually a suspicious background that needs tidying up. Every single one I've ever known about is in some sort of trade basically or skilled labor that they delude themselves into thinking is *art*. They love to pretend that they don't need to do what they do. Charleston is overpolluted with the type." She has jumped to disagree too quickly, and in a way that betrays that she does believe the beginning of the story of Jerry's time in New York with his socially prominent renegade friend, but wishes she didn't. There is in her voice a flippant tinge of what Mrs. Lamm recognizes as jealousy. It is a tone of voice she has heard often in her life, and it reminds her of when they were children and her sister would say she didn't want something when she very much did.

"Jerry has never done any such of a thing," counters Mrs. Lamm. "He has never tried to pretend he was something he wasn't."

"You must be out of your mind. That boy has tried to be everything except what he is ever since I've known anything about him. Up to and including trying to pass himself off as some sort of crazy lady assassin," says Mrs. Lamm's sister.

"He has tried in every way possible to improve himself, but he has never pretended that he was anything but what he is, a poor tenant-farmer's son," Mrs. Lamm lectures. "As for the trouble he's got himself into, there will be, I am sure, an explanation in the fullness of time."

The conversation pauses for a silence long enough for both women to know that they have had a tiff. Then Mrs. Lamm perks up and smiles sweetly at her sister. "Just so you know and can compensate, it is a sign of a weak and fearful mind when people want to hear a story and then don't believe it when it veers off from how they'd like it to be," she says.

"Oh, for heaven's sake, go on," says Mrs. Lamm's sister.

"They lived in a real odd part of New York among some outlandish types of people, hermaphrodites and men in women's clothes and women in men's clothes and perverts and Communists, I think. And actors, too, according to Mr. Coy of New York, but not anybody you would have ever heard of.

"At first Jerry took up with these people knowing very little about them beyond their names, then there were calls from a very well-spoken mother with this real high-toned accent like they have in old movies about high society. And the mail was not the kind of mail that people living in such a way as they were, in such a place, got. Requests from charities and invitations to weddings and deb balls on very good stock. Newsletters from fancy schools. Then one day there was mail from the Social Register Association asking for an update of Mr. Handiford Pepper Crompton's information. He sent the form back after changing his name on the form from Mr. Handiford Pepper Crompton to Miss Dynel Fall, a name sometimes used by the now Mr. Coy of New York when he was dressed for the train station, so to speak. Which they duly printed, Mr. Coy of New York said when he told me that part, and it tickled him so good that he snapped his fingers in the air over his head.

"Then, he says, when Jerry asked, as anyone would have, why Handy lived the life he did, he claimed that he lived this debauched life because it was a life lived among the kind of people for whom who he was and what he came from and how much money he had was meaningless. In so many other situations he could never know whether it was being a Crompton that got him in and kept him in whether he succeeded or failed.

"With sex, success is measurable, is what Mr. Coy of New York says, and he tells that part like he is telling about somebody who has given his last dime to a good cause."

At the jail, Jerry has told Maggie the story Mrs. Lamm is telling her sister.

He adds, "Well, of course it is an impossible thing to ever be sure of. Silliness really to expect it, especially for someone like Handy whose family connections would be at the top of the list of interesting things about him to most people. Unrealistic for anyone to expect that they can decide why they will be liked or pursued. I, for most of my life, certainly never had much to recommend me except what I aspired to," says Jerry.

"I'm not sure that is true, Jerry," says Mrs. Labrette.

"You know it better than anyone," says Jerry. "The qualities people liked about me were most often the ones I made up—acquired, admired in others and decided to attach to myself. Except for you, everybody in Branch Creek, the women at least, are that way, and I wouldn't be surprised to find out that it is true of every place on earth."

"I have never been as good as you make me out to be, Jerry," says Mrs. Labrette. "And I don't know if I agree with you at all. It is most often the one characteristic we would change first in ourselves that is usually the most winning. That is certainly true about you."

"And what, do tell me, is my most winning characteristic?" asks Jerry.

"Innocence," Mrs. Labrette replies.

And in Branch Creek on the porch in the glider, Mrs. Lamm has explained to her sister a similar theory of desirability, which her sister is certain represents and proves further the delusions rampant in Branch Creek.

"Huh! If you are liked it is in spite of what you aspire to, I would imagine," Mrs. Lamm's sister retorts.

"What a mean and hateful thing to say," says Mrs. Lamm. "You yourself are made up of all the things you try to be and all the ways you hide what you don't like about yourself. Like how you pretend you don't want to know something when you do and pretend you disapprove of what I'm telling you because you know it will make me tell you more if for no other reason than to irritate you.

"What has this to do with anything? Of course it is true what you say. So true it doesn't bear repeating. Do tell what happened next," says Mrs. Lamm's sister peevishly.

"Well, as you might expect. Well, no *you* wouldn't, but as those of us who know Jerry might have expected, he caused the boy and his family to make up with each other. It started on the telephone. From a quick I'll see if he's here, the conversations between the mother and Jerry over time became longer and more friendly, and they got interested in each other. They would talk about Handy together—discuss his likes and dislikes and tell each other things about him that neither one had known before. It was Jerry who got back the mother's son for her. She was grateful. Jerry was taken in by the Cromptons. Asked to their big old house on Nantucket Island every summer. Had all the holidays with them at their big old house in Boston. Went abroad with them to their big old house in Paris. And the boy—Handy, I mean—nearly became what his family would have thought of as respectable. The two of them lived together with the blessing of the Cromptons. They believed that Jerry was the reason why they had their son back, and they determined never to lose him again no matter what. They accepted and then approved of their son's happiness, and they used their high social position to make sure that their friends and acquaintances either did the same thing, or made a good show of it. The inner circle, those closest to the Cromptons, took the attitude that if the Cromptons thought it was all right, then it was, and others who didn't think much of people like Jerry and Handy fell in line, too, for they did not want to get on the wrong side of the Cromptons.

"The two of them, Jerry and Handy, became the first like themselves to be invited into Society as a pair and not as extra men. They were asked and came as a couple, and at many a dinner table in many a fine apartment would a man find himself with either Jerry or Handy seated on one side and a lady on the other, their presence so threw off how things were usually done. Mr. Coy of New York claims this was the end, in all but the stuffiest of houses, of the man-woman, man-woman seating that had been the custom in New York since the beginning of time."

Her sister shifts impatiently in the swing. The chains holding it to the porch ceiling squeak and groan as if to express the occupants incredulity. "They can't have been the first of their kind to cross the threshold of such houses," she says.

"I'm sure you're right, but the fact that they have become the stuff of legend, as they say, for people like Mr. Coy of New York is the point.

"Of course it worked out fairly well for everybody involved. What had been a right closed-off group of people could now tell themselves they were opening up to the world as it existed. Contradict the notion that they were an intolerant and hide-bound group of snobs. Mr. Coy of New York says these kind of people love to find somebody passably acceptable among the unacceptable and take them up. It was a great opportunity for Jerry."

During the time between when he was taken up by Handiford Pepper Crompton and the events that ended that time, Jerry continued to write to Maggie. He told her about every place he went and what he did, and he described the houses and furniture and pictures and the food to her in the most excited, childlike way. He was the little awestruck boy again, like the day his mother died. Only now it was not a table set with brought-in dishes and linens and a sad room brightened by funeral flowers but the world he had to dazzle him.

He wrote to Maggie that he had begun to notice a pattern, and he told her he had seen the mocking hand of God operating in his life. He asked her why every time he suffered what most people would call a crushing loss, something that he wished for above all else came to him, often before he even knew he wanted it. "When they take something away from me they seem to give me something." The double funeral had brought him a double reward, he reasoned. He had lost what he cared for most at the time, but the loss had freed him, he wrote, so that the tragedy seemed to him to lead directly to where he was, on his own in the big world he'd found. Now, as a result of his misfortune, he had come to believe, he loved and was loved, and he was living a life better than any he had first learned to dream about from Maggie and the ladies.

He believed this would be the end of his journey, as love

often is the end of all searching—the rest of life—the answer to the question, What are you going to do? Love something or someone. It was a happy time again for Jerry.

Sit in the room in the jail with Maggie and Jerry as together they explore the limits of love.

"We were a hit. People thought we were beautiful. I often wonder if it was they or I who was fooled," says Jerry.

"Who, Jerry?" Maggie asks.

"Everybody but me. Or only me and no one else," Jerry says.

Maggie looks at him now with a relaxed, slowly blinking, patient receptivity, for she believes he has put aside his flippant bravado and started telling the truth, needs and wants to tell it. She settles into the hard plastic chair, and, as when he was a little boy and chattered so excitedly about some new luxury that he had not known or jabbered breathlessly in anticipation of a day with her and all that it promised, she listens as she had always done before. Then she had been proud of him and of herself, and now it is with something like pride with which she sits and hears him trying to find, if not meaning, sense in what has happened to him.

"Handy looked like something that, if you were to turn over a frozen leaf in an icy enchanted forest, you would find kneeling underneath, looking up at you. Beautiful in that way, I mean. Blond and cold, and some thought cruel and outrageous, but I knew better. It was deformed courage," Jerry said. "The two of us together were knockouts, more than we would have been apart, and I had people tell me that they invited us in some cases because it was such a pleasure for the guests just to look at us. It was the allure of two people who seemed so contented, the lack of doubt and the absence of loneliness that they were attracted to, I think. There was this writer who noticed it. I memorized what he said."

To help himself remember what had been written about him and Handy and to tell it to Mrs. Labrette exactly, Jerry sits up straight and turns his head slightly to one side as if he were listening for something important coming faintly from far away that only he would be able to hear. Then it comes back to him.

"That writer said, 'To see them cavorting in the sun on the beach in Southampton is to remember innocence, and to hold on, sometimes for a full minute, to the hopeless hope that you could once again be who you were, even though you are now old and finished and afraid and have seen everything you thought worth seeing and done over and over all the things that make you think you are happy. Youth is before you. The two are in possession of that which you seem to remember you once had and they, generous and beautiful, hand it back to you—return that which you need most in order to go on living—the nearly forgotten memory of how you once were.' That was what this writer said about us. Handy thought he was foolish and told him so, but still the writer printed it in a story. It was supposed to be about us."

Jerry relaxes and sinks back into the chair, almost cocky, as if a test had been put to him and he performed perfectly.

"But what is it he is talking about except just what I said before? We were happy. That's all. And everybody could see it was so."

They had been something of an attraction and were well known in those places where the Cromptons kept houses precisely because it was a Crompton who was flouting convention. When they were on the beach, small crowds would gather and watch them. Lone, lovely, aspiring men, and women too, would put their blankets down in the vicinity of the boys, as they came to be called. On the chance that they would be noticed by Handy and Jerry, that they might get one of Handy's gorgeous, cold smiles or have the luck that the two boys might saunter over and linger for the afternoon as they were known to do sometimes. But always, at the end of the day, each, responding to a look from the other or some subtle signal undetectable to anyone else, got up, brushed the sand from his backside, smiled again and walked away from the poor, thwarted hopefuls who watched the two climb the dunes to the beach club Handy's family belonged to. There, they changed, and went home for cocktails on the rose-rambled porch of the Crompton house, then dinner at which, perhaps, they might even mention briefly someone they had met that day, but the only consolation an afternoon in the company of the boys could possibly offer was that maybe the less desirable but still perfectly companionable might, since these two beauties had been briefly interested, attract someone else not as fine but good, or that another of the disappointed ones might console himself with one like himself, only to find the attention would bring no satisfaction, of course, for it was youth and beauty in love with each other that they were really after—Handy and Jerry.

"But sometimes if a person was being particularly obnoxious and persistent, Handy would offer himself for money and he'd take it if they'd pay," Jerry says. "'I'm interested in their limits,' he'd say, 'and mine.'"

It was of course not always so enchanted an existence. There were troubles, and in spite of the happiness the Cromptons' acceptance of Handy and Jerry brought them both, there were times when Handy would be drawn back to the precariousness of that unwise life he was not willing to completely give up. It was during these times that Jerry would feel most severely the difference between himself and his own upbringing and that of Handy's. There was in Handy, Jerry learned, a rashness that, although he was attracted to it in his lover, he could not imagine for himself—a lack of fear of consequences, or perhaps ignorance of such a thing as consequences, which separated the two of them. Jerry saw these attributes in one form or another in all the rich and privileged people he met through the Cromptons. In his poor little country-boy mind all Jerry could do was worry that Handy's recklessness would bring tears and regret and even annihilation, whereas Handy, with the sense of imperviousness to risk that his sort can have, saw no reason to deny himself even the most momentary deliverance from ordinariness and boredom, however dangerous it could be.

At the jail, on another day, on another visit, listen to what Jerry has to tell Mrs. Labrette of love's limitlessness.

"When Handy would be impossible like that, I put up with it. It was a fair trade for what I got from him—what life around him and his family offered. He was what he was when I met him and fell in love with him. I didn't know then he had this other life of privilege. I only knew he was being kind to me and giving me love of a sort I'd never had and doing things to me to prove it. One person doesn't make another feel the way he made me feel when we were in bed if he doesn't love him. I hadn't had much experience, but I could tell when I was loved. When I got to New York, he was the one who took me in. I read once about how a bird hatched out of the nest will attach to whatever it is that helps it be born, whether it is a person who has kept it warm and helped it out of its shell or whether another kind of bird has sat on the egg. It will belong to something other than what it is, and I bet it thinks it is something other than what it is. It was like that for me. The other stuff, the houses and the trips and learning and his family, that wasn't what made him worth the trouble that he certainly was. That stuff was just a bonus. It was being taken in. You have to love to be taken in, and you are in love the moment you decide to let it happen. And if you can't understand that you can love and be loved by someone whom the rest of the world would see as unlovable, then you can't ever be loved at all, I think."

While she listens, sitting in her chair across from him, an expression, faint but unmistakable, of sorrow and distress, as when a familiar pain that had subsided returns, stiffens Maggie's face. Her hand raises as if to silence him, then drops to her lap, and her face softens as if a drug has taken effect.

"I think you are right," she says, and nothing more.

"I loved him because I had to, because I learned to love first by loving lost causes. And because I had been loved as such, by you. Was it worth it? And then some," he says as the guards come and end the visit that has been another long one.

Iced tea has been brought out onto the porch on a lacquered tray, and Mrs. Lamm and her sister stop talking until the maid sets the tray down on a wrought-iron fern stand and goes back into the house.

"Then men started to die," says Mrs. Lamm. "Nobody they knew very well at first, but eventually it was like bombs going off all around them—and they keep on dying."

"As always," says Mrs. Lamm's sister.

Come, not to the jail anymore, but on Visitors' Day to the prison, where Jerry, after having pled guilty, is serving his time. He continues his conversations with Maggie. She comes often and always dresses up, just like the wives and children and mothers of the other men. The little girls who come to visit their daddies or the men they know as their daddies wear Sunday dresses with frills and bows in colors bright as penny candy. Their hair has been cared for like a garden—sectioned off, orderly as a map and tightly plaited right to the scalp and held in place with ribbons and colorful barrettes. The little boys are cool and fresh in new shirts and long pants. Their shoes are shined. It is rare that a child much over sixteen visits, and why that is Jerry and Maggie only wonder. Maybe by then, Jerry has said, they have learned to be embarrassed by the place and their father. But not these children. They light up when they see their daddies, and many of them are carried out crying when the visiting time is over. Their mothers are dressed up, too, but not for church. They display themselves like a big plate of rich food just out of reach. They do not mean to tease or frustrate, but to hold out hope to their men. They are dressed as if for a nightclub, in clothes that hide a promise they will not be able to keep this day, in this place—but sometime soon, they seem to say with their low-cut necklines and smooth shoulders and their hems high like raised windows. They wear sparkling earrings and necklaces, night jewelry.

It is Visitors' Day. A day that all the prisoners look forward to, but Jerry especially. He longs for and anticipates Maggie's visits, but he enjoys the other visitors, the little girls and little boys and their mothers and grandmothers turned out as for whatever occasion would be of most importance and happiness for them. It isn't a depressing place at all, he thinks, but as joyous a place as he has ever been in and so full of gallant children and generous and proudly dressed women and unconquerable love that he is choked with pride and heartache each time they come.

"They all try so hard," he explains to Maggie, "and of course it works. They try to be happy and they are, with their pretty clothes and snapshots of missed birthdays and the food they bring to have together with someone they love. That is why it is so unhappy when the day is over, because it has been so joyous for everybody here. The love rises like a flood and fills the room by the end of the day, and ten minutes before everybody has to go home and we have to go back to our cells, you could drown in it," he explains. "It makes me proud to be among them."

Maggie dresses beautifully every time she comes, and today she is separated from the others only by the quality of what she is wearing.

The other dressed-up women smile approvingly at her, acknowledging an unspoken bond between her and themselves—the kinship of those who take the time and go to the trouble to make the best of things.

Maggie and Jerry talk, and more and more of what happened is revealed to her.

"When people started dying, Handy found a calling almost," says Jerry. "He used his money to help. He broke trusts, and got money from his parents and from their friends, and he helped to set up organizations that took in the sick and fed and clothed them and defended them in court against all the persecutions. I was beside him. I did everything I could to help, and knew how because of you. Apart from a scent or seeing somebody who looked like somebody I knew here, what was happening up there in New York was the first thing that really reminded me of home. The way some good people, with nothing to gain, asked no questions but just tried to take control of the situation, and, regardless of who the sick were and how they had gotten that way, put aside all their squeamishness and tried to figure out what to do. It was the first time I saw clearly from where I had come. What my tribe consisted of, or the tribe to which I wished to belong. It was not a question of belonging to women or men or belonging to a family or whatever is the opposite of that. What I found out was that the world and its people are, as far as I can tell, divided into two tribes, not in conflict necessarily or at odds somehow, because the other tribe, the one I didn't want to belong to, the ones who neglect and are indifferent, didn't seem to even care about opposing anything. It is hard to work up anything like hate for people like that. It got very simple for me. The world divided along the lines of those who are willing to help and those who are not. Between them are the deformed. Finding the helpful was like finding you and the others again—Mrs. Lamm and poor Elizabeth Anderson—Elsie Moye, even, always trying to help in a way that will call the most attention to herself. It was like that day when you all pitched in to clean and cook and to bury my mother, and it was as blessed to find it up there in New York and under those circumstances as it had been down here. Maybe more so because this time I knew what I was looking at. Before, when I was a little boy, I hadn't known that it was kindness and goodness, not just relief, I was experiencing. And I don't know, as awful as it was, it made me want to let you know that one of the things I'd learned from your kindness was how to find home quickly. I made up my mind to come back here when I could and bring Handy with me."

Today Maggie is hearing something she understands. Today they are in the same club. "Your letters to me at this time were as though written from a war zone," Maggie says. "I remember one, I showed it all around, where you described going into an apartment to find two men lying side by side in their bed where they had died holding hands. And some didn't wait for the disease to take them, you said, especially the ones you knew from the good families. You said it was so often a gun to the temple for people like that rather than the shame and indignity of dying from that awful disease in the way they knew was coming."

It is in this way they talk. Reminding each other of, discovering together, marveling during brief lapses into silence, at the goodness of people.

Watch how the story of Jerry and Handy travels from place to place as Mrs. Lamm's sister, back in Passiflora, South Carolina, passes it on to her friends, who know nothing of Jerry and Branch Creek, except what they have heard on the news. They know they know very little from that. It is when the news people depart that the real story begins, and to have one in their midst who is connected by blood to a woman in Branch Creek who knows Jerry and also is friends with the woman in whom he confides is a more reliable source of truth than anything they might see on TV or hear on the radio. She tells about Jerry again and again, and all her friends are eager to know the story.

Here she is at her card party held every Wednesday afternoon at the Passiflora Country Club.

"And especially then with his ability to run a house and his belief, formed by his association with all those women in Branch Creek, that it is an important, even noble, calling, Jerry kept life during these periods from descending into nothing more than a sordid struggle for the two of them. It is when he has to improvise that Jerry is his most effective."

She has learned that by repeating as near to exactly as she can what her sister has told her, she establishes authority and gives her listeners the impression that she knows firsthand what she is telling them. It is, stripped of her occasional opinions, exact enough.

"How he learned to not just make do with very little but to live in what you could call style of a sort, the ladies had firsthand knowledge of. I myself saw this talent take shape over time in Branch Creek with my own eyes.

"It was when Handy's money meant life or death for people that Jerry saw a way he could pay back in some way all that Handy had brought to him—when they had to make a separate life for themselves, isolated from the safe, refined existence they had with the Cromptons," says Mrs. Lamm's sister.

"They lived on very little. Handy, coming from a family for which the possibilities seemed endless when it came to what he might choose to do, and where success in so many areas is assured and where it is axiomatic among such people that it is not only deserved but a moral obligation as well, seems to have decided to give it all away. Well, what can seem like experimental roughing it for someone who has always been underpinned by that kind of money is, for a boy like Jerry, a harsh return to the nightmare of insecurity from which he had hoped to have awakened."

Here, she is embellishing on what Mrs. Lamm has only touched on. The people of Passiflora are much more interested in people like the Cromptons than the people of Branch Creek are. Handy's family, for them, would be an integral and interesting part of the story, possibly the most interesting, and she and others who tell it after her will especially want to convey that they understand the upper classes as well as they understand themselves. Her assessment is more or less correct, which is a compliment to the way Mrs. Lamm suggested, alluded to or took for granted how someone who had been brought up in a family like the Cromptons might think and feel. It again shows that the women of Branch Creek have learned something from Jerry, and that the self-satisfied even separated by class and distance can know each other.

At another Wednesday afternoon card party she is telling more about Jerry. "All his ways of protecting himself from the painful and fearsome realities of his life came back to serve him well, and there was nothing about how he dealt with Handy's almost reckless generosity that was flip or larkish. At no time whatever did Jerry view what was happening as an amusing adventure with a rich, eccentric young man who on a whim of a different kind might just as easily remember all his advantages and use them for himself and one other person whom he cared about. No, Jerry went into battle against uncertainty, as you would know him capable of as I do, if my sister were yours.

"Was it to measure Jerry's love, appraise his courage, some upper-class test to see if Jerry had naturally and unaccountably the qualities by which people who are born into Handy's group recognized each other—pluck, bravery, imperviousness to discomfort, rash indifference to risk, noblesse oblige, disarmingly polite candor—all these things that, when observed in an outsider of possible interest to someone of Handy's background, in some way are proof of their own unfailing judgment and of the worthiness of certain members of the less fortunate classes? I'd say so. But then what good is love that has not been tested and in more brutal ways than these?"

She trumps the trick—lays down her hand. "The rest are mine," she states, without the slightest suggestion of triumph in her voice.

"I keep thinking he was trying to rid me of some kind of moral fastidiousness that he sensed in me," says Jerry. His eyes are downcast, and he has a confused scowl on his face as if he does not and never will understand what he just said.

"The disapproval of the one who loves you most is the hardest to bear, you know," says Mrs. Labrette. She leans forward and lowers her head, trying to look into Jerry's face. "Why do you think he would have tried to do such a thing?" she asks.

"I think then"—and Jerry stops and looks up hopefully at Mrs. Labrette like a pupil with what may or may not be the right answer—"he could have loved me for always and settled down and stopped doing some of the things he had to do from time to time. When I didn't care anymore, he could stop it. Like that."

Mrs. Labrette straightens and looks back at Jerry blankly, and he cannot tell from her face whether he has answered her question correctly or not. He waits but she says nothing, so he reassures himself by pretending an attitude of confident boredom.

"Who knows? It is a situation that has been faced before," says Jerry. "I guess I was the lucky one he chose to work it out on."

Mrs. Labrette settles into the uncomfortable chair. "I don't like it when you get like this," she says disappointedly.

"Like what?" says Jerry with a look of mock innocence.

"You know exactly how you are being," says Mrs. Labrette.

"It's hard," Jerry says. "What I have to tell you."

"I expected it would be," says Mrs. Labrette, and she reaches across the table and places her hand on Jerry's. "No touching, please, ma'am," says the guard politely but firmly. Mrs. Labrette withdraws her hand.

"It's Miss Maggie, Jerry. Tell me," she says.

Jerry looks around the room as if to find something he needs. He settles on Mrs. Labrette and begins.

"The way he lived—always trying to see how far he could go—how he needed to do crazy things and get into situations where his money and family didn't set him apart or protect him, that certainly was not something I was glad about, but I could take it because I thought with time I could talk him out of all that—convince him that he was just looking for the person who could change him—who would just tell him to stop, and that I was that person. Convince him there were limits, and there were, but not in him.

"There was this man Handy met. He was a social figure, friendly with politicians, and he owned an entire eighteenth-century village," Jerry continues. "It was not in any way as significant as Williamsburg, for example, but it was his, and he had restored the houses and shops and barns with his own money. The restoration had been carried out by experts—accurate in every detail. There was no electricity or running water—nothing that wouldn't have been available in late-eighteenth-century America. The fabrics had been copied from prints and paintings of the period and woven on specially built looms.

"During the day, it was open to the public. University

history departments would have conferences there. Professors came to study. There were tours and demonstrations by artisans working with antiquated tools and methods. Nearby was a prison, and this man"—here Jerry leans close to Mrs. Labrette's ear and whispers the man's name, for he is from a family the name of which even the prison guards would recognize—"developed a program for the well-behaved prisoners. He provided housing and work in the village. They learned dying arts—glassblowing, furniture restoration, obsolete ways of laying brick and such as that, and they could get released early if they behaved." Jerry pauses and smiles ruefully. "Dying arts. Sounds so hopeless a thing to be involved in. The story of my life, isn't it? Or yours."

Mrs. Labrette nods benignly, not in agreement, but to acknowledge the jab. "I suppose much of what I do seems frivolous to you now," she says.

"No. I'm sorry," says Jerry. "It's gotten to be a kind of habit. Anyway, there were citations and awards and personal letters from presidents and governors. There was a framed picture of the Queen and this man together and a letter to him from her with the royal crest, where she expressed gratitude and admiration. For what, she did not say, but she had granted him a special coat of arms for his carriages.

"He had an estate next to the museum village; a huge house and stables and a coach house for his collection of antique horse-drawn vehicles, which was considered to be the finest private collection in the world except for the Queen's. He and one other man are the only people on this side of the Atlantic who can put together a full postilion. The other man lives in Canada. He started out as a butcher, which I just love. In Europe, it is pretty much only royalty capable of such a thing."

Jerry has seemed the most like himself to Mrs. Labrette talking about the coaches and this man's house. He is excited by what he has to tell her, with a touch of the know-it-all that has always been, she remembers, a sign of his delight whenever he found a new form of luxury he had not known of before.

"You may not have known that there is a small, exclusive, but very active group of people whose passion is driving. That is what the sport is called—driving, no matter if it is just a simple cart or a full coach with four horses and liveried footmen. This person belongs to that group in this country—has served as president. He's loved by coaching people not just because he is an authority, but he uses it as a way to raise money for historic preservation all over the country. There are charity coaching events in Newport and a big event in Virginia every spring to raise money for some of those James River plantation houses."

The guards listen. They do not hear this kind of talk in the jail as a usual thing, and they seem almost proud to have Jerry for a prisoner. The formal, hawklike vigilance relaxes, and they carry themselves less like men who do boring and dangerous work. They stand straight, but not rigidly, and there is a new calm efficiency in the way they go about their duties. At times they are courteous. Jerry and Mrs. Labrette have sensed a guilty loosening as they hover nearby trying to appear indifferent, their studied nonchalance revealing more interest in Jerry's story than if they sat down at his feet to hear it. Whenever guards from some of the other parts of the prison are around, Jerry's guards treat them with hospitable condescension.

"He had re-created for himself, there in the Pennsylvania countryside, the life of an eighteenth-century English duke. When I saw it, I did not know that it was possible to live as he does—in such splendor—that there was anyone left who had the money to do it."

As though to look on or even remember such a place was

a luxury for which payment was required, and not with money, the expression of wonder and admiration that has been on Jerry's face is overtaken by a dazed, numb look. But Mrs. Labrette has seen this expression before and knows it is not one of dazzlement, but that what he is knowing now has changed utterly from what he was knowing an instant ago. It is the expression she saw on his face in the hours after his mother's death and again in the days following the tragedy at her own house.

"The whole vast extravagance of it was a respectable cover for his real life, which took place at night and on special weekends when the village would be closed to the public. Then it was his own private playground. The charity, which no one could question, was a convenient cover for his other life—an experiment in the limits of depravity. It was without exception the grimmest, most hopeless place I have ever been to in my life.

"They met at a bar, of course, this man and Handy. A place on Eighth Avenue in New York where well-off men go to find boys. Handy would go there with our friend Hugh who was there doing business, shall we say? Handy loved it when he was mistaken for someone for hire. 'I could earn a living if I had to,' he'd say. He let this man think he was there for the same reason the other boys were. There was a 'date' as it is called, and money changed hands. That kind of thing happened to Handy. He would always give the money away to someone on the street.

"Of course the man figured out pretty quickly that Handy was not what he was passing himself off as. These people, I mean Social Register types, not hustlers, can always recognize each other as surely as they can make you feel welcome and excluded at the same time. There is some barrier between them and all but their kind—nothing you can put your finger on but it is there as smooth and strong as silk.

"He asked Handy to a weekend in Pennsylvania. Said it would be 'amusing.' The man told Handy his name, and they established enough connections and found they knew enough of the same people to satisfy themselves that each was who the other had thought he was. That's something else those kinds of people can do with just a few frivolous, cryptic remarks and signals that you wouldn't even notice. It's like telepathy."

"But that would be true of most social groups, even, I imagine, among what you call the hustlers as well," says Mrs. Labrette evenly.

"It isn't the same," says Jerry impatiently. "Anyway, Handy accepted the invitation, and he told the man he had a friend, me, and the man wanted to know if I was attractive.

"'I told him you were hot' is what Handy said to me. So we were both invited, only Handy told the man he'd have to pay. Handy wanted to be there in that way, you see, as a hired plaything. He got a kick out of the idea that someone like himself, someone who the others would have thought could pay would instead be paid. Kind of naive when you think about it. That was what I could never get used to. Even in the most depraved circumstances, he always had this purity about him. Innocence. Maybe it was just complete self-confidence, or was it simply a trick of the trade he had learned from the pros—how some of them fake innocence so that the men with whom they are doing business feel they have to pay for defiling such guileless-ness?

"On Friday afternoon a car and driver were sent to pick us up. The car was a Rolls-Royce," Jerry says, and he stops and looks directly at Mrs. Labrette to see if this impresses her.

"How nice for you," she says.

"When the door closed, it was like being sealed in a tomb.

The driver was a former prisoner. He had been in this program started by"—Jerry looks around the room—the guards are listening—"Mr. Jones, we'll call him," he says to Mrs. Labrette. He shifts his eyes toward the nearest guard, then back to her so she will know that she is not to repeat Mr. Jones' real name anytime anyone besides the two of them can hear it, and when the guards realize that a secret is being kept from them, there is not on one face any appearance of irritation or resentment. They go on about their business, still listening intently to what Jerry tells Mrs. Labrette, and they accept with resigned sophistication, like the gentlemen they are learning to be, that they are not to know the name and that the story will be no less interesting because of it.

"This driver was Venezuelan and lived with his wife and baby in a dependent house near Mr. Jones' residence. 'I have a big one,' he said. 'Is way to get a head in the world,' and he laughed in the most aggressive, humorless way, like someone who wants you to know they're smart enough to get a joke. It was I who didn't get it. It was as though he and Handy had cooked up a prank just to make fun of me. I looked up at the rearview mirror and saw the driver looking back at me. He was wagging his head up and down, so stupid, agreeing with himself."

Mrs. Labrette brings her hand to her mouth as though she is about to be sick, and Jerry cannot account for why, instead, what shows on her face are the effects of a smile hidden behind her hand. Her eyes go merry and her cheeks swell, and he hears a laugh gurgling in her throat. She is trying not to let it come out, but it sounds as though she will choke on it.

"I don't know why you think it is funny. Handy thought it was funny, too. I think I knew then there would come some reason why we couldn't last," he says pointedly, and

Mrs. Labrette composes herself, like a girl who has been scolded for misbehaving in church.

"I had always thought that there was a world so different from what I knew, that I would not recognize anything about it. I had wanted that. You know it's true. I have always had this faith that what I wish for is better than what I have. I still have it. Naive of me, it turns out, but it has been a way up. I wandered into something menacing, sophisticated and arch and mistook it for what I had asked for. I thought I was ready for it.

"Handy seemed to be as happy as he had ever been, comfortable as you would be in your pew in church. He laughed along with the driver and encouraged him. 'Really. Do tell,' he'd said. And the driver became besotted with him. 'I coming to party. I find you. You look for me.' He was so confident. Handy told him, 'I'll look for no one but you.'"

"It is true that people like Handy seem to belong wherever they are or wherever they are seems to be the natural place for them," says Mrs. Labrette, just to say something. "I've always admired those who have that quality."

"Well, he was at home in his own dissolute skin," says Jerry. "When we got there we were taken directly to the host, who was by his pool. The driver started shedding clothes as we made our way to meet the host. By the time we arrived at the pool, the driver had undressed, and he went over to the chaise where Mr. Jones was sprawled out, and straddled him and bounced up and down. It was dirty, silly pretend sex. Childish and disgusting. He moaned in the most exaggerated way with the intention of being comic. 'Ooooh, Poppy, Poppy, Poppy.'"

Again Mrs. Labrette puts her hand to her mouth as though to be sick, but Jerry sees her eyes both twinkle and fill with panic like one who has been found out.

"Do you want to hear this?" he asks.

It appears to him that she is trying to say no. She shakes her head quickly, but a short and hysterical laugh shoots out of her. He takes it for assent.

"Then he made that disgusting 'Ooooh, Poppy' sound again, and Mr. Jones just giggled this mincing little tee hee the whole time the driver was bouncing on him. Then the driver turned around and straddled Mr. Jones, and he slapped the driver's buttocks so limply that it didn't even make a sound. 'Isn't he tcho divine?' he asked, and I said nothing, but Handy said, 'Yes, tcho,' mimicking Mr. Jones' way of saying it. And Mr. Jones narrowed his eyes and looked at Handy as if to say, 'I'll get you,' and Handy looked right back at him in the same way.

"Then the driver got up and walked toward the house, and the filthy, ridiculous flirtation dropped as though he were an actor exiting the stage. He picked up the clothes he'd shed, took a cigarette from his shirt pocket, lit it and walked directly into the house with no intention other than leaving, like he was just knocking off for the day.

"'I'm saving myself for hundreds, anyway,' Mr. Jones said. It was cold and impatient, and it frightened me. Handy just smirked at Mr. Jones, and he smirked back at Handy, and this time it was like they were sharing a bitter and sad secret. I've thought about the two of them and how they played this game many times since then, and I think in the end all there was in it was bottomless apathy, boredom. They both seemed to see that they had discovered that the secret of life was a joke on everybody else—that only the two of them got it—that the way to get through life was to bore yourself to death, so that when death came you were not only ready but wanting it.

"Their eyes locked, and then Mr. Jones looked so longingly at Handy that I thought he would weep. It was as if he had realized that what he had spent his whole life and used up his youth and beauty and allure finding out was already known by someone still young, someone who still had it all, and I saw something else I hadn't wanted to see. It was this dissolute, oily, lust-bloated man being overtaken by the recognition that he would never have that kind of power again—that it was too late—that he was old and would die no longer able to live up to his own pathetic and depraved standards. He was like a pretender next to the real thing. Would it have made him feel like a fool to see in Handy what it had taken him all his life to come to? Or could he delude himself a little longer precisely because it seemed to have turned out that his reality was one only a person with his life before him could afford to accept? In other words, had life passed him by, or could he still hope?"

Jerry stops talking and looks at Mrs. Labrette as if he expects her to answer the question. But instead, she turns her head away, hides, it seems to Jerry, as if a story of disillusion could be read in her face, too.

"He reminded me of a good used piece of furniture in a grand, not quite tidy room," says Jerry airily, and laughs a short light trill, and waits for Mrs. Labrette to face him again. She does so with an amused smile.

"Everything about him was expensive or had been, but there was surrounding him also this cavalier neglect and wastefulness, like mopping the floor with a mink coat or using a sterling silver pitcher to catch a leak in the ceiling. There seemed to be everywhere evidence of a grudging remembrance of how things ought to be done, but there was also exhaustion, a feeling that it had all been too much trouble and therefore had been dispensed with.

"We were taken to our room, which was in the gate house. The gate house was two towers connected by a windowed archway, and our room was in that part. From it you could see who came and went from the place. It was very nicely furnished, with a pair of pretty little silk-covered recamiers, one under each bank of windows, and the windows were curtained with blue toile printed with French lords and ladies and musical instruments. What looked like thick stone walls flanking each side of the gate house were stables, and you could hear below from time to time the horses snuffling and neighing. I would have been happy to stay in the room with Handy all weekend.

"We sat in one of the recamiers below the windows and watched the guests arrive. They came all afternoon, and each guest was checked off a list by Mr. Jones' driver. Some arrived in chauffeur-driven cars. A man who lived nearby arrived in an open carriage pulled by a matched pair of grays with a liveried coachman, and two liveried footmen sitting bolt upright at the rear facing backward. The carriage slowed and was waved through by Mr. Jones' driver. As the carriage pulled off, the footmen blew a fey kiss to Mr. Jones' driver. Like a salute.

"All afternoon the guests arrived. They would glide through beneath us and wave and smile at the driver, and they were dazzling in every way, with expensive shirts and brilliant white teeth and glossy hair.

"There were several swimming pools on the estate and a lake, and around three o'clock in the afternoon Handy and I put on our trunks and went down to the lake for a swim. Oddly, there was no one there, so we stripped. When Handy came out of the water, he was excited to the point of what I can only call exaggeration. 'I am unrelievedly priapic. You're going to have to milk me,' was what he said to me. He laughed, and again it was so innocent. You would have thought he was asking me to toss him a towel. He said, 'I'll never last like this. I'm like a closet case at camp.'

"I said I was sure that would be fine with everyone, but

I did what he wanted right there by the lake, hiding in this thick drooping willow tree."

Mrs. Labrette's expression remains serene, passive, the only sign of discomfort a red bloom spreading over her face. She shifts in her seat, pulls her skirt down over her crossed knees then lays her hands one over the other on her lap.

"Do you want me to go on?" Jerry asks.

"Yes, I think you have to," she replies. "It is harder, though, when it's about you. When I have to picture you in it."

"When we got back to our room, a handwritten invitation to dinner was waiting. We dressed and went down the stairs to the gate, where we were driven in a carriage to the main house. The dinner was held in an allée of giant oaks, which stretched out from the back entrance of the house to where the hill dropped off toward a small river below. Completely private. Unless you flew over in an airplane, you could not see anything going on behind the facade of the house.

"The table was enormous—covered in white linen to the ground and set with so much china and silver and crystal that it seemed impossible that anybody else on earth could have any. And do you know what the centerpiece was? It was very much like yours, only there was someone naked standing in an enormous shell, like Neptune, and the hippocampi were naked men with these horse heads, and everyone was on an enormous mirror representing the sea and in that mirror the guests could see the naked men from every possible angle. It was this living, dirty version of the table you set the night my brother was burned alive. It was as though another sick joke had been staged for me, but all of these men seemed to think of sex as a joke anyway, as something hilarious, and I don't know why, but that surprised me. I hadn't known anything but how serious it is and meaningful, always, even with a stranger."

"Do you still think that way?" asks Mrs. Labrette.

"I still want to," says Jerry, and they are quiet for a moment, almost as if the conversation has come to an end, as if the point of it had been reached and understood and agreed upon by both.

"But there is more," Mrs. Labrette states simply, and Jerry continues.

"The highlight of the evening was after dinner—a coaching party through the estate. There were footmen, naked except for their boots and tailcoats and hats. The coachman wore his whip. Anything to amuse. Nearly all of these men, having spent a lifetime of frivolity, were hard to please—quenched and thirsty at the same time. I had never been around such people, for whom nothing was ever enough. And when it overtook them, as it did so soon, it was the boredom that was more disgusting than anything else. At one point along the route, as we approached a steep rise in the road we began to hear hunting music, and as we made the hill at the summit, revealed before us were sixteen naked French-horn players in the branches of an enormous old oak tree. Underneath the tree were *tableaux vivant*, scenes of stable boys being debauched and such as that. Before long the organized entertainment had been so effective in arousing the guests that it became not only unnecessary, but a nuisance, and everybody just had at each other all over the place. In the woods, all over the house. I saw a ménage à trois on the roof. One man was tied to the chimney.

"Handy and I floated through this until, toward midnight, Mr. Jones came to us. He said, 'It's time for you to sing for your supper.' He told us that he had a friend who had come late and missed most of the evening. He had been in the city on business or whatever. The man was waiting in a bedroom upstairs. Mr. Jones had gotten together an outfit for Handy, black leather pants with no seat in them, a harness with metal studs, and a leather mask that covered his whole head. There were zippers in the places the mouth and eyes were, and he put a leash around his neck. He told me to take off my shirt, and he gave me a leather mask, but it only covered half of my face. 'You are to lead Handy into the room, hand the leash to the person on the bed, back out of the room and shut the door behind you,' Mr. Jones told me. We went up the long staircase and found the room Mr. Jones had told us to go to.

"I whispered to Handy that I wouldn't do this. 'I can't,' I said. 'I'll walk home if I have to.' And from underneath this mask, muffled and irritated, he said, 'Don't be dreary,' and I don't know, it made the whole thing sound meaningless and harmless and kind of funny even, so I just decided to get through this day and hope we'd never be involved in something like this again.

"The door was cracked, I pushed it open. The room was lit by lots of candles. At the far end of the room was a bed with a canopy with silk curtains. There was a man on the bed. His hands and feet were tied to the bedposts. I remember he was bound with black electrical cord. He raised his head and looked toward us, but it was as if he could only see shapes—forms, not people—his face was dumb with lust and anticipation.

"It was Handy's father, Mr. Crompton."

Mrs. Labrette holds her hands up in the air as if she is trying to stop Jerry. "No," she says, but Jerry does not know if she means stop, or this can't be. He speeds the story, the words racing from his mouth as though to get it all out before Mrs. Labrette runs out of the room or faints or has the guards take him away.

"My grip tightened on Handy, but I couldn't say a word. I was so afraid that Mr. Crompton would recognize my voice. We could run, I thought. We were masked and he would never know we had been there. Then in a thick French accent which I had never heard him use, Handy said, '*Vous pouvez vous retirer.*' It means, 'You can go now.' It is how a French lady would dismiss a servant. I couldn't move. On the bed, Mr. Crompton was writhing slowly, almost imperceptibly, like a constrictor that has captured its prey and is just waiting for it to die.

"When I still didn't move, Handy whispered, 'Do as Monsieur, our host, has asked,' and then I knew he meant to go through with it, so I backed out of the room and closed the door."

Mrs. Labrette rises from her chair and without a word goes to the door and stands waiting, always the lady, until a guard comes and opens it for her. Another guard joins her and escorts her from the room. Jerry watches her walk down the hall. She does not look back. The other guard comes to take Jerry back to his cell.

"I think you're on your own now, buddy," he says to Jerry.

"She'll come back," Jerry replies. "I've only to ask."

"I sure do know about things I never thought I would," Mrs. Lamm says. "I'll say that much for being mixed up with Jerry."

Linger by her porch for more. She has nearly lost her sister, who is so irritated and bewildered that she has become an unpleasant audience, and Mrs. Lamm wishes for a listener of quicker perceptions and one who is not so naive about frailty—so tied to her need to believe in the good sense and rationality of people. Mrs. Lamm's sister has put her needlepoint away for the afternoon, for she has been unable to concentrate much on counting stitches and changing thread. The napkin she has been working on has a red leaf and a green berry due to her inability to keep her attention fully on what she is doing. She is still sitting in the swing but bolt upright with her arms across her chest, incredulous and irritated, at Mrs. Lamm's preposterous accounts of Jerry's life in New York.

"It is a ludicrous story, there is no doubting, but the fact that you, my own sister, would repeat such an obvious impossibility, let alone untruth, and in such filthy detail, is evidence of a twistedness in your mind that I had not known of. You've made this up. I would not have thought you capable of it," says Mrs. Lamm's sister.

Mrs. Lamm straightens up like an electrical shock has come through her, and a look of triumph comes over her face. She has been given exactly what she wished for. A chance to say something she loves to say.

"Be gone witch, you have no powers here," she tells her sister, bold as brass. "It happened, and there is not a thing you can do to change that, and besides, you believe it, or want to listen to it at any rate, or you'd have flounced off this porch a while back. So sit still and hear some reasons."

Mrs. Lamm's sister rolls her eyes and wilts. Resigned, she leans back in the swing and squirms to find a comfortable position she can settle into—one in which indulging her sister's outlandish tale will be made bearable.

"Now, the man who gave that party was not named Mr. Jones. His name was Larky Hamilton. 'Larky' was a nickname given to him when he was a young man. But you have no doubt heard of the Hamiltons, and he is one of them. They put the green on money." She is silent for a moment. She looks over at her sister as if taking her measure. She puckers up her lips and twists them to one side of her face, deciding if she ought to tell her sister what she thinks—what she believes—is the meaning of what happened to Jerry in New York. Does her sister even deserve to hear? she wonders.

"Well?" says her sister, proving to Mrs. Lamm that her sister, if not worthy, is grudgingly attentive. It will do.

"Here's my theory," says Mrs. Lamm, and the words come out of her mouth as though she had been trying to see how long she could hold her breath. The pleasure of telling her sister something only she knows about runs through her like a chill. Every muscle in her body adjusts. It is the equivalent of a pitcher's windup, or the adjustments a golfer makes before he drives the ball down the fairway.

"Larky Hamilton knew what he was doing when he sent Handy into that room." Mrs. Lamm says this conspiratorially, narrowing her eyes. She raises her chin defiantly, daring her sister to disagree. "As sure as you're sitting on that swing, frowning. He knew who Mr. Crompton was, and he knew Handy was his son. What neither Mr. Crompton nor Handy knew was that they both knew Larky Hamilton. What if Larky had been in love all his life with Handy's father? Fell for him when they were even younger than Jerry and Handy, and never got over it? Never was able to place that love somewhere else, and it turned in on him and caused what happened? Let's say they'd been little boyfriends in college and Larky thought his life was settled. Well, the Cromptons of that day and age might have learned to accommodate a lot of peculiarities, but not this kind yet. And as it turned out, Mr. Crompton had leanings in more directions than just Larky Hamilton's. Larky learned them all, see. Like Mr. Crompton became an obsession with him. Left by Mr. Crompton all those long years ago and knowing of Mr. Crompton's oddities, Larky had the perfect hold over him. It could all be done in a friendly way and for old times' sake, and things would be arranged by a person Mr. Crompton knew; someone who understood, was from his own social class and, he thought, accepted what we'll call his broad tastes as far as perversions were concerned. Mr. Crompton trusted in Larky Hamilton's discretion. Larky had him." She snaps her fingers quick as the flick of a whip.

"He lived his life thinking up how to either get him back or get back at him—after a while he didn't care which."

Although she doesn't realize it, Mrs. Lamm's sister's head has tilted to one side during the tale, and a look of almost spellbound wonder has slackened her features. She sits waiting for Mrs. Lamm to go on, and when she doesn't, the silence brings her back to herself like a splash of cold water.

"You cannot know this," she says dreamily. Then irritably, "It is ridiculous for you to discuss the private lives of these extraordinary people. People from good families, I would point out, your social superiors," says Mrs. Lamm's sister.

"It's what Mr. Coy of New York thinks, too. It's got you listening, and it sounds possible, doesn't it?"

Mrs. Lamm's sister says nothing. If she were honest, she would have to admit that she is interested, so she remains quiet and petulant.

"Larky just had to think up a way to either get him back for good or get back at him in a way that would most satisfy his revenge," says Mrs. Lamm. "Larky probably thought Mr. Crompton wouldn't let himself be in love with him. Could do it, even wanted to do it, I bet Larky thought. Was rich enough to live any way he wanted to, but in the end just didn't have the courage. Mr. Coy of New York is always saying that you'd be surprised not how much the rich indulge themselves, but how much they don't. That would have been how Larky would have seen it, I'd imagine."

"You really have gone off the end of the limb and have fallen beyond the drip line," says Mrs. Lamm's sister almost agreeably.

"It's a theory," says Mrs. Lamm. "What Larky Hamilton couldn't imagine was that maybe Mr. Crompton really did want a more normal kind of wife." She throws her head back and laughs so loud, it sets a dog to barking across town. "I meant to say *life,* a more normal kind of life. That he found a girl, and fell in love with her, and that just settled things for him. Less confusing for Mr. Crompton, coming from the kind of background he came from and considering the expectations and obligations that went along with such privilege. And let's say he really loved the woman he married and loved the children she gave him. So much the better. And what if there was this little secret perversity or a little group of them that had to be dealt with from time to time? He had Larky, who he knew was in love with him and wouldn't betray him for the world. And Larky was a person who was in a position to arrange for Mr. Crompton to indulge himself from time to time if he needed to. So let's say that in the beginning Larky arranges for him to be with a young man once in a while. Maybe he and Mr. Crompton even try it a few times, but Mr. Crompton is unenthusiastic and finally unwilling. This would gouge out the wound in Larky Hamilton a little deeper, wouldn't it? Then one day there is at one of these parties someone not quite so common, someone sort of like Larky was as a young man, and Larky sees Mr. Crompton go crazy for such as that. He has another piece of information to file away for his revenge. And of course, moving among the people he moves among at both ends, it is only a matter of time before he runs into somebody like Handy. Just as surely, something would have put him onto the idea that Handy was Mr. Crompton's son. First, it may have been a physical resemblance that Larky noticed in Handy. He would have been so familiar with the face he had loved all his life that he would have recognized any part of it in someone else. And one day, surely real names are exchanged and the shock of it hits Larky but he doesn't even blink, and I bet it was like a knot came loose in his heart. It was perfect luck, so much so that it seemed providential to him, and he would have thought it tempting fate not to use what had been put smack-dab in his hands."

"You should think up stories for the movies. Science fiction," says Mrs. Lamm's sister.

"Oh, hush. You know yourself it is the least likely thing that could have happened that is in most situations usually the truth," says Mrs. Lamm.

While her sister puzzles visibly over Mrs. Lamm's aphoristic statement of plausibility, she continues, "So, he plans a party, but at a time when he knows Mr. Crompton can't come until very late. That way he can have Handy and Jerry there. They won't have to see Mr. Crompton. Let's say Mr.

Crompton never attends these parties as a guest. That would be indiscreet and dangerous for him. They have always done it the way it was done that night. 'Come by late, I've found one for you' would be how Larky might have always put it. And Mr. Crompton would spend his day and evening thinking about what was to come. So the big night comes, and the party goes off well, and at the end of the evening Larky asks Handy to perform one last service for him—a special friend who can't be seen in such circumstances. Handy agrees and Larky sits back and waits for the disaster. His plan is simply to reveal the father's shame to the son—to see Mr. Crompton exposed. But the joke, if you want to call it that, is on Larky Hamilton and Mr. Crompton. Handy trumps them both."

"Ab-surd!" says Mrs. Lamm's sister.

"It's possible," says Mrs. Lamm, leaning back in the glider and looking contentedly off to the end of the porch where her crepe myrtle is this year in full, unbelievable bloom—beautifully deformed with flower heads as big and deep pink as half a watermelon.

"Only you could imagine such ridiculous filth," says Mrs. Lamm's sister.

"Oh, plenty more could," Mrs. Lamm says.

The guards have gone back to their old ways, vigilant, unfriendly and by-the-book. They have heard enough of what at first they thought was sophistication. Now they mean to ban it from their minds forever. They are less polite to the lady even, because she sits and listens and doesn't tell that man what they think he ought to be told. They still do as she asks, fetching glasses of water, opening doors for her, but she has always asked for little. They still let her stay longer than the prison rules allow, but the gallantry is gone from their indulgences, and they perform their duties with a visible sense of superiority. They are no longer impelled by her fine manners and absolute kindness toward them, but make sure that what she wants happens, because she is a woman of influence with friends, who, if she complained, would cause trouble for them.

It is part of their job to hear everything the prisoner says when Mrs. Labrette is with him, but they now listen from a distance, as far away as they can get from the two.

Mrs. Labrette has returned to hear the rest, because Jerry has asked her. "I need to know if I was right," he said to her over the telephone, and that, as Jerry had known it would be, was the lure.

"We waited in the hall, Mr. Jones and I, and listened," Jerry says. "We heard the door lock. No sound of surprise or shock came from within the room, nothing to make you think Mr. Crompton had discovered who he was with. It was quiet in there for a while, which for me was a relief. Mr. Jones was listening like he was about to be attacked. Then there were sounds—just rustlings at first—the tap of something being put down on a table or the thud of something being dropped to the floor. The squeak of the good old joinery. There was a low sound from a throat that in any other situation would have been taken for lamentation.

"When Mr. Jones realized that Handy was going through with it, he looked at me as though I had caused what had happened, as though I had somehow been the reason his attempt at revenge against the man he loved and who would not love him back had turned on him. He was the one who had been made a fool by Handy, but he seemed to convince himself almost instantly that I was the one on whom the joke had been. He looked at me as though I was to be both pitied and despised, and he said, 'I suppose I am very sorry for you.' Then he left.

"I waited until it was over. Listened to it all until there

was silence, which seemed the silence of death after long suffering.

"Finally the door opened, and there was Handy just standing there. He had not removed the mask. Mr. Crompton was still tied to the bed. Then Handy turned to face the bed and he reached behind his head and untied the mask and pulled it off and flung it toward Mr. Crompton. It landed at the foot of the bed. At first Mr. Crompton did nothing, just looked straight at his son with no emotion, as if he were reading a sign or something, then suddenly he burst out laughing, and just kept laughing. I thought I was going to be sick.

"Handy said, 'Let's go,' and walked past me and down the stairs. I looked back at Mr. Crompton—I don't think he knew it was me, and then I grabbed the doorknob and I slammed the door, hard, but I could still hear him in there laughing. So I ran down the stairs after Handy. In spite of what had happened and even though I knew now that Handy was sick with something I would never understand and could not help him with, that he was probably crazy with it, I went down the stairs after him."

"I've heard all I will hear," she says, and she stands up to leave.

"There is no more," says Jerry, and he rises.

For a moment they stand silently, each looking to see what the other will do, like a doctor and a patient after the bad news.

"You were right to go after him," says Mrs. Labrette, and she watches as the guards take Jerry away. The visit is over.

Mrs. Lamm on a visit to Passiflora. Sitting on her sister's screened-in patio. Looking out at the golf course of the Passiflora Country Club.

The click of a club hitting a ball is heard shortly after a

man tees off in the distance, and regularly, as if out of nowhere, shiny white balls like freak hailstones drop from the blue sky and land on her sister's back lawn.

They are sitting on golf balls. The cushions on the patio furniture have been covered in a barq cloth printed over and over, crowded with, a golfer from the turn of the century wearing knickers, driving cap and sweater vest in a matching argyle pattern. He has hit the ball, and it is flying off into the air. Looking at the repeated pattern of golfer and golf ball and eye-crossing plaid makes Mrs. Lamm feel like she is having a spell.

She thinks about the vast differences between Branch Creek and Passiflora. She keeps her thoughts to herself as long as she can, but when finally she is no longer able to and just has to say something, she tries to be disapproving in an agreeable way.

"These new houses are easy to keep clean, I bet. And economical to heat and cool, I imagine," she says to her sister in a tone she hopes will in a gentle way announce how tacky she thinks it is to live inside the grounds of a recently organized country club. "Everything spanking new. Even the antiques are new. Reproductions are just as pretty, aren't they? And you don't have to be all the time worrying that the maid is going to scratch it or somebody is going to set a glass down and leave a circle. I would love to have new things, but we're already practically buried in all that stuff from I. C.'s family. You can't imagine what a responsibility and burden it is to be handed down such things. Many is the time I wished I had married somebody like you did, who hadn't been burdened with a whole lot of past."

Her sister's maid comes out to the screened-in patio, carrying a silver tray with two bottles of cola. The maid's name is Tempie, and Mrs. Lamm likes to point out to her sister the irony of having an employee with a name that suggests such impermanence. She does this subtly, she thinks.

"You know good and well it is short for 'Temperance,'" her sister snaps every time Mrs. Lamm says the name and looks confused.

Under each bottle of cola is a small linen cocktail napkin, which is how they serve soft drinks in Passiflora; in the bottle with a good napkin to wrap around it so you don't get your hands too wet or too cold, whereas in Branch Creek everybody would rather perish from thirst than to drink out of a bottle anywhere but at a ball game. In a glass, Mrs. Lamm thinks. Please! And a little paper napkin, for the Lord's sake. And to top off the pretense, Tempie is wearing a uniform, something you would see in a French farce, although Mrs. Lamm is not exactly sure what a French farce is, but she has heard people use the term when they are ridiculing this kind of maid's uniform.

"New, new, new," she sighs. "Don't you just feel lucky?"

"If I had any such thing as luck, I wouldn't have a sister," says Mrs. Lamm's sister.

"Would you ask Tolerance to bring me a glass, please, or a paper cup or a canning jar, anything," Mrs. Lamm whines.

Her sister gives Mrs. Lamm a look that would fry an egg, but the glass is brought, although it isn't glass. It is heavy plastic with a thick hollow bottom in which a little golf course has been enclosed somehow. There are little flags and little men swinging golf sticks, and tiny golf balls rolling around that you can try to get to roll into the holes. As if you didn't have anything better to do, Mrs. Lamm thinks. She pours the cola out of the bottle into the plastic tumbler, but she does not drink from it. In front of her is a low cocktail table. The legs are fashioned from golf clubs, its feet number-one woods. The top is glass and painted to look like a course, complete with sand and water hazards and clubhouse with a bar called the 19th Hole. She sets the tumbler of cola down on the cocktail table. She will leave it there and not drink it as a lesson to both hostess and help.

"Can we talk about Jerry?" asks Mrs. Lamm's sister.

"Why, of course, if that is what you want to talk about. You sure do enjoy hearing about him, it seems," says Mrs. Lamm indulgently.

"Well, I have theories of my own that may be borne out, and it seems like a fitting time, while you are so busy pointing out the flaws in my house, myself and my maid, to find out just how he came to know so much about decorating and such as that and turned you all into such intolerable snobs," says Mrs. Lamm's sister.

"I haven't done a thing in this world but compliment everything around me since I got here. Except the cola in the bottle, but all the rest I think I have been very nice about," says Mrs. Lamm. She gives the patio a sweeping glance. "There are those who wouldn't be," she says not quite under her breath.

She waits to see if what she just said gets noticed, but if her sister has, she lets the remark pass. Mrs. Lamm shifts and wiggles into the sofa, crosses her legs and pulls her skirt down over her knee.

"That was the funny part," she begins. "The joke was on us, or on Elsie Moye, to be more exact. As you know, Elsie was always in direct competition with Maggie for Jerry's heart and soul. It was a useless and hopeless waste of her time, of course, but it never seemed to get through to Elsie Moye that he had long ago attached himself to Maggie and all she stood for. She was continuously trying to think up ways to dethrone Maggie. And I don't to this day know why. It was useless. Maggie didn't even see herself on a throne or at the top of some social ladder or anything like that. We don't even have such a thing in Branch Creek."

She removes the napkin from underneath the plastic glass of cola. She had not noticed before, being so preoccupied with getting something to drink out of besides a bottle, but now she sees that the cocktail napkin is machine-embroidered with a kind of coat of arms; all golf business, crossed golf sticks and three balls and a flag and something in Scots. And a little bit of plaid dabbed into the design, of course. She fingers the emblem, looking down her nose at it, eyes lowered, with a faint smile on her lips, then she puts the napkin back under the plastic glass.

"As I was saying, we are plain people in Branch Creek, so it was odd that Elsie Moye thought there was some sort of competition going on. I guess just because she had more money than any of us, she thought it was not fair that she couldn't run things. Anyway, she's the one who made it possible for Jerry to go to New York. The idea was he would go for a year and enroll in a school where they taught about decorating. She agreed to bankroll him. He never went. To the school, I mean. Got mixed up with that Handy Crompton, and that was that. Jerry bought an old Emily Post at a secondhand bookstore. It was written in the twenties. He read every last word of it, and that's how he always had a few little odd bits of information that the rest of us hadn't ever heard of, so out of date that they seemed right to us. I think he went to the museums, and he certainly saw how to do, being around those Cromptons and their friends. But he just used Elsie's money for fun. I'm not sure she even knows this.

Four to six golf balls plunk onto the grass unaccountably, for there is not a golfer in sight. They stand out on the lawn like white mushrooms. Another ball thumps the roof over their heads and then rolls off into the border of pink impatiens planted all the way around the house. Easy flowers to take care of, Mrs. Lamm thinks, contrasting them to her own capricious roses and temperamental azaleas and nearly belligerent cape jasmine. There is, she believes, an indication of character in the difference between her gardening and that on display here, but Mrs. Lamm lets the thought pass without wrapping it in words and lobbing it at her sister.

"Doesn't it jangle your nerves to have those golf balls dropping out of the sky all day long?" she asks.

"What would jangle my nerves if I let it is you," says Mrs. Lamm's sister. "So he took Elsie Moye's money and used it for an adventure. I like that. I'm going to have some fun with that."

Jerry and Handy were driven back to the apartment on their street where the trees are higher than the buildings. The same driver who had come for them brought them back. They rode all the way in silence. The car crossed the Hudson River on the George Washington Bridge. Off to the south lay the city, huge, black and scowling, like a low-approaching thunderhead. It was still dark. There were only a few lights on in the tall buildings, as if a secretary who couldn't wait to get home or a sleepy, slipshod janitor had forgotten to turn them off. In the east behind the crowded skyline there was a weak, lusterless glow in the bottom of the sky. Day was retreating and night was falling all over again, as if the sun had taken a look at its work and decided, Not today—like a hungover, depressed, but usually responsible middle-aged man who one morning wakes up, looks out the window and then for reasons he only vaguely understands, turns off the alarm, pulls the covers over his head and, in spite of his throbbing temples, goes immediately back to sleep, never knowing that he will not wake again, ever. Never knowing that this is his last day on earth, and he will spend it avoiding his life.

On the bridge, midspan, Handy moved closer to Jerry and took his hand, and they both sat up straight looking slightly off to the south where the city was.

"Home?" said Handy in the manner of a child not sure he is calling a thing by its right name.

Jerry did not turn to Handy but continued to look at the city and the light behind it that could not decide whether to come or go.

"Home," Handy said again, this time with the assurance of the child who, not having been corrected, assumes he has rightly identified what he was not sure of.

Jerry waited and was still and did not speak until they had crossed the bridge and were skimming the edge of the city in the black car.

Then finally, "No. Where we live," he said.

The driver turned off the West Side Highway onto Twelfth Street. Among the meat wholesalers and storage warehouses were bars and sex clubs. Places you could get what you wanted and leave the person who had given it to you there. The car swanned up the street overtaking men going home alone. They walked quickly and purposefully, as if they had just gotten off work. There were boy-girls in high-heeled shoes, walking cautiously over the uneven sidewalks and across the street, which in some blocks was still paved in cobblestones.

The car stopped for a light. On the corner, standing completely still, was a boy-girl in a tube top, jeans and sandals. His head was lifted and his ear tilted to the sky as though he were listening for the answer to a question. His face, lit in the sickly yellow of the street lamp, had a saintly look of ill health and suffering.

"Open the window," Handy said.

Jerry pushed the button, and the barrier of tinted glass lowered, giving off a morbid buzz.

"Good evening," Handy said. The person did not move, but continued to stand perfectly still and stare into the heavens. "You will find it can hold out longer than you," he said. "And when you break, which is assured, it will still have nothing for you."

The light changed and the car moved off. Jerry closed the window.

"What could he have been looking at?" Handy asked, more to himself than to Jerry.

"Just stoned, I imagine," said Jerry. "Why did you bother him? I think it was cruel."

"I suppose it was, a little, although it was not my intention to be so. He just made me think it is never good to look up. I was talking more to myself, really," said Handy.

"But he didn't know that," said Jerry.

The sky had brightened a little over them and lit a path leading ahead at the top of the buildings corresponding to the streets they took. Jerry looked up. He could only know they were moving along, but he could not tell where they were going. He tried, by watching the sky and by feeling when the car turned or stopped, to stay oriented and aware of exactly where they were, how far from where they lived, but it was impossible.

He looked at Handy next to him, beautiful, the same.

"I have not changed," Handy said, as if he knew Jerry was worrying that he had.

"I did not think you had," Jerry said. "Maybe that's the sick part. If I have changed, I don't know it. I must have, but I can't tell how. But Handy, I want to know why," Jerry said.

"I'll only say this. He had it coming. Believe me," Handy said.

The car turned onto their block, and between the buildings the sun had just risen over the East River, shining so brightly that it could have been a locomotive racing down the street to collide with them.

"I do believe you," Jerry said, as if it were the last sentence he would speak before they were hit.

The car stopped at their building, and the two climbed

the stairs, Handy leading the way, up to the apartment. Jerry made food, eggs and bacon, and he made coffee, light and sweet. They ate it all quickly, so he made some more, and they ate that. Then the sun was up and shining on the green treetops outside the window of the little kitchen.

"In the daylight, a night is hard to remember, isn't it?" asked Handy. "You can almost pretend it was never there."

"But it was there. There was a night last night," said Jerry.

"Yes, there was," Handy said. "Shall we pretend there is to be no day?"

"How?" asked Jerry.

"I will show you," Handy said, and he took Jerry by the hand and led him into the bedroom, and there, with the authority of one who has visited the far reaches of his limits, delighted Jerry in ways he had not known were possible.

They did not sleep until night came again. The next morning when they woke up, Jerry told Handy that he would never leave him no matter what. That even if he should find out that Handy had killed, he would try to save him from the consequences.

"Why?" asked Handy, as though he thought it would be a stupid thing to do.

"Because everybody should have one person who would do anything for them," said Jerry.

"I don't think you will ever have to do anything as drastic as that for me," Handy replied.

"And everybody should have one person they'll do anything for," Jerry went on as if he had not heard Handy.

"But it is good to know," said Handy.

The summer before the winter when Jerry's little brother rocked over face-first into Mrs. Labrette's guest-room fireplace, Mr. Chiffon made what turned out to be the last effort to reclaim his son from the tribe of women.

There was a man named Henry Hampton running for the United States Senate, and although Mr. Chiffon didn't know much about politics and did not see that it had ever done much for him, this candidate had mailed a letter addressed personally to Mr. Chiffon asking him to come to a rally. The politician had signed it, "Yours in Christ," at the bottom, so Mr. Chiffon decided he would attend.

"I feel like I got to go," Mr. Chiffon said to Jerry, "and you're going, too."

The rally was to be held on a Saturday night at the race-track in the county fairgrounds over in Toisnot. All the week before, Jerry did his housework and tended to the garden and looked after his little brother and his daddy in the careful, efficient way he had always done, but every day he had a new question for his daddy about the coming Saturday.

"Will I still be able to spend the day at Mrs. Labrette's?" he asked soon after his daddy told him they were going to the fairgrounds on Saturday night. The answer was no.

"How are we going to get there?" Jerry asked late on Tuesday when his daddy came out of the field for supper. He had been worrying all day that they would have to go on the tractor. The ride into Branch Creek on Saturdays had started to embarrass him. He and his little brother being pulled in a rattling tobacco truck behind his daddy's old tractor just didn't suit him now, and he thought he'd die of shame and boredom if he had to go the ten miles in such a way to Toisnot.

The answer to that question was that they were going with a man who had a pickup truck. It was somebody Jerry did not know, but he looked forward to riding in the back of a pickup truck at night.

On Wednesday he stopped in the middle of pulling beans and went to find his daddy out in the field behind the house, dusting the tobacco. "Are we going to take the baby?" he asked. Worrying about Saturday made him forget that his daddy was easily angered by too many questions, particularly when Jerry asked questions that seemed to be saying he thought his daddy wasn't being careful enough, had not reasoned through a situation thoroughly, that some important detail had been overlooked.

"Hell, no, we are not taking the baby!" His daddy stood up on the tractor and kicked the duster hopper, which had clogged up. "Quit worrying, Miss Annie. I got it all taken care of. Jasper's wife is going to stay here and look after the baby. This is a man's meeting we're going to. You think you can quit prissing around long enough to act like a little man? Now go to the house and get supper. I got it all worked out." He moved off down the rows, white clouds of poison huffing out from either side of the tractor.

On Thursday and Friday Jerry's mind was so filled with questions that he could hardly do the things he needed to do. He dropped a five-pound bag of flour on the kitchen floor and spent the better part of an hour just trying to get enough of it back in the bag so he wouldn't have to tell his daddy that they were out of flour. Although he stood right over the stove the whole time tending to them, he nearly burned the sausages he was frying for their supper because he didn't turn them soon enough, distracted with wondering whether there would be any other boys his age at this thing he was going to. And twice he was thinking so hard, he almost didn't hear the raspy breathing that meant his little brother needed his head propped up. A thousand questions were on his mind about what exactly would go on at the rally. What was the man they were going with like? Would it be boring? But the one that kept coming up over and over and was the question still left when he had settled the others was, Would this be something he belonged at? Would it be a place where he could imagine himself being before he got there, and when he left, would it be a place he would think about himself having been to the way he liked to go back over a day spent with Mrs. Labrette, or, when alone high up in the top tier of the tobacco barn, he planned and imagined everything he intended to do before he died? But Jerry knew there was no use in asking his daddy that question, for he couldn't even have understood what Jerry wanted to know, let alone give him an answer.

When Saturday came, Mr. Chiffon went into Branch Creek in the morning, but he did not take Jerry and his little brother along. In the afternoon, he came home. Jerry was sitting on the porch when his daddy returned high and happy in the tractor seat. He cut the engine just outside the shed and jumped down from the seat while the tractor was still moving. He was carrying a bag of fried chicken from a take-out place. The tractor rolled to a stop under the shed without running into the side of the barn. It was a trick he had not done since Jerry's mother had died.

"I got something from town for us to eat," said Mr. Chiffon. His voice was strange to Jerry—light and excited.

He even walked differently—straight and brisk, like an important man.

Jerry followed his daddy into the kitchen. He unpacked the bag of food and served it up on plates while his daddy sat waiting at the table, telling Jerry all he had to do before they went to the rally.

"Make sure you feed the baby and get him situated so Jasper's wife won't have to tend to him much more than just setting while he sleeps. You put on one of the shirts old lady Labrette bought you and one of the nice pairs of pants," he said. He sat up so straight at the table and talked fast, and it made Jerry a little mad. For the first time ever, he seemed like a man who could have looked after all of them better than he had been doing.

"This here is a great man we're going to see tonight. He wants to get things back to how they used to be, Jerry. That's what I heard uptown. He don't like how things have changed down here, and he wants us to go back to God and the old ways," Mr. Chiffon said. He got up from the table and went into the bedroom, then came out, then went back in, and he kept coming in and going out of the room as he talked, each time with one more piece on of what he intended to wear. "And he's going to start by keeping the colored people out of the schools and stopping colored people and white people from marrying each other."

Jerry didn't know that what his daddy was talking about or that what this man they were going to see meant to do was something that needed doing. There wasn't a single colored boy or girl in his class at school, and he didn't know of any white folks marrying colored people.

"Pa, there aren't any colored people in the school," said Jerry.

"There is other places, and it's coming here, boy. Goddamn! It's coming. That's what they're talking," Mr. Chiffon said.

He buttoned his shirt all the way up to the top button. His neck stuck high out of the shirt, and the knot of bone at his throat pulsed like the wattle of a turkey trying to keep cool. Jerry watched him put his shirttail in and pull his belt so tight that his pants ruffled around his waist.

"How will this man stop what is coming, Pa?" asked Jerry. He had gotten dressed and was wearing a light blue knit shirt and a pair of blue seersucker pants that Mrs. Labrette had bought for him. His daddy was in the kitchen, combing his hair in the little mirror on the shelf over the sink. Jerry sat down at the table and waited for his daddy to answer the question he had asked. When his daddy was done, he turned to Jerry as if to get approval—the way a man who has had a wife for a long time will do, not because he particularly wants to know what she thinks, but because she has made him show himself to her so many times that it is a habit with him. Jerry didn't say anything about how his daddy was dressed.

"By getting in there and taking over!" Mr. Chiffon shouted. "When he gets in there you'll see how he's going to do it."

Jerry sat still and watched his daddy move about the house. He looked like most of the men Jerry saw up and down the streets of Branch Creek and surrounding towns, skinny, brown from working in the sun, tough and stringy as burnt meat. In his clean but sorry clothes, he was still who he was. If I had a house of my own, I'd make him go to the back door, Jerry thought. Then he looked down at his own clothes and knew right away that if what his daddy was wearing to this thing at the fairgrounds was all right to wear, then what he had on was not, and he was glad of it. He'd go to this thing with his daddy, but it would be the last time he'd do something he didn't want to do. He might have to take a beating or two, so he would, and then he'd start to be all the time exactly what he wanted to be instead of just at Mrs. Labrette's and when he was alone, and he thought about when he would not have his daddy anymore and all it felt like was waiting.

"I'm ready," Jerry said.

"Me too," said Mr. Chiffon.

They went out onto the porch and sat down in separate chairs to wait for their ride. The front bedroom window was open, and Jerry could hear his little brother gurgling and snorting inside. His daddy sat silently jiggling one knee up and down. He reminded Jerry of a panting dog. Nothing passed on the road in front of the house. The asphalt was so black and clean and the iridescent broken white line had just a week before been repainted. It looked as if no car had ever passed the house and none ever would. Jerry started to cry.

"What you crying at, boy?" his daddy asked.

"I don't want to go," Jerry said.

"I know you don't," his daddy said. "But you're going."

Jerry looked at him and did not see anger as he had expected, but a kind look, and mixed in with it some sort of knowing, not like he understood, but like he had accepted what he did not. Jerry stopped crying and wiped his eyes with the back of his hand.

"It ain't been fair for you," his daddy said.

"Pa, I'll go. I want to go. I don't know what ails me, Pa. I want to go now. It's all right," Jerry said, for he did not want to hear his daddy being sorry for him. It made him feel crowded and like something a little bit sickening had brushed up against him.

"It'll be fun, boy, you'll see," Jerry's daddy said, and the kind look left his face, and he looked like somebody who had finally found out that he was not going to get something he had been hoping a long time for.

They sat quietly, gazing off in the direction their ride was to come from. The corn was growing high on both sides of the road, and soon they saw the roof of a green truck coming toward them. The truck burst out of the corn where the field ended, slowed only enough to make the turn into the yard, swerved around and slid to a stop at the front steps. There was a tin plate with a silhouette of a naked woman on the front bumper. The man driving was so much like his daddy that Jerry didn't pay any attention to him. There was a woman on the seat beside him, fat and ugly and poor-looking, but in the back of the truck, sitting on the wheel well, leaning on his elbows, was a boy about Jerry's age. He was grinning in a way that made him look happy and mean at the same time. He had on a white short-sleeved shirt and what looked like almost new blue jeans. His hair was blond and had been misbehaving in the wind. Another breeze blew it up in front. His forehead was whiter than the rest of his face, and in his eyes was this look of knowing some things he ought not to know—things he wouldn't tell you unless you begged him or were strong enough to twist his arm or gave him something he thought was an even trade.

The woman climbed out of the truck. When she walked in front of it, the man driving blew the horn just to scare her. She scowled, and waddled up the steps and into the house.

"Let's go, boys!" he shouted.

Jerry's daddy let out a high-pitched howl to celebrate.

The blond boy looked straight at Jerry, laughed then smirked. Jerry's daddy got in the truck, and Jerry climbed in with the boy. There was a bale of hay just under the back window of the truck, and Jerry sat down on it. The man driving blew "shave and a haircut, two bits" on the horn, and they pulled out into the road. Jerry watched the broken white lines of the road shoot quicker and quicker from under the truck as they picked up speed, until they were coming out so fast he couldn't have counted them if he had tried. For a while the boy sat silently, just staring and smiling and smirking at Jerry, and he wondered if the boy might be a little bit slow or not exactly right, but then the boy got up from where he was sitting, and crouching low as if moving around in a canoe, came and sat beside Jerry on the bale of hay.

"What's your name?" he said loudly. The beating of the wind and the speed of the truck caused the words to fly off behind them as soon as they were heard, like a note read and thrown away.

Jerry had to holler his name twice before the boy understood him.

"What's your name?" Jerry asked the boy.

"Davis," he said. "Ever been to one of these things before?"

"No," Jerry said.

"They're bullshit. I been before. Bunch of boring bullshit. Long old talking and sometimes grown men running around in white robes and cone heads praying and burning shit. But they get so worked up, you can run off and get into some trouble sometime."

"What kind of trouble?" asked Jerry.

"Smoke, for one thing," said the boy, and like a magic trick there appeared in his hand a pack of cigarettes. "And cuss and once in a while a drink of whiskey or something like that."

These were things Jerry had never wanted to have any part of until now. He watched the boy hide the pack of cigarettes in the hay.

"They don't care what you're doing," he said, tossing his head all big and wonderful like a horse refusing to take the bridle. "You ain't ever been where they don't care what you're doing. I bet you been watched over like money."

"No, I hain't. Haven't," said Jerry. "Been watched over like that, I mean."

"Ah, come on, I can tell. You ain't done much you ought not to done. I'll fix that," Davis said. He looked Jerry over, starting at his feet and moving right up to the top of his head. "I like your fancy pants," he said.

"Somebody gave them to me," said Jerry.

He was happy. It was as if something he had tried to hide about himself, something so hated, something that he had spent so much time thinking about and trying to figure out ways to get rid of had been recognized, and this flaw had been pointed to as what made him wanted by one he had never hoped he could even wish for; as if he had always wanted brown eyes instead of blue and someone had told him they wished they had eyes like his. Like that, he'd found his blessing and it was cursed.

The two boys rode in silence, looking off for long stretches in opposite directions at the scenery whipping past. Then, unable to stop himself, Jerry would turn to look at Davis, and sometimes Davis would look back at him, and they would say nothing, but they would grin at each other and Davis' face would go red, more the shy one now, and Jerry the one bold and shameless as an idiot.

When the truck pulled into the fairgrounds, the parking field was nearly full already. Orange clay dust fogged the air and coated the vehicles. The sun was down, and there was only the idea of daylight in the sky. They had to park far away from the racetrack.

Jerry and Davis followed their daddies through the tight maze of parked cars and trucks toward the racetrack in the distance, which was all lit up as if something was being dissected inside it. There were flag poles across the top tier of the grandstand with Confederate flags flying. Fiddle music was coming over loudspeakers. As they picked their way between the cars and trucks, they were joined by more and more men and boys. Neither they nor the others with whom they were gathering spoke. It was as if everyone was approaching something secret and holy, and all sharing a single prayer that they had learned to pray when young, whispered low, lips barely moving and, although inaudible, known by each to be what the other was murmuring, the way in church you know that the creed you are professing is the same as that of the worshiper pews away, even if you cannot hear him. *We have a secret. We believe in our secret. Our secret which art in secret, secret be thy secret.*

Jerry stopped in the narrow space between a truck and a car. He felt his stomach roll, and he thought he might be sick. His daddy and Davis's daddy and Davis had not noticed he had stopped.

"Pa!" he called.

His daddy stopped and turned around, looking in all directions.

"I'm here, Pa," said Jerry, raising his hand.

"I can't find you, boy," said his daddy.

"Here," said Jerry, and he jumped up so that his daddy could see his head above the truck he was behind.

"Come on, boy. It's starting. We'll miss it," said his daddy.

From the grandstand a great cheer went up, and a band started to play "Dixie," and the crowd was singing and hollering.

"I can't, Pa. I'm sick. I'll go back to the truck and wait for y'all," he said.

"He ain't sick," said Davis. "I'll go get him."

Jerry waited. He could not see Davis coming after him. He appeared around the front of the car. His eyes were big and afraid.

"You really sick?" he asked.

"I don't know," said Jerry.

"Come on, it'll be okay. I told you, we'll get out of there before long. Then we'll have some fun." Davis was whispering.

Jerry didn't see anything around that looked like any fun. This was not the fair with its games and rides laid out around the grandstand. But then Davis put his hand on Jerry's shoulder and looked straight at him.

"I'll stay right with you. I won't go nowhere without you," said Davis. "Let's go now."

He got behind Jerry and followed him closely, as if to herd him into the grandstand, saying "left" and "right" and "Go behind that green car" and "Watch out for the mud hole," until they found their daddies. Jerry fell in behind his daddy and Davis', and Davis kept following Jerry, near and careful.

They reached the grandstand and got in the slow-moving line of people at the gate.

"Damn, I bet we won't get a seat," said Davis' daddy. "I sure didn't think there'd be this many folks come."

Inside the gate there were girls dressed as Southern belles in pastel dresses with hoop skirts and wide sashes tied in huge bows at the back. They were holding out baskets to collect donations. Davis' daddy pulled out a dollar and threw it into one of the girls' baskets, and Jerry was surprised to see his daddy do the same. Jerry studied the girls and the dresses. One girl's hoop skirt tilted up, and he could see she was wearing tennis shoes. He was even more sure that there would be something here, unreal and cheap. Another of the girls had her hair up in a bun, and she had pinned a plastic gardenia blossom in it, and Jerry thought that was sad and stupid, too.

There were people giving away buttons with the candidate's picture on it, and there were tables with pamphlets. Their daddies took the buttons and some of the pamphlets. Davis was still behind him, so Jerry looked back at him and made a face with his tongue sticking out, and Davis laughed and said, "Quit it, quit it now," so Jerry kept doing it until Davis laughed so loud that his daddy looked back to see what was going on.

"Y'all behave," said Davis' daddy.

He turned back around and walked importantly, like someone had made him the boss, so Jerry imitated him, and that made Davis try so hard not to laugh out loud that he got choked and started coughing.

Jerry had been in the grandstand before. At fair time he'd gone there to see a man on a horse jump from a high platform into a tank of water. The walk up the ramp from the dark below into the light-filled arena was exciting to him. To come up onto a scene in progress—the stage with people in bright artificial light, and green grass and red dirt seen in color when outside the lit-up place it was night, and all the people banked high in the bleachers looking down—was still exciting at first, even if what everyone had gathered for turned out to be dull or irritating.

In the bright light Jerry could not see at first. He shaded his eyes with his hand. A long stage had been set up on the grassy infield behind the red dirt track. He squinted, trying to make out what was on the stage. It looked dirty, like something he'd have to sneak off to look at in secret. A doctor in his white coat and stethoscope was on the stage with posters on an easel. He held a microphone in his hand and with a stick pointed to different views of a muscular, nearly naked Negro man, and said things about how the man was different from white people and more like a monkey or an ape than a human.

"Here. And here," the doctor said, pointing to the man's brow and nose.

On another poster were pictures of just the Negro man's head from the front, side, top and back and pictures of noses and lips, some black and some white. On a table beside the doctor were different kinds of hair. The doctor picked up some hair that had come from a Negro, and said it was good for scrubbing pots. The crowd laughed and applauded at the things the man said.

They had to go high up in the bleachers to find seats. The two they found were not together. The men took those, so Jerry and Davis had to sit on the steps at the end of the row.

"This is better," said Davis. "Easier to run off." When the doctor was done, a preacher came on the stage and prayed a long, boring prayer. At the "Amen," the fiddle struck up "The Star-Spangled Banner," and as the flag was raised on a pole in the infield, the crowd sang the anthem. Then the crowd said the "Pledge of Allegiance." Their daddies leaned out and looked down the row at the two boys, so they had to stand and say the Pledge.

The band struck up "Dixie" before the crowd could sit, and the hollering and singing started up again, and a white Cadillac convertible with a sparkling sign that said Courtesy of Gold Leaf Cadillac on the door drove onto the track. The candidate was sitting up on the trunk of the car like a beauty queen, waving. He was wearing a blue suit, and his hair was dry and neat. When he smiled, his white teeth were visible even from high up in the stands. The car made a single pass along the length of the grandstand and then cut across the track and back to the stage. In the wild cheering, Davis grabbed Jerry's hand.

"Let's go!" he said. He ran down the steps and Jerry followed, not looking back to see if his daddy had seen him go. They ran along the front row to the ramp leading out of the grandstand.

"This way!" shouted Davis. Under the bleachers were rows of food stands, shuttered until fall and the fair, and Davis ran behind them until he reached the last stand at the end of the row. In a small space between the wall of the stand and the side of bleachers he stopped and leaned against the wall, gasping. Jerry followed and found him, and before either had caught his breath, Davis, putting his hands against the wall on either side of Jerry's head, lowered his face toward Jerry's and kissed him on the lips then pulled back and looked him in the face.

"Never been kissed," he said, smiling.

"My mama and Miss Maggie," said Jerry.

"My mama," Davis repeated, laughing, and lit out running again. Jerry ran, too, following him through the maze of cars. They ran because they had to and they could, like colts. Davis ran and leapt, his legs still wheeling in the air. Jerry ran and did not get tired or winded.

From the grandstand they could hear the voice of Henry Hampton, and although they did not care or try, they couldn't have understood what he was saying if they had. They could hear cheers coming from the crowd, but what each listened for was the yelp of the other. They ran and ran, each place they ran to in the crowded parking lot looking exactly like where they had just run from. Jerry got lost in the puzzle of vehicles and tramped-down grass of the field.

Then he couldn't see Davis and stopped running.

"Davis!" he called.

"Jerry!" said Davis more calmly.

"Davis?"

"Jerry."

"Davis."

Following the sound of his own name, he found his way back to the truck they had come in and to Davis. When he got there, Davis was in the back of the truck, and with the hateful Henry Hampton saying things they could not hear but could tell were bad and mean, and the sound of the hateful crowd cheering as if to urge them on, they sinned in every way they could think of, their only worry, getting caught. They stopped when they began to hear voices nearby and engines starting up. When their daddies came back, Jerry's looked angry, but Davis' didn't seem to mind that they had run off, so Mr. Chiffon didn't say anything to Jerry.

"We're going to another meeting," said Mr. Chiffon. "We're taking you home. Davis can spend the night with you."

Jerry's eyes sidled up to Davis'. Neither of them spoke or even moved for fear that their delight would show.

They slept in Jerry's narrow bed after having exhausted themselves giggling and playing a game Davis knew that he called What's This I Found? And while they slept, during the night or in the dark part of morning—no one ever really knew exactly—in the next county over, some men, robed and masked, broke into a house where a Northern college boy and his Negro friend were sleeping together. They had come down to show poor Negroes how to vote. Some of the men dragged the white boy out of the house and forced him onto a bus to New York.

Years later, not until after Jerry had tried to shoot Henry Hampton and served his time and had come back to live in Maggie Labrette's house, a bulldozer excavating land for a new high school out in the next county over scooped up a load of dirt. When it swiveled to dump the red clay aside, some bones and the remnants of a T-shirt and underwear tumbled out of the bulldozer's bucket. Tests confirmed that the remains were those of the other student.

After the weekend at Larky Hamilton's, Handy stopped hiding from who he was, if hiding it had been. He had his hair cut in the prep-school-boy mop of his adolescence and reactivated his account at J. Press, where his file, a record of his growth from short pants to trousers to a first tuxedo, was pulled out and updated—the period in which there had been no entry was discreetly not explained or represented by even a blank line, and the file was simply continued underneath the last entry, which recorded his measurements for a custom-made blazer and some gray trousers—"No explanation necessary. Glad to see you back, sir. Hope your absence was for pleasant reasons." He bought chinos, shirts with button-down collars in light blue, pink and white, some cashmere, cable-knit, crewneck sweaters, a new blue blazer and some new gray slacks, brown loafers, black oxfords, even some plaid boxer shorts—Black Watch. So accoutred, he became more provocative and outrageous than he had been.

He found, however, that people are less tolerant of outrageous behavior if you look normal than if you are hugely eccentric in your dress and manner.

The effect of his change of style, as far as it had an effect on Jerry, was that to the everyday mind and sensibility, he and Handy appeared, from the outside at least, to be a model of respectability—a credit to all men who live together under the same roof and sleep together in the same bed. The old man on the ground floor, who owned the building, acknowledged them from his window overlooking the street with a smile and a wave in winter and a pleasant exchange in warm weather when the window was open. Often they would return to their apartment and find a plastic grocery bag hanging from the doorknob, containing homemade cookies or a banana bread wrapped in aluminum foil. This was from an old lady who lived beneath them. In the hallway or on the stoop she would stop Jerry.

"It is since you came . . . ," she would say, raising a hand and lifting her eyes to heaven to indicate what it had been like before he had moved in with Handy.

He did not tell her that Handy was worse in a different way; that he seemed now to go out of his way to offend strangers with his winks and comments and his blatant coquetry toward men who were not apt to be tolerant of it. In a taxi once, waiting for a traffic light to change, he rolled down the window and blew a kiss to a couple of policemen in a patrol car. The policemen pulled the taxi over and told both of them to get out. They were patted down, checked out. One of the policemen asked Handy what did he think he was doing.

"I so admire what you policemen do. How you protect us all, and truth be known, I've always had a thing for a man in a uniform, and I must say you wear yours well, officer," he said to the more attractive of the two.

What could you do with someone like that? Jerry asked himself. And the policemen were not charmed or amused as Jerry had seen them be to more outrageous types.

"Don't I look good in mine?" the other policeman asked menacingly, turning around to show off his uniform.

"I can't decide which of you is more handsome," said Handy.

What could you do? The policeman looked furtively up and down the street, then backing Handy up against the taxi, punched him in the stomach.

In all that charm and daring, affront costumed in conformity, was his end.

It happened because of a movie. Handy hated the movies, hated going to see them.

"The pictures are always bad," he would say, "and the audiences unruly." He had some sort of curse on him when it came to the movies. Jerry could seldom convince him to go, but when he did, he regretted it. It would put Handy in a bad mood right away. Before they left the house, when Jerry was looking in the paper for times and locations, Handy would get irritable, which took the form of rushing rather than dawdling through whatever they had to do— eat, bathe, dress—to get ready. But he couldn't say he wouldn't go, and Jerry appreciated that, loved him for it, and knew that it was one way Handy had of loving him. But he hurried through everything. He would have run the projector at double speed if he could. They would find themselves in the semidark movie house early, waiting for the picture to start. Handy would talk to the previews. *Coming Soon* was projected or announced from the screen, and he would make sounds like he was having an orgasm. In one picture there was a particularly long and spectacular train wreck after which the audience clapped and cheered. Handy waited until the applause had stopped and then loudly passed his judgment on the scene.

"Pre-posterous," he spat.

Either Jerry and he were always getting up to move, or everyone around them was.

Once, in a nearly empty theater, a seven-foot-tall man with enormous hair sat directly in front of Handy just as the movie started.

Once, a lady sat down beside him with a foul-smelling TV dinner, which she opened and ate loudly.

If there was a bum, a victim of Tourette's, the mother of colicky twins, a masturbating autistic or a leaky, gaseous geriatric within commuting distance of the particular movie house they were going to, he, she or it would make a special point of sitting behind, beside, in front of and, once, on top of Handy.

So on a hot summer night, Jerry convinced him that the movie theater would be the most comfortable place. Handy picked the movie. It was one that had been getting lots of publicity and had caused hard-shell Baptist, Pentecostals and Catholics to form picket lines in front of any theater where the movie was playing. What offended was the depiction of Jesus as a man with appetites.

"It puts forth the idea that He—what?—had a past, shall we say," Handy said, looking up from the listings. "If we must go, let's go to that one."

The rush began. Handy was ready long before Jerry, standing by the door, impatient and irritable. Jerry ran around gathering his keys and his wallet, so hurried that he started out the door, shoeless.

"For God's sake," said Handy.

Jerry locked the door. Handy was already clumping down the stairs like a fussy child.

At the movie house a long line of people were waiting to be let in for the next showing. Protesters held signs and passed out pamphlets, but the movie had been out for a while so there were fewer than there had been. A red-faced man in a dusty blue suit held a ragged open Bible in one hand and patted the air with his other while he preached the end of the world in a sad high-pitched voice full of regret.

Jerry bought their tickets while Handy waited at the curb.

They walked along the street passing the others waiting for the movie.

"A very tony crowd, don't you think?" said Handy as they got in the line. The couple in front of them, a pretty blond girl and her clinging boyfriend, turned and looked at Handy, the expression on both their faces flat and disapproving.

"What horrors await?" said Handy, staring back at the two. The girl smirked and the boy rolled his eyes.

"Come on, please," said Jerry. Handy looked at him innocently and smiled. The impatience and boredom went out of his eyes, and he kissed Jerry lightly.

"I promise I'll be mostly good," Handy said, and then pushing his face toward the backs of the couple in front, added, "Just for *you.*"

Up ahead a group of young men all in the same purple-and-gold athletic jackets were working their way down the line, talking to people and handing out tracts. They were big and healthy and looked as though neither a thought nor a doubt had ever occurred to any of them. Smiling and friendly looking, they seemed to be enjoying what they were doing. In the line people either took the pamphlet or shook their heads politely and smiled apologetically. There were few candidates for conversion, so the crusaders made their way quickly down the line.

The audience for the earlier show had let out, and soon the line started to shuffle forward. They were moving toward the group of athletes. When they reached them, one, the biggest, approached Handy.

"Brother, have you found Jesus?" he asked, narrowing his eyes and looking at Handy as though he knew the answer was no.

"Is she lost again?" Handy said, lisping flamboyantly.

Jerry saw the couple in front look at each other. They

were trying not to laugh, but it was plain they thought what Handy had done was funny and provocative and foolish.

"What did you say?" asked the athlete. His buddies had gathered behind him now. Their muscular shoulders broadened like cobras. They stood huge, ready to defend their faith.

"It was a joke," said Jerry, stepping between Handy and the athletes. One pushed him back. Ahead of them the line moved forward. Behind them people were peering over each other and stepping out of line to see why they weren't moving. People started complaining. "Knock it off, guys." "Come on, let's go." "Take it someplace else." A couple of ushers had come out into the street to see what was happening. The athletes backed off. The line started to move forward.

"If I see Miss Jesus, I'll tell her you're looking for her," Handy said over his shoulder.

"Stop it. Stop it. I mean it," said Jerry urgently.

He looked back. One of the athletes had his arms locked around the teammate Handy had taunted. Another was talking to him in a way that looked as though he was trying to calm him down not with Christ-like admonitions but with a plan of action.

When they got inside, Handy showed no sign of having been at all intimidated or frightened. Jerry's heart was beating so hard, he could hear it.

The couple who had been in front of them were in line to buy popcorn. When the boy saw Handy, he gave him the thumbs-up, and nodded his head, clearly impressed now rather than annoyed.

"Way to go, man," he said.

Jerry and Handy found seats in the quickly filling theater, and the movie began.

Immediately Handy didn't like the picture. He talked out

loud to the screen when something annoyed him, and pointed out to the dismay of those around him flaws, improbabilities, anachronisms and lapses of logic in the story. He was glared at and shushed repeatedly by several people in front, and a lady across the aisle finally threatened to go get the manager.

"I don't think my presence here is appreciated," Handy said finally, as if to imply that, were it true that the audience would rather not hear his commentary, he would never understand why.

"Do you want to leave?" Jerry whispered, in almost more of a command than a question.

"I thought you'd never ask, darling," Handy said full-voice.

"I'm not going," Jerry whispered.

"Very well, I will see you at home, and you can tell me how it all ends," Handy said. "I've heard there is some unpleasantness with an ex named Judas." He rose from his seat and clambered over the others in the row, apologizing elaborately to each person he squeezed past. He exited the theater to applause, which he acknowledged by gently nodding his head left and right like a royal on a walkabout.

Jerry stayed until the end, and left with the others. Outside it was still hot as day. It felt like the inside of a tobacco barn, high up, just under the tin roof. He walked across Sixth Avenue and headed east down Bleecker Street toward home. The doors and windows of the cafés usually opened to the streets were closed. Inside late-nighters ate in air-conditioned comfort. A few patrons, seemingly immune to the Malaysian heat, were braving the outdoor tables.

When he reached his building, the old man on the first floor had the window open and was sitting by it in front of a table. An electric fan and a small TV were on the table. From where Jerry stood he could see a rerun of *The George*

Burns and Gracie Allen Show strobing through the blades of the fan.

"Good evening, son," said the old man. They had never told each other their names.

"Good evening, sir," said Jerry.

"How was the movie? I heard you leave, and I heard your friend complaining, so I knew that was where you were going," said the old man.

He reached over to the TV and turned the volume down. "Where is your friend?"

"Upstairs, in the apartment. He left early," said Jerry.

"Ah. Yes? And I did not see him return," said the old man regretfully, as though he had been waiting for Handy to come back.

Jerry climbed the stairs and opened the door to the apartment.

"Handy!" he called. He intended to have it out with him this time. This time it had been too much. They might have been really hurt. "Handy!" he called again.

There was no answer. He looked in the bedroom and the bathroom, but Handy was not there.

Jerry turned on the TV and watched George and Gracie. Perhaps Handy had gone out for a conciliatory pint of that ice cream Jerry liked so much. He'd never had that kind until he came to New York, and even if Branch Creek had everything and New York had but that, it would be reason enough not to go home.

Gracie said good night. Jerry watched another rerun, and when that one was over, Handy had still not come home. He was out at some bar or probably already gone home with someone. He'd still do that kind of thing. It was rare, but irritation such as he had endured at the movies could send him off into the night. He called it "picking up a big scary man." He might even be doing it to punish Jerry for not being brave and clever enough, or just for wanting to go to the movies.

"I don't know why I—" he said out loud, but stopped short of what he was going to say.

But I do, he thought.

Then there was a bump at the front door that shook the wall. It scared Jerry. He went to the door and looked through the peephole, but could see nothing. He heard scratching sounds. When he looked down at the place where the scratching seemed to be coming from, there was blood oozing in under the door.

He opened the door quickly and, at first, couldn't make out what he saw. His first impression was that someone had dumped a slaughtered calf at his feet. That it was some sick warning from someone Handy had probably offended in some way.

Then he knew. He pulled Handy into the apartment and left him lying inside the door just long enough to call for an ambulance. When he went back, Handy was choking, so he held him up, held his head in his hands so that he could breathe easier.

"Who was it? Who did this?" Jerry asked. His tears fell into Handy's blood, but like oil and water, the two did not mix. The tears formed little pools and floated on the surface of the blood.

"Those poor young men who couldn't find Jesus," Handy said weakly.

He died before the ambulance arrived.

Lunch at the Passiflora Country Club with Mrs. Lamm's sister and her golf-lady friends. Half-empty old-fashioneds gleam icily around the table like amber votive lights. A waiter they all know is nearby, fluttering and perching.

"Those boys, the ones who did it, in the purple-and-gold

jackets, got no punishment to speak of," says Mrs. Lamm's sister. "Somehow the lawyers got the trial moved to New Jersey, claiming they couldn't get a fair hearing in Greenwich Village. They all testified under oath that Handy provoked them further when he came out of the movie by insulting Jesus again, then propositioning them one by one. Every last one of them said Handy grabbed their private parts and squeezed so hard that hell flew in them and they couldn't remember much of what happened. Plus, he was found blocks away—had made it up to his apartment. They maintained anything could have happened between the movie and that apartment house. And of course the life he led wouldn't have stood up to the once-over it would have gotten if the family had pressed things. Which, understandably, they didn't want to do. He was dead. It was all unpleasantness, don't you know, that they would just as soon let pass."

The lunches arrive, and are put down one by one in front of the ladies. When everyone is served, they eye each other's plates, and as always each wants the lunch of another and the complicated exchange of dishes that is their custom begins.

After Handy was killed, Jerry left New York the way he had come—on a train, with five hundred dollars in his pocket. When he got back to North Carolina, he sent Elsie Moye's money back to her with a little interest and a note thanking her and saying that he had learned all he needed to know without having to use it. He lived in Raleigh, and with the good taste he had acquired from longing for the things he had not been born with, he was able to show certain kinds of people how to want things they had not known how to want and do things properly with what they accumulated. It was then, and perhaps still is, assumed that anyone who had lived in New York for even a brief period knew better about how things ought to be done than those who had not. So that when he returned to Branch Creek, he had some money. He opened the florist shop and became the arbiter of good taste, which has been so often spoken of.

But he had not forgotten what he had been through and the things he had heard and seen. His anger had become as savage as his taste was refined. It was now the years between the beginning and the middle of the plague, and he watched people die from it at the same time that he saw them killed because of it, and he heard the twisted, hateful talk, no different for its evil effects than what he had learned to loathe and fear at the fairgrounds when he was a boy. Every time he heard that what had happened to Handy had happened again to another young man, or when he heard of an old bachelor gentleman found robbed and murdered with slurs upon his manhood carved into him with a knife, another bead on the tally flipped to that side of his heart where revenge was deposited, and the closer someone came to paying for all the wrongs. He thought often of justice and looked for examples of what he had learned from Maggie and church. He remembered his mother saying that right always prevailed. But he could never find what he hoped for. He read on his own during this time and found that if right prevailed it was because of those who had taken it upon themselves to right wrong and punish its doers.

Then one day he heard Senator Henry Hampton on the radio, giving a speech. God had brought his retribution upon homosexuals, Senator Hampton intoned. He said that modern science had proved conclusively that the brains of these people were different from normal people. They indulge in unspeakable acts that involve drinking blood and urine and eating feces, he said. He said they have plans to take over the schools. They will win your children over to their hideous ways. He said that the government gave them your taxes to disseminate information on how to perform the acts that had brought this curse of disease upon them. He said that they ought to be registered and tattooed in a prominent place so that everyone would know what they were. He said that you better wake up now and do something about this before it is too late, and he said that the best way to do this was to keep him in office. He said it looked like we were getting lucky, that God was on our side and had sent a plague to afflict our enemies. He said he would protect you from this evil as long as there was a breath in his body. He said he would put up the good fight until this evil scourge had been wiped from the face of the earth.

The day after that speech on the radio, on the other side of the state, what had happened to Handy happened to someone else. That afternoon Jerry drove to Raleigh to shop for a conservative red suit, accessories to match and a pistol.

"He threw himself onto the mercy of the court and got the minimum sentence in what they call the mitigated range—a little over three years, I think."

Mrs. Lamm's sister is standing over the first tee of the Passiflora Country Club course, getting ready to hit the ball. Standing around her are her golf-lady friends. They all have had their hair made blond and then streaks of believable gray put back in. They are dressed more like men than women, wearing Bermuda shorts in sherbet colors, and knit shirts, and ringing their frosted hairdos, white visors embroidered on the crown with the club insignia. The sun, over time, has lined and speckled their faces. The skin on their legs is brown and drooping.

"He had learned to fear words, and he had seen as a child what the kind of people who followed that Senator were capable of, and that was what motivated him. Plus, Maggie had him some clever lawyers who brought all this stuff in about how he had made something of himself, considering what he'd come from, and the awful thing in New York with that friend of his. Do you know what he said at his sentencing when he was allowed to address the court? 'I fell asleep. I stayed at the movies. My aim was bad. The sentence is more than fair. I'll serve it gladly.'

"The judge was, in my opinion, lenient."

She swung the club expertly, and the little white ball sailed off into the sky, arced, and landed commendably close to the first hole.

In the last year of Jerry's imprisonment, Maggie's health began to fail. Her heart, on which she had been so hard, finally started to resist her demands of it. She was not able to make the trip to Raleigh to visit Jerry as often as she had in the first two years, and at first, he feared that she had lost patience with him, that she had decided his troubles were his own and of his own making and that she had washed her hands of him. But he had been wrong, for although she was not up to the car trip, and the strain of sitting with him in oppressive and physically uncomfortable surroundings was something that Parchman had warned her against, she continued to write to him, and she had none other than the Governor fix it so that she could call Jerry once a week and talk to him as long as either one of them wished. She never abused the privilege— always waited until Saturday, the day that had been agreed upon, and their conversations seldom went much longer than an hour, but both looked forward with an almost adolescent fervor to the gossip and good cheer each provided for the other. She kept him up on the doings and goings-on in Branch Creek, and from the prison he continued, through Maggie, to advise and counsel, direct and bully the ladies of the town in matters of beauty, taste and culture. An enormous project was the sesquicentennial of the incorporation of Branch Creek. From the prison he oversaw every detail, from the schedule to which the actual day of celebration was ordered to the flowers planted uptown that spring in preparation for the coming event. "Old-fashioned flowers," he directed the Women's Society, "sweet william, cockscomb, parlor maple, four-o'clocks, touch-me-nots. The things women of the early mid-nineteenth century would have put out, beautiful but hardy and practical, nothing temperamental," he instructed. "They had not the time for it."

He prescribed picnics in the town cemetery, as would have been the fashion of the time, and he forbade a marching band of any sort with its anachronistic blare to sully the festivities. He had books on costumes and food and manners of the period brought from the university library, and he pored over them in his prison cell. His research was thorough, and the effect was a celebration of charm and authenticity, which is still spoken of with pride and awe.

On the main day of the celebration, standing in a horse-drawn carriage festooned with ivy and roses, Maggie made a speech thanking all those who had worked so hard to bring the day about, and at the end she told the crowd, which had gathered from all over Toisnot and the surrounding counties to see how things of this sort were done in Branch Creek, that there was one person to whom the most credit was due. She read a proclamation from the Governor himself that congratulated Jerry Chiffon and conveyed the gratitude and respect of the town, the county and the state. She accepted the proclamation herself on Jerry's behalf.

"I know we all look forward to the day when he will be among us again," she said. The horses were unhitched from the carriage, and, led by the Congressional representative from the district, the men of the town drew Maggie to her house on Central Avenue where a reception was held that overflowed her formal rooms onto the porch and eventually spilled onto both the front and back lawns.

When the day was done, she took to her bed never to rise again.

Lyman went before her, a year later. Parchman, who had crossed the street to the Labrette house for one of his regular visits to attend to Maggie's failing health, found her husband dead on the porch in his wicker chair, with his hat on.

Jerry was let out of prison in time to attend Lyman's funeral, which was held at the house. From her bed through the open door, which led into the wide hall, Maggie could watch the service that had been set up there for her. Hugh Coy came from Raleigh at Jerry's behest to do her hair, and Jerry himself fashioned, not from commercial florist flowers but from what grew in her own back garden, the one floral tribute Maggie would allow.

"I never thought such a thing could be said, but that funeral was about the most beautiful occasion of any kind I have ever seen in this town or any other, for that matter," remarked, of all people, Elsie Moye Beamon.

Parchman made himself a comfort to Maggie, coming often to administer what help he could and staying longer than was necessary for what was required medically. They talked together about the past like the last of a dying breed. She, when she was able, received her doctor while she was propped up in bed on lace-trimmed pillows, the pale-blue silk of the hand-embroidered loopy *L* monogram faintly glowing in the curtained light, labeling her, even though he was gone, as still Lyman's wife. Parchman would remain in the tufted chair that he had drawn close to her bed to go about his examination and treatment. Inclined toward her, his elbows on his knees, he watched her, and even when alone, they spoke elliptically, in an encoded, private manner.

She spoke of times gone by and mistakes and decisions made.

He spoke of what might have been. He told her something she had not known.

It had seemed a certainty to Maggie's parents, J. Robert and Hattie Bonner, that they would remain childless, but in her fortieth year Hattie had Maggie.

As is often the case with parents who have waited so long for a child, when the Bonners finally had their little daughter they treated her like the blessing they thought she was. She was watched over by her mother and father and a twelve-year-old colored girl named Callie, who was brought from one of J. Robert's farms to come live on the lot.

Every day the baby was bathed in rosewater, rubbed in olive oil, dressed in little white organdy gowns, then laid in a bassinet skirted with enough pink-and-white French tulle to outfit a ballerina. If she whimpered, both the mother and the nurse turned from whatever they were doing and ran to her, and whoever reached her first lifted her out of the bassinet and did what little it took to soothe her—a bounce or two, a few soft clucks, a gentle pat on the back. Nothing was allowed to trouble the baby for long.

As she grew, they seldom had reason to scold her, and if they did, it was only in the mildest way, as though offering advice more than reprimanding her.

"Oddly enough, sweetheart, you'll find you tire less easily if you sit up straight," Hattie might say when the little girl slumped. Maggie developed not into a spoiled and willful young girl, but rather gained the confidence and sweet, thoughtful ways of one who has never been criticized, never had love withdrawn, always had her spirit indulged, her personality encouraged and has been given all the things, within reason, that doting parents with money can provide.

She never got dirty, and her clothes were always tidy. She looked cool on the hottest day. In the winter she had furs and woolens and an inner warmth as well, so that she never hunched and shivered against the wind but stood with her shoulders lowered and her head erect, and over her cheeks came an apple-blossom pink that could have as easily been caused by sitting just far enough away from the fire to be comfortable as it could have from being out in the cold.

Her parents never heard her insist on anything, because she had never known that there was anything on which she needed to insist. The things she was lavishly provided with were all the things she might long for if she, like less fortunate children, had to wish for what she didn't have.

She wore handmade dresses smocked so closely that Mary Moye, who could not manage such fine needlework had to tell her daughter, Elsie, that the dresses were a sinful display of pride on the part of the Bonners and that Elsie, being a Moye and having nothing to prove, could and would do without them.

Maggie's sweet nature and kind, polite manner made her the favorite of all her little friends except for Elsie Moye. On Maggie's sixth birthday, at the party given to her on the front porch of the house in which Maggie would one day marry Lyman and stay to live with him, little Elsie Moye exhibited what would in one way or another be her reaction to Maggie for the rest of her life. She had a fit, and "fell into the middle of it," as Hattie Bonner would say. The rich cake and ice cream and too much excitement were blamed, but just before the tantrum, Callie found Elsie hiding behind a porch chair with the biggest present among the many Maggie had been given. Elsie had gotten as far as getting the ribbon off. Callie pried the package from Elsie's avaricious little hands and put it back on the table with the other gifts, but when it came time for Maggie to open it, she walked sweetly over to Elsie, as if approaching a sick old lady, and placed the package at her feet.

"You can have this one, Elsie," said Maggie with nothing but generous happiness in her tiny voice. Little Elsie Moye kicked the box so hard it slid half the length of the porch, then she leaned forward in the little festooned party chair, spread her knees and vomited onto the floor a swirl of what had been white, pink and green cake icing. Even so, at the end of the party, little Maggie asked if Callie wouldn't take the present over to Elsie's house and leave it. This was done, but it was not appreciated by little Elsie, who couldn't have cared less about the present when she realized that Maggie didn't want it herself. Nor was Mrs. Moye impressed, but rather saw the gift as an embarrassment and an affront to herself and to Elsie, and she thought that Hattie Bonner had chosen to highlight their shame rather than tactfully ignore what had happened at the party.

Maggie grew in sweetness and perfection, and a sight seen in the town on Sundays, which made those who saw it think Branch Creek might be a bit tonier than some other places, was the Bonners, husband and wife, in the front seat of their car with little Maggie in the back, her erect, primly hatted head just visible over the car door, looking straight ahead. She seemed more like a princess, who will one day control things herself, being carried to a great occasion by palace factotae than a little girl off to church with her parents.

Everyone in town thought she had probably been ruined by J. Robert and Hattie, and they waited to see that she had been—waited to see an act of selfishness or some petulant back talk signaling the failure of the kind of overprotective yet lenient upbringing she was getting. The proof did not come for a long time, then in her sixteenth year—she remembers the day—the boy who lived across the street, Parchman Anderson, whom she had probably seen every day of her life, on this day suddenly distracted her.

It was autumn but still warm. She was sitting on the porch, reading, and he came around from the back of his house across the street with a rake and started getting up what few leaves had fallen red and gold onto the lawn that October, imitating April, had turned a new green once again. There were no clouds, and Maggie remembers a sky bluer than usual, and the sunlight through the turning leaves made everything look bright and sharp-edged to her, as if she had a fever. The Anderson boy had only made about two swipes over the grass with the rake when he paused and, still looking down at the ground, turned his head slightly to one side as if he had heard a rare bird call or someone had spoken his name. Then he lifted his head, and it was not that he had lifted it to look at her, but that seeing her had stopped him from looking elsewhere for what he thought he'd heard. He smiled broadly and quickly and waved to her as if she had greeted him, then having performed the expected courtesy, went back to raking the leaves.

That was all it took. She was not contented anymore. And although she continued to behave in an agreeable sweet manner, there came upon her a slight edge of irritation that accompanied her thoughtfulness and sincerity. She learned what wanting was.

She continued to go out on the porch to sit long past the seasons of warm weather in the hopes that he would come out. She would stare for hours at the house across the street, and when he did appear she would try not to look at him because it made her cry now to have him so close and not know how she felt. When she was not on the porch, looking for him, waiting for him, she thought of him in ways she could not tell anyone about. She imagined him bathing, and she pictured him waking up in the morning, and she thought of the back of his shirt collar and the gap between it and his neck. She could spend a morning remembering some little thing about his face or how his hair, golden and gleaming, rushed from his temples over his ears.

He was a year ahead of her in school, and there she only caught glimpses of him throughout the day. Every day he walked home from school, and although Maggie was picked up in a car, she learned to pick him out from the other boys by his confident, ambling gait. She would catch sight of him in the side mirror after the car had passed, and every day she held him there like a snapshot until the car turned onto Central Avenue. When she got home she would hurry to the porch and sit and wait until he appeared alone, strolling down the opposite side of the street. Sometimes he would speak, say hello or utter odd, almost poetic observations on the weather—"It's lavishly hot, wouldn't you say?"; "The damp is very droll, don't you think?" or, with oriental simplicity, "Rain, I believe." And she would spend hours trying to figure out just what he meant.

Other times he walked in silence and looked down and gestured sparingly with his hands like an actor going over lines in his head, and she wanted more than anything in the world to know what he was saying to himself.

She got sick from the cold, and then lay in bed and worsened with jealousy. She was jealous of his shoes, the ground under his feet, the air in his lungs. She got up from her sickbed too early and returned to the porch to watch and wait for a glimpse, a nod, a smile. Her parents worried mightily. Maggie told no one how she felt, but only she believed she had a secret. Her mother and father knew it had to be something as bad as love to make her change from the pliable, pleasant daughter she had been to such an unhappy, oddly behaving girl. Then her health relapsed, and Dr. Anderson himself came.

"This is no joke. You are perilously close to pneumonia, darling," he warned. "You stay in that bed until I say you can get out of it." She breathed in deeply the entire time Dr. Anderson attended her, thinking, *He* smells like this. There is air coming from his father that *he* has breathed.

In a week some white chrysanthemums arrived. Maggie recognized the flowers as having come from the bed that Mrs. Anderson kept covered from the frost every fall well into November. With the bouquet was a note from Parchman. *I miss seeing you shiver,* it read. She sent back a note. *I have not stopped.*

She became moody and short with her parents, even in public, and people thought that the results of her upbringing were now apparent. Maggie stopped going to church because Parchman didn't go. She knew he aimed to be a doctor like his father, who was a man of science and had passed his lack of tolerance for religion to his son, having seen firsthand the limits of Divine intervention. Still, Parchman's father attended and supported the Branch Creek Methodist Church, for he knew few would have had confidence in his ability to heal if he did not.

For a Sunday or two, her father made her go, threatened to use a switch on her if she did not, a thing he had never before imagined doing, so she went and cried and sniffled all through the services and sat firmly in the pew during the hymns and responses and embarrassed her mother and father so that they gave up on trying to get her to attend. In public they made light of the situation, jokingly calling Maggie the Prodigal Daughter. Privately they grieved and placed their trust and hope in the scripture that promised that if you raise the child in the way she should go, she will not depart from it.

It was one Sunday when both their parents were in church and after she had stopped loving God as much as she loved Parchman that he finally ambled over to Maggie's side of the street. She was on the porch, and he came out of his house and headed purposefully in her direction with a confident smile on his face, as if he had been dared to go see her and was daring. He would have been hit if a car had been coming, for he looked neither right nor left when he stepped out onto Central Avenue.

When he reached the porch he simply said her name, "Miss Bonner," as if stating a fact. He stood below her on the walkway, a slightly amused look on his face, as though he was trying to make a decision that didn't much matter to him.

"May I sit?" he asked, and not waiting for an answer, climbed to the top step, sat down, leaned back against a column and blew a sigh through his lips that Maggie thought conveyed both self-satisfaction and relief, as though he had done something he had been wishing he would do.

"I'd imagine we are the only people in town not in church," he said.

"Why don't you go?" asked Maggie earnestly.

"Because everybody else does," he replied with a knowing smile, as if he were talking about someone who didn't impress him much.

"And I always went because everybody else does go," Maggie said, laughing. "Now I don't because you don't."

"Wouldn't it be grand to always do only what you want to do with someone who only wanted to do the same things?" he said.

"I would do anything you want," she said.

He said nothing but looked at her quizzically, examined her as though to make sure it was this girl who had uttered such a promise, and when he saw her looking back at him with a clear, confident gaze, he moved up onto the porch not amorously, not shyly, but with the enthusiasm of one who has found a mind he loves more than a heart—discovered a spirit more exciting than a body. He was hooked.

They would turn themselves and the town inside out in their passion for each other. Branch Creek was now a place from which to launch grand and exotic adventures and find the dimensions of a love unlike any other that had ever been known.

But every town, however small, has several of these epic romances going on at any given time, and only the smitten imagine there to be any greatness in their adventure. It is the practical parents and relatives who see the folly in it. In the case of Maggie and Parchman, both sets of parents were against the thing. Sensible and circumspect, the Andersons and the Bonners saw only unhappiness in the union of a dreamer like Parchman and a beautiful, sweet but gullible girl like Maggie, who had been raised to be cared for and indulged.

"Boys poetic like him grow up to be men who take to the bottle usually, or worse," said Mr. Bonner to his wife. "And I'll be damned if I'll see my daughter, whom I have raised to expect a life free of that kind of worry, reduced to working in a shop or hired out to keep some old lady company." Of course he never seemed to factor in Maggie's inheritance, which he himself knew the value of. That alone could have kept as many alcoholic husbands as she might ever want to waste herself on in good whiskey for life, and Hattie Bonner knew that, with the money both Parchman and Maggie would have someday, it would be something other and worse than want that would befall the two if they were to marry.

"They'd grow to hate in each other the very things they think they love now," she said to Callie.

"I think that boy just loves her loving him," said Callie.

On the Anderson side of the street, it was thought that although Maggie was a perfectly nice girl as well as a beauty, being local, she would not do. It was Branch Creek itself that they wanted to be sure the boy escaped, at least for a time long enough to know if it was a place to which he wanted to return. Although she embodied what was best about where they lived, it was a wider world they wished for their son to know something of before he made any lifelong decisions.

"She'd hold him back," said Mrs. Anderson simply, and her husband agreed.

But both sets of parents were too smart to demand that Maggie and Parchman stop seeing each other. The two sweethearts continued to meet and keep company, seemingly with the consent of both families but in reality each side was always looking for signs of a change of heart or an opportunity to instigate one.

Mr. and Mrs. Bonner hovered and could always find some reason to be in the front of the house whenever Maggie and Parchman were on the porch together. The windows were flung open in warm weather, and Callie was sent to dust the sitting room and hear what she could, and she was given authority to intervene on her own if what Maggie's mother called an emergency happened. But she came to be an unreliable chaperone, falling herself for Parchman's high-minded and romantic talk almost as hard as Maggie had.

"He's coming back here to help poor folks, Mrs. Bonner," she informed her employer. "I heard him say so."

"I do sincerely hope that is true, Callie," said Mrs. Bonner. "But I doubt that anyone could sustain such high ambition without a strong foundation of faith underpinning it. Parchman, as you know, has none."

As for Maggie, the more Parchman talked, the more she listened and believed in what he had to say.

In good weather she sat in the swing and he sat in a chair and told her what was wrong with the world. And rather than evoke pity in her or outrage, she was happy and contented because she knew that he would fix things.

"I wouldn't be surprised if that boy wound up governor," Callie reported.

Sometimes Parchman would sit in the swing with Maggie, or, if inside, on a sofa next to her. Her mother tried to catch the two in a situation for which she might justly demand that they be kept apart. She'd come around the end of the house to the porch rather than from inside, or she'd bustle into the sitting room unexpectedly when they were there, but Mrs. Bonner always found Parchman turned toward Maggie, one knee bent between them, one foot on the floor, an elbow on the back of the sofa and a hand in his hair, the other hand in his own lap and enough space between them to allow him to look into Maggie's eyes, not adoringly but to be sure she understood what he was saying.

"They don't seem to be courting at all," Mrs. Bonner said to Callie. "It really does look like they are discussing religion or a book—some such thing as that."

"Oh, you can fall just as hard if not harder for what comes out somebody's mouth as you can for what they look like," replied Callie ominously. "And they can fall hard for you for loving that." She had married a preacher and knew. "He's smart and kind, and he's got some ideas different from anything she's ever heard, I can tell you that."

"Like what?" asked Mrs. Bonner impatiently, as if to assert that not only were the boy's ideas probably unimpressive but that there was no such thing as one idea different from another, so Callie didn't try to tell her.

Parchman and Maggie found ways to be together outside the watched porches and hovered-in sitting rooms—ways which could not be denied them. At Christmas they started attending church again, and it was thought by many in the congregation, their parents included, to be a sign of the irresistible lure of the Christian faith.

They volunteered to co-chair the White Christmas program. Every year a needy family was found, which was not difficult. The recipients were most often tenants of one of the church members. Food and toys and clothes were donated. A program of carols sung off-key and a reenactment of the Nativity was performed in the church a few nights before Christmas. Costumes were homemade from sheets and towels, and the stable and animals cut out from plywood, then painted in flat, unshaded colors. The church was lit by candles, which effectively blurred the amateurishness of the presentation enough so that even someone who knew better might find it moving. After the program the co-chairs—this year, Parchman and Maggie—delivered the donations to the selected family. It was the first time anyone other than adults had performed the service, and, as skeptical as the membership was, they could not deny the precociously high-minded reasons Parchman told them were why he and Maggie should be the ones to do the job.

"One day we must take over," he argued. "It is never too early to learn what our responsibilities will be. It is Miss Bonner and I who must someday carry on." It was exactly what the congregation wanted to hear, and Parchman knew it.

Maggie couldn't wait for that night to arrive, for it would be the first time she had ever had a chance to be with Parchman without her mother or Callie lurking. They were to use Dr. Anderson's car. Parchman would drive.

The evening came, cold and damp, and the church was full. The carols were sung with, if not musicality, fervor, and the children presented the tableau of Mary and Joseph and the usual cast of characters. The angels, white-robed and tinsel-winged, sang "Silent Night" while the members of the congregation, who in their devotion and awe half expected the doll in the manger to coo at them, reverently stepped forward to the altar and laid their contributions, wrapped in white tissue and tied with white ribbon, underneath the white-flocked Christmas tree. Some had tears in their eyes, some sang softly, all were full of the spirit of giving and bathed in the festive, watery light. A prayer was said, a benediction of communal complacence. Many were moved, and as they were filing up the aisle after the prayer, Cleo Lewis, a poor girl from out in the country who had started coming to Branch Creek Methodist after her family had been helped by the members in just this way, said, "You could near about believe that old story was happening again tonight somewhere close to us." And those who heard her say it nodded reverently.

Then, with the contentment bestowed upon them from knowing that what has been done is at least not wrong, the church people, warm with atonement, but hungry, regathered in the Asbury Room for punch and every kind of cookie and cake and cupcake that the women knew how to make. Chocolates and sugarcoated pecans were piled high in cutglass bowls, and in the middle of the main table, big as a washtub, sat Julia Labrette's silver punch bowl, wreathed in holly and magnolia leaves and brimful of lime-sherbet Methodist punch. The preacher, dressed as Santa Claus, bounded into the room when least expected, and children ran screaming with terror into their parents' arms, but one by one he lured the suspicious little ones to his lap with a present from his sack, wrapped in bright red paper. The children were convinced that the man was who he claimed to be when they opened their presents and found to their amazement that they all had gotten something they liked.

Upstairs in the sanctuary, Parchman and Maggie carried the contributions from underneath the tree and loaded them into the trunk of Dr. Anderson's car. There had been a true outpouring that year, and it took many trips back and forth. So they could be alone, Parchman told everyone who offered to help to go and enjoy the party. Each time Maggie, loaded down with packages, passed Parchman in the aisle, she smiled at him, and he smiled back, and she blushed and thought she'd faint, and she wondered if what they were doing was wicked, if somehow their secret motive tainted the good deed. He worried not at all.

The trunk and the backseat of Dr. Anderson's car were full. Maggie got in and moved over in the front seat to be close to Parchman like she had seen other girls do with their boyfriends. He put an arm around her like those other boys she had seen with the other girls, and she felt, along with the satisfaction of doing a kind thing, excitement and content-ment—how wonderful it was to be like everybody else—to not be so perfect, to have reasons other than right ones for doing a good thing, to have a secret, to be complicated.

It was a dry and not at all picturesque affair—the face-to-face bestowal of the donations on the family selected by the church. Maggie and Parchman were in a hurry to unload the car as quickly as possible so that they might have some time to kill in ways both had been imagining since they'd hatched their plan. And it was just as well that the thing take place in a hurry, Maggie thought, for the family only made an insincere show of gratitude.

"Y'all can come help us unload this stuff," Parchman said to the parents, and they did so without enthusiasm, as though it was a job for which they were being paid poorly. The toys were wrapped, and those held little interest for the man and woman. They peered appraisingly into the boxes of food and clothes without a glimmer of happiness, as if what they had hoped might be in the box was, as they had expected, not there. The woman squinted through a veil of smoke from a hand-rolled cigarette held between her teeth.

"She's looking for a carton," Maggie said softly and disap-provingly to Parchman.

Inside the house there were only kerosene lamps giving off a cold, oily light. There was no sign of Christmas in the room, just an old bedstead and a table, and a coal heater in the corner. Around the heater four children huddled in shabby coats that were a record of want—the youngest, a little girl in the most worn one—then a boy in a coat that would one day be put on the girl—up until the oldest child, a boy about six years old who wore a coat not new, but less used than the rest.

"Here's some stuff for y'all," said the father.

The children did not rush to the boxes and tear into the presents happily and greedily as most children would have, but approached them almost warily, the oldest boy first, as if to protect the others from some danger that the boxes might hold, then slowly, carefully, they began to draw things out of the boxes. They removed the wrapping timidly, and looked up at their parents and at Maggie and Parchman as if to see whether they were doing something they oughtn't. When they finally opened a present, they would stare blankly at the toy truck or puzzle or coloring book they'd found inside the white paper. They didn't know how to play, but only held the toys and turned them in their hands, admiring the shape and what little color shone in the lamplight.

Maggie's heart might have been broken by the scene if she had not been so in love. In spite of the misery around her, she saw only Parchman clearly, buttoned up in his wool overcoat, his white collar and silk tie lapping up what little light there was in the room, and on his face not pity but a look of triumph, as though he had proved a point, and the cold room and dark walls and joyless children were there only to make him right and show how different he was from everybody else he knew. She thought that was something to admire. This very kind of misery is what he will fix one day, she thought.

The good deed took less than half an hour. They did not

go straight home, but stopped just outside of town by the bridge over Branch Creek to be by themselves for just a little longer.

"It was not how I thought it would be," Maggie said sadly.

"I don't think I was too surprised," said Parchman.

"We ought to do more than we do," she said.

"One day we will," he said.

"We will?" she asked.

"Yes, *we*," he answered.

Aside from being together unchaperoned, they did nothing that they needed to be ashamed of, but there were only the two of them to insist that this was true, so when Elsie Moye, out for a drive with some other girls in the new little roadster she had been given as an early Christmas present by her besotted father, saw Dr. Anderson's car pulled off by the side of the road, and knowing Parchman and Maggie had left the church in the car, went back and told everybody who would listen what she had seen, Maggie and Parchman were not believed.

In those days in Branch Creek such a thing as Elsie Moye was telling about Maggie and Parchman was thought to be at the very least not quite fine. Most of the time it meant ruination for the girl. Steps had to be taken if Maggie's reputation was not to be permanently damaged, and How many times had a young man of promise been distracted and had his future ruined by an incautious, love-struck young girl? was the rhetorical question asked by many in town. And within a day, it was as though an invisible wall had been built down the middle of Central Avenue in order to keep Maggie and Parchman apart.

For a while the two lingered, as if hopeful, in front of their houses, on opposite sides of the street, sitting by the window, each gazing in the direction of the other, Maggie often in tears. Callie was told to draw the curtains in Maggie's face if she came upon her staring toward the Andersons' house.

"Don't explain, don't say a word to her, just close those curtains as many times a day as you have to," instructed Mrs. Bonner.

At school, every teacher knew to keep them apart. Clubs that had been coeducational were divided and held separate meetings. In some organizations the result was a membership fewer than was required for a slate of officers. Lunchtime for the junior class was staggered farther behind that of the seniors so that Maggie and Parchman hadn't even the opportunity to pass each other on their way to eat. Such was the power of the Bonners and the Andersons.

To be together they started going to church again. There, they could not be kept apart. They joined the choir, they joined the Wednesday-night Bible study group. From eight o'clock on Sunday morning until one in the afternoon, they were in the Branch Creek Methodist Church together. They set the altar, trimmed the candles and got the chancel ready for eleven o'clock services. In between, they attended Sunday school. They could not sit together during the service. The Bonners and the Andersons sat directly across the aisle from one another, so Maggie and Parchman could not even turn their heads to smile at each other without being noticed. But each knew the other was there, and each breathed in the holy air together. After services, they tidied up the chancel, replacing hymnbooks to the backs of the pews, gathering the printed "Order of Service" folders that had been left behind. They served the coffee and donuts in the Asbury Room after the sermon and then cleaned up. No one could say a word, because it was the Lord's work being done, of course, and work that no one else had ever liked doing. Only the preacher, a young unmarried man, pale, skinny and sepulchral, was unambiguously pleased, for he knew nothing of the kind of thing that Maggie and Parchman's parents were afraid of. The two young people seemed to have an enthusiasm for helping out, and that relieved him of the endless begging and cajoling he'd always had to resort to in order to get certain day-to-day chores done. He beamed at the sight of Maggie and Parchman quietly, discreetly busying themselves around the church, so obviously in love with each other and with Christ, and one love feeding the other, the preacher believed. It was as if they did not want even God to know what they were doing lest they be accused of pious pride. Then, of course, the One More Thing happened, and even the preacher accepted that the church was not the place for two infatuated young people to discover the limits of their love. In the church basement they were found out.

"I was going to get a broom, I think, and I've forgotten why, and when I opened the door they were in the closet together," he told Mr. Bonner.

"I ask you this, preacher. Did you see anything to suggest she might be ruined?" asked Mr. Bonner. "And would you know what you were looking for?"

Mr. Bonner had no more trouble making a preacher answer his questions than he did anyone else.

"No! There was nothing, nothing," sputtered the preacher. "Really nothing at all to suggest anything other than a kiss at the worst."

But it was enough for the Bonners and the Dr. Andersons. Parchman was sent straight off to an Episcopal school for rich Southern boys in Virginia. It was already late September, and it took some doing on Dr. Anderson's part and a fair amount of money, some of which, it was said behind many a gloved hand, came from Mr. J. Robert Bonner.

Now when a girl knows at the young age Maggie was when

she settled on Parchman what she wants for life, she is likely to change her mind later, but at first Maggie was like a war widow, tragic, grief-stricken to the point of dementia. She stopped eating for a week, cried most of the time and said she wouldn't have anybody if she couldn't have Parchman.

At Thanksgiving he came home from the boarding school, and they were allowed to see each other as long as one or another of the parents was near. When they finally had a chance to talk, Maggie was surprised that the first thing Parchman said to her was to ask if she had ever heard the Brahms intermezzi.

"No," said Maggie.

"Then you have not lived," Parchman said, rather arrogantly, Maggie thought. "A gang of us went over to Richmond to hear Rubenstein."

At Christmas he brought over a package for her. Inside was a collection of phonograph records of the Brahms, and she listened to them constantly on their outdated Victrola, trying to hear what Parchman must have heard.

It was during this Christmas holiday that he first mentioned that near his boarding school there was a girls' school called Laurel Hall.

"We have these mixers, they call them, and it is ridiculous. They make you go, but they won't even let you out on the porch for a breath of air unchaperoned, so don't worry," he said.

"Really," said Maggie, and she imagined Parchman on a porch surrounded by rich, smart, beautiful girls from all over the country, and it was not jealousy she felt but exclusion. There were these girls, and there were Brahms and Richmond, and time and waiting and distance. There were places in his mind she could not occupy, and she started to fear, then believe, that most of the time he thought of other, higher things than her now.

For this, she cut him dead. When he came home for the summer, her grief over being separated from him turned to anger and resentment, and she tortured him whenever she got the chance. In church, looking neither left nor right but straight ahead, confident, uncaring, beautiful and cruel, she breezed past the pew he and his parents occupied. He sent notes across the street, which she sent back unopened.

Then Lyman Labrette, son of a land-rich family out in the country and five years older than Maggie, returned from the war. With the consent of her parents, she let him call on her, and even take her for rides in his father's Cadillac. She made sure Parchman saw.

Finally, in spite of their parents and the town and Maggie's unfathomable cruelty to him, Parchman crossed the street to her house. He called her name, and she came out onto the porch. Standing in the yard below her, tears rimming his eyes, he asked her a simple question that to anyone but a jealous girl would have been profession and proof, as ardent as a poem, of love.

"Why are you doing this to me?" he asked, and when her only answer was to lift her chin higher and fix her gaze off to one side, intentional heartlessness and embarrassment mixed in her pretty face, he turned, and, shoulders hunched, head bowed so low he appeared to be in prayer, arms crossed at his waist as if to cradle the dying heart inside him, went back across the street to his own house.

The pleasure it gave her, this act of cruelty to a being over whom she had power, frightened and sickened her. That night she asked God to take from her the feeling, and she vowed to spend the rest of her life overcoming the sin she had committed. Kneeling by the side of her canopied bed as if at an altar, she prayed, "Cure me of this cruelty, Lord, and for the rest of my life I will stay away from anything that loves me too much."

God did as she asked, and she kept her promise.

She's all right now, people said. They may even be friends one day, and tell at gatherings, their spouses as amused as they, how in their youth they nearly drove each other as well as their parents and the town crazy.

"He's the kindest, most polite man in the world," Maggie's mother said of Lyman. "Courtly even, and you wouldn't expect it coming from the son of Mr. Will B. Labrette."

"And there is all that land and money," said Maggie's father with a chuckle.

For Maggie, Lyman was still and quiet, and he was good to her in such a way as to make her see that there would never be anything higher in his mind than her.

He feels lucky, she thought, and he shows it.

Lyman went off to Raleigh to the agricultural college and took the two-year course in farm management, a program set up for the sons of big landowners. The first year, he came home every weekend.

"I wouldn't want anybody beating my time," he said to Maggie flirtatiously.

The next year, Maggie graduated from high school and went to a college for rich girls that was within courting distance of where Lyman was a student. They kept company, and the parents were happy. She made her debut Christmas of that year, and immediately wedding plans began.

In the spring they were married. Parchman, away at the University of Pennsylvania School of Medicine, could not attend the wedding. For a present he sent a subscription to a series of concerts in Raleigh, two tickets to eight musical evenings. Maggie could not get Lyman to attend. She always had to find someone to take the spare ticket, and it became a gentle but nagging reminder, like worrying about a disease she was not at all likely to contract, that the person who would most gladly have accompanied her to the concert hall in Raleigh was Parchman.

The first Christmas of the Labrette marriage, Parchman came home, and a package with a tag—"To Maggie and Lyman"—was found under their Christmas tree. When she opened it, inside was a phonograph record of Stravinsky's *Rite of Spring,* and she went immediately to the record player and put it on.

"Good God," Lyman said, and left the room. That was all.

Maggie listened through to the end of the record and then listened again, and when Parchman came to their Christmas-night open house, she told him she liked the music.

"Liked it," said Parchman. "There is more to it than liking it."

She had liked it not enough and in the wrong way. That evening, he told her about his work in the Pennsylvania hospital where he was a resident. Cases of diseases among the poor from the coal mines that were thought to have been conquered were showing up.

"And for no reason, except poverty," he said bitterly.

He looked directly into her eyes, and she looked back to see if she could see what it was he hoped to find in her so that she could supply it, but every time he told her something, she sensed that she had not appreciated what he said in the way he wanted her to.

Lyman saw it and plainly pointed out what the situation was.

"That man is still in love with you, darling," he said one day.

There was not a glimmer of anything in what Lyman said but information, pure and reliable.

"It doesn't bother me one bit," he said. "He'd be a fool if he wasn't."

He was that sure of himself, and that sure of Maggie, too.

But it got her to thinking.

Parchman turned, as she might have expected if at the time she had understood the limits of love, but she knew the right thing to do was to give him no hope. As he realized what she was doing and how correct and seemingly easy for her it was, Parchman became more embittered. If he met the two of them at church or uptown, making sure Maggie noticed, he would ask Lyman a question about something he knew Lyman would not understand or care about.

"You're the educated one, Parch," Lyman would say. "You tell me, old boy."

Parchman would look at Maggie and smirk. And he'd try to embarrass Maggie, too. "Did you hear the opera on the radio?" he asked her one day when they met on the street outside the Branch Creek Bank and Trust. Elsie Moye was there and claimed she had heard it and that she thought it was marvelous.

"I didn't know it was on," Maggie said.

"Elsie, darling, we are among the philistines," said Parchman.

Elsie simpered, and acknowledged his comment with a patient smile meant to convey pity, which, of course, she did not have.

Then after a year of this, a Laurel Hall girl whom Parchman had met briefly during his time at school in Virginia, showed up in Branch Creek, hired to teach the first grade. Her name was Elizabeth Randolph. She was a descendant of the famous FFV but from a collateral branch in which the money and power was what she herself described as a historical memory. She moved into the teacherage and for the first time ever that anyone knew about, in the afternoons and early evenings, violin music was heard coming from that house. She could paint, and a landscape she had done of the creek for which the town was named was bought by Parchman at an auction to raise money to buy a new velvet curtain for the school auditorium, in which Elizabeth then started to stage little plays acted in by the children of the town.

Parchman invited her to supper at his parents' home on a warm evening in the spring, and after they had eaten, he escorted her across the street to meet Maggie and Lyman. Maggie was enchanted.

"You can tell that girl is accomplished," said Lyman. Maggie immediately took her in and on, and it was easy work introducing her to the Central Avenue crowd. All were impressed, for as should be clear by now, the people who matter had an unerring ability to recognize quality when they saw it.

One night after Parchman took her back to the teacherage, he looked across the street as he always did when he came and went from his parents' home, and he saw Maggie sitting on her porch alone.

"Good evening," he said.

"Parchman, good evening to you," said Maggie. "Come and sit for a few minutes, will you?"

He crossed the street and sat on the top porch step where he had sat so many times before, his face lit by the watery light of the street lamp and the light coming from the hall through the front door.

"I am so happy for you," said Maggie. "I believe you have found the right girl."

He did not reply, and when Maggie looked to see why, she could see even by that dim light that he was staring at her as if he could kill her. She said nothing more, and he stood up and went home.

The next thing anybody in town knew was that Dr.

Parchman Anderson and Miss Elizabeth Jane Randolph were to be married.

The wedding was in her family's old home out on the farm from which they had for centuries acquired their livelihood and prestige. To Maggie, Parchman looked as though he were drowning, except when their eyes would meet, and then a look she could only call defiant came over his face, and it was as if the whole wedding had been put on to show her—a bluff that would be called off if she gave Parchman the right sign.

All during the ceremony she held Lyman's hand and in her mind gave thanks that she had married him.

There is nothing above me in his heart, she thought.

The wedding has been told of and that is as accurate an account of the day as any.

Upon their return to Branch Creek, Parchman's father handed his practice over to his son, and he and Parchman's mother moved to their old homeplace in the country. Parchman and Elizabeth took over the house on Central Avenue. Elizabeth continued to teach for a year, but soon the expectations of a village doctor's wife required that she give up her job.

"It would be considered rather thoughtless and perhaps a bit greedy for a married woman to take up a job that might mean a livelihood for a woman with no husband," Maggie told her diplomatically.

The trouble that came between Elizabeth and Parchman surely started early on and was gradual. The telephone in the Anderson house had to be heard, and a special bell was installed. At night every time it rang, Elizabeth was jolted awake—her heart beating so fast and hard that she thought it would explode, and during the day she would jump when she heard it and cry out in a small, startled way, and her small white hand would flutter to her head and skim through her hair as if the noise had disarranged it. And the patients coming at all hours of the day and night, she could not seem to get used to.

"It isn't snobbery or disgust, I don't think," Maggie said in Elizabeth's defense, "but the too-nearness of suffering that she is helpless herself to do anything about."

For a few times in the beginning of their marriage, Parchman asked her to go with him on his calls and she tried to help but was more often a hindrance. It was all too much for her, something she never would have dreamed she would have to experience. When she timidly dared to resist, he made her go, but she too often had to be doctored herself before they got back home. Parchman grew to despise her weaknesses. He became short with her, then bored, then cruel. He could be heard throughout the neighborhood, cursing and railing at her, and a common sight for Maggie was Elizabeth in her flower garden, digging and pruning and intermittently taking a dainty handkerchief from her dress pocket and holding it to her eyes.

It was during this time that Parchman first started asking Maggie if she would go with him on his calls. He had changed, hardened, and Maggie knew why.

Every time he shouts and curses her, Maggie thought, it is because she is not me. When he was brusque and cruel with his patients, Maggie was glad she was there. She believed the unhappiness in the Anderson house was because she had broken his heart so long ago, and at night she prayed that helping heal the sick and bury the dead atoned in some small way for what she had done. She helped those who could be helped get through Parchman's treatment, and those who could not met their deaths a little more gracefully than if she had not been in attendance.

Maggie and Lyman tried to have children, but after five years of marriage they had not been blessed. Maggie assumed it was her fault, that something was wrong with her body. She went to Raleigh to a specialist, but the results of the examination were inconclusive. Lyman had come through the war without a scratch. He was sure their childlessness was not his fault, but he loved Maggie and never blamed her.

"If life is to be lived without children, so be it," he said to her, then added, "but it is not to be lived without you."

In that fifth year of their marriage the Tobacco Board asked Lyman to go to Argentina for six months. Maggie would be left alone for the first time in her life. It was not something she had ever thought she would have to face, and she didn't look forward to being without Lyman for that long.

None of what happened was planned.

A few days after Lyman left, one night around midnight she woke up to the sound of a car horn blowing continuously, as if stuck. She put on some clothes and went out on her front porch. The sound of the horn was getting louder quickly, so she knew something bad had happened. As the car got closer, the glow from its lights narrowed into a pair of purposeful beams aimed straight down the street. The car skidded to a stop in front of Dr. Anderson's, and a man ran out and banged on the door so loud that every house on the street lit up. The man was excited and talking loudly. Maggie could hear a lot of what he said. A bad wreck. One dead already. Teenagers from another town, on the way home from a basketball game. There had been drinking.

"You got to come," she heard the man say.

She went inside and got a sweater and hurried across the street. She was in the Anderson driveway, and Parchman pulled the car up, but didn't stop. He leaned across the front seat and opened the door for her, and she got in. They followed the man who had come to get help. When they got out of town, the car ahead turned onto the worst road in the county—a crooked two lane to a little town called Oakville that followed the course of a winding river. Maggie dreaded where they were going. There had been many bad wrecks on this road. A long blind curve had been the thrill and end of many who, drunk on beer or love, had tried to impress themselves or some girl, thinking in their besotted state that if Fire Ball Roberts and Tiny Lund could take a curve at one hundred miles an hour, they could. Or if a driver didn't know the road, the curve could sneak up on him before he knew it was there. People walking along the road in broad daylight had been spattered because they hadn't seen the car coming and had not been seen by its driver until it was too late.

They followed the twisting road ahead of them, and Maggie watched the headlights of the other car sway from side to side in a wide arc, sweeping over the woods and fields as if searching for an escaped convict.

They started into the long curve. The first sign that there had been an accident was black tire marks so wide apart that she could tell the driver had not slammed on the brakes and lost control of the car, but had gone into a sideways skid. The marks stopped abruptly in the road as though the car had vanished. A purse sat upright on the pavement by the skid marks.

Where the curve in the road was the sharpest they saw a patrol car, its red light flashing almost gaily. Parchman pulled up behind it and they got out. The officer came toward them.

"Ma'am, this isn't anything you ought to see," he said, but Maggie ignored him and followed Parchman.

One searchlight on the patrol car was shining up into a live oak tree. Up in the top of the tree was a body folded backward over a limb, the heels touching the back of the head. The spine had been snapped in half. When they got closer to the tree, Maggie could see drops of blood falling like garnets from the end of the branch the body hung on. She could hear the droplets hitting the leaves on the ground below. A boy was sitting underneath the tree, senseless with shock but not a scratch on him. He was talking to his dead friend up in the tree about the game.

The other light on the patrol car was pointed at the wreck. The car involved had rolled many times before it landed in the field. The front end had been driven into the ground as if it had fallen from the sky. Before they got to the car, they found one girl lying dead yards from where the car had come to rest. All her clothes had been torn off. She looked as though she had been sanded. She was rolled up, her face staring out from between her legs as if she was giving birth to herself.

When they got to the wreck, they found another girl. Her head was wedged between the door frame and the windshield. Her breath was cut off. She had turned black. Parchman got into the wreckage and went to work on her. Maggie pulled on the door, and when she did, it moved a little and she saw the girl's face lighten almost immediately. The girl could get air as long as Maggie held the door, so she hung all her weight on it and the girl breathed. Once, without realizing she had done so, Maggie let up on the door.

"Goddamnit, Maggie, hold that goddamn door!" yelled Parchman.

She pulled down harder. Parchman told her everything he was doing.

"I'm giving a shot of adrenaline. Her right leg is severed at the knee, I'm applying a tourniquet to the thigh. Hold on, honey. Hold on, darling. You are my brave girl."

Maggie had never heard Parchman talk to a patient like that, and when she looked up, she saw that he was talking to her, and she felt as though she could have torn the metal from around the girl herself.

Finally two ambulances arrived, and a fire truck. The firemen cut the girl out of the car, and she was carried away in the ambulance, alive.

The firemen raised the ladder up to the top of the tree, but before they could climb up to get the body, it tumbled through the branches, arms and legs wheeling as if the boy were alive and knew he was falling. The body hit the ground with a thud.

"Every bone in his body must be shattered," said one of the firemen.

"You could fold him up like a blanket," said another, shaking his head. They put the dead boy and girl in the other ambulance and drove away.

Parchman examined the unhurt boy. When the patrolman put him in the car to take him home, he was screaming and beating his head with his fists, and Maggie knew he had come to his senses.

A tow truck arrived, and Maggie and Parchman watched it pull the wreckage away.

Maggie followed Parchman back across the field and got

in his car with him. He turned around in the road, and headed back toward town.

It was then that Maggie noticed the sky for the first time that night. It was black, crusted with stars, cold, and she started to shake not with fear or exhaustion, but with excitement because of the way Parchman had spoken to her at the wreckage. She looked over at him. His face was lit golden by the dashboard lights. She stared at him until he looked back at her. Neither one spoke a word. Up ahead, a dirt path branched off the paved road, and when they got to it Parchman turned and drove until they came to a place where the woods closed in on both sides of the path. There, he stopped and switched off the engine. He turned to her, held her wrists in his hands for a moment, then pulled her to him. They loved each other while the indifferent stars wheeled in the sky.

It was morning when they drove back into town. Parchman let Maggie off in front of her house and went home to Elizabeth.

Maggie got into bed and slept, and when she woke up it was noon. In the daylight, the night before was hard for her to believe.

She tried to put the night behind her. She prayed long and hard at the side of her bed for God to restore her to the promise she had made to him before she was married. She hardly left her room for three days. Callie brought in food and worry, and although she begged Mrs. Labrette to tell her why she was praying all the time, Maggie just shook her head and waved her maid away.

"I got to figure out how to get in touch with Mr. Labrette way off in South America," she said to Mrs. Lamm's maid. Then on the afternoon of the fourth day, Mrs. Labrette emerged from her bedroom, dressed and groomed in her usual perfect way. But there was something more subtle in her customary pleasing, elegant deportment. There was in her face the look of one with a secret purpose that only she knows exists and that when it is accomplished, although others will see the results, only she will know that the outcome accessible to all was the concealed intention.

She's having a baby, is what Callie thought, and she don't even know it yet.

In a little more than a month, Maggie knew, or was sure enough to panic in the middle of the night and run across the street to Dr. Anderson's. He took her into his office at the back of the house and examined her underneath the bright lights. When he had finished, he looked up from the end of the table and simply nodded.

"I can't have it," said Maggie.

"I won't help you not," said Parchman.

Maggie got dressed, and Parchman put away his instruments and removed the sheet from his examining table.

"You can have it," he said, staring directly into her eyes.

A calm, almost happy expectancy overtook her. The next day she wired Lyman in Argentina and gave him the news that they were to be parents, that he was to be a father. His response was one word.

Overjoyed!

When Lyman returned, he was more careful and kind to Maggie than he had ever been before, if such a thing was possible, and he went directly over to the Andersons to speak to Parchman.

"Now, look, old boy. Can you handle this? Because I'll take her to Raleigh if need be," he said.

"This is a situation that has been faced before, Lyman," said Parchman patiently. "I'm up to it."

"You're sure?" said Lyman. "I'm not a man to be given a promise that can't be kept."

"I can handle it," Parchman insisted. "And by the way, congratulations."

Lyman went home assured. With his lawyer he set up provisions for the baby.

"It'll never want for anything, Maggie," he told his wife proudly.

Then gradually regret returned and overtook her again. She carried her baby in shame. She brooded, sitting by the window and staring out across the street at Dr. Anderson's house. When she saw Elizabeth come out into her yard, Maggie would duck back away from the window and draw the curtains, not to keep Elizabeth from seeing her, but so she would not have to look upon the woman she was betraying. When she started to show the signs of her condition, Maggie stayed confined to the house most of the time, as was expected of a mother-to-be, and it suited her. On the few occasions when she did have to leave her house, she hurried out of one door in through another, scurrying, furtive, as if afraid that the light of day would somehow reveal her secret. Lyman believed her behavior was a manifestation of the mysteries of motherhood. Her absence from the public life of Branch Creek surprised none of her friends, but was viewed as the proper sort of modesty a woman in her condition ought to have.

Fear overtook her. At her appointments, Dr. Anderson spent more time calming her panic than seeing to her physical health.

"What if . . . ," she would start, but could never finish the question, unable to think of an outcome as awful as the unspecified, premonitory terror in her heart.

"It will be fine," Parchman repeated again and again.

At home alone and stone-still at her kitchen table, she imagined the child in the house with her every day. This lie, this truth—this constant evidence of her deceit and sin. She imagined it playing in the yard in full view of Parchman and Elizabeth, both the wife and the child not knowing, and she knew she could not stand the unbearable burden of an evil lifelong fiction. What looks would pass between her and Parchman, and how long before the child would grow to reveal who its parents were? Would Lyman each day see more clearly what she had done to him?

God is testing me, she thought. Testing my promise. She cried all the time.

"Mr. Lyman, I never saw anything like this," Callie said.

Lyman worried and called Parchman every other day.

"What ails her?" he railed into the telephone.

Callie took Maggie over to see Parchman and would wait in the backyard until she came out. Sometimes she was better, sometimes not.

In the fifth month Maggie started to feel the baby move, and by the seventh month, a calm came over her more worrisome to Lyman and Callie than any of her behavior before had been. She became as serene and unemotional as a medieval painting of the Virgin Mary. She sat in her boudoir chair, at the dinner table, on the front porch swing enthroned, erect and unblinking while Callie and Lyman hovered around as if waiting for some revelation to come from her.

"It won't be long now," said Callie.

Across the street they would see Parchman framed in the living-room window, motionless, staring toward the Labrette house.

"Like a buzzard, if I didn't know better," Callie said to her other maid friends who worked on Central Avenue.

On a Saturday night in the middle of the eighth month, Maggie's time came. Lyman took her across the street and Parchman examined her.

"It is a while yet," he told Lyman. "Go on back home."

Then at three in the morning, Maggie screamed out from her bed, and Lyman ran to get Parchman.

When Lyman had gone, Parchman took his medical bag from the table by the back door and emptied it of everything except what he would need to deliver the baby. He got in his car, drove across the street and backed into the Labrette driveway.

Lyman was on the front porch, waiting. "Why did you drive the car?" he asked irritably.

"Just a precaution. You never know," replied Parchman. Lyman's face tightened with fear and worry.

"Go to the kitchen and wait," Parchman instructed.

Alone in the room with Maggie, he stood at the end of her bed.

"What will we do?" Maggie whispered frantically.

"Who do you need now?" he asked.

"You," she answered.

"How much?" he asked, his eyes narrowing, cutting into her.

"Now, only you," she replied.

"I have a plan," he said.

Every hour, Lyman came from the kitchen to the closed bedroom door.

"Is everything all right?" he asked.

"Yes, Goddamnit," barked Parchman.

Parchman waited like a hunter. When he could see that the baby was near, he came out into the hall and shouted for Lyman.

"There is trouble. Go get Callie," he said.

"Is Maggie all right?" Lyman asked, more a threat than a question.

"Do as I said. Go!" Parchman shouted. When he saw the car leave and take off down the street, Parchman returned to the room.

The baby came easily. When he had cleaned it and wrapped it up, Parchman brought it over to Maggie.

"A boy," he said.

"I can keep it? Can I keep it? I can keep it. Let me. Let me," she said, her eyes tear-filled and beseeching.

"Look at it," he said. He held the baby near her, but when she reached for it, he drew it back as if he were trying to tempt her from the bed.

"The eyes," he said.

"They are blue," she said.

Parchman placed the baby at the foot of the bed and leaned over close to Maggie's pale sweaty face.

"What color are yours?" he asked.

"Blue."

"And Lyman's?"

"Blue."

"And mine?" he asked, smiling down at her.

Maggie frowned almost irritably and tried to raise herself from the pillow, then wincing in pain, fell back and gave up.

"Brown. Why are you doing this to me?"

"It is simple Mendelian genetics, dear. In as soon as two months he could have my eyes. Perhaps it will take seven months, a year. Oh, there is a slim chance he might have blue—do you want to take it? Want to wait every day for that surprise? Much more of a chance he will have mine," he said.

She turned her face to the wall silently.

Parchman wrapped the baby in a soft warm blanket and put it in his medical bag. He took the bag out to his car and carefully placed it on the backseat.

When Lyman returned with Callie, Parchman was on the porch, waiting for him.

"You had a son. It never drew a breath," he told Lyman.

Lyman lowered his head and punched his leg with his fist. He looked up to the porch ceiling and then at Parchman.

Callie stood motionless at the bottom of the steps. She lowered her head to pray.

"Can I see?" asked Lyman.

"You don't want to," said Parchman with an ominous finality that silenced Lyman. "I'll take care of everything."

"Is Maggie all right?" he asked.

"Yes," said Parchman. "Wait. I'll let you know when you can see her."

He went back to Maggie's room. She lay motionless in the bed.

"There is no other way," said Parchman.

"I know," said Maggie, staring at the ceiling. "It isn't possible. I couldn't do it even if it was."

Parchman said nothing. He leaned toward her as if to kiss her. She snapped her head toward the wall, and he backed away and left the room. He went to the kitchen where Lyman and Callie were waiting.

"You can go to her now," he said.

He left the house and got into his car. He drove out of the Labrettes' driveway. He took the baby out into the country to one of his farms where lived a couple, his tenants. The wife had borne nothing but deformities incapable of living. The week before, another had come and mercifully failed to breathe. Parchman had delivered it.

To these people he brought Maggie's baby.

"Say anything ever to anyone about this, and I will throw you off this farm and make sure you never get work on another," he said. They were happy to have a child and glad to do what their landlord told them, even though they had to.

It was neither for revenge nor mercy that Parchman told Maggie the truth. He had no motive of which he was aware, no insistent inner voice that compelled him to make things right or give a dying woman a chance to know the full significance and consequence of a decision she had made in her youth and, later, for long periods had almost so forgotten that the sin of it seemed not to have imposed any discernible retribution on her. It just simply seemed to him now to be the end of the story.

The day was as bright and green and flower-filled and scented as had ever been, the windows to Maggie's bedroom flung open and the warm, wormy breeze undulating her voile sheers so that they looked like enormous jellyfish.

There had been a long silence, a portentous break in what had been and what was to be, when simply, quietly, as if pronouncing the diagnosis of a disease neither fatal nor curable, Parchman, looking down as if in prayer, murmured, "He's ours, you know."

When he looked up to face Maggie, she had her arms stretched out and to her side, braced, the bedcovers clenched in her hands, her face pale and tense, as if the bed were racing out of control down an icy, steep declivity into a wall of stone. Then, as if injected with a lethal dose, she wilted, hung her head and Parchman watched as tears, large as sudden summer raindrops, fell audibly on the white sheet across her lap.

"I could have kept him," she whispered. "There would have been so much less"—but the word did not come to her—she did not say what there would have been less of— "if I had kept him."

From then on, she refused all treatment for her heart. Parchman begged her to let him continue what he could do, but she would not.

"Why, Maggie?" he asked her, cradling his own heart as he had done the day she sent him back across the street to his house without a hope.

"Perhaps it is a chance to show some courage," she replied.

She phoned her lawyer and instructed him to change her will, leaving the house, its contents, all the Labrette money and what the law called after-acquired property, not to the Branch Creek Methodist Church, as her wish had been in the past, but to Mr. Jerry Chiffon.

On a morning less than a month later, Callie went into the bedroom and found Maggie dead. She was lying bent over at the waist, her face buried in the covers. Her left upper arm lay by the side of her head, and her hand was outstretched and open before her on the bed, as if humbly waiting for something she wanted above all things to be placed in it. It was thought she had probably raised up in the night and reached toward the ceiling, then collapsed forward.

Everybody but Maggie and me turned on him. Well, by everybody, I mean Elsie Moye Beamon, but what she thought didn't matter any more than it ever had. She and Maggie are both gone now.

One of the first things he did after Maggie died was buy that old falling-down house he had grown up in. I. C. and I couldn't believe it, because Parch has never sold so much as an inch of his property. I don't know how Jerry got it out of Parch. Jerry never lived in it. Never intended to, but he had the house remodeled, taking away all the modernizations and the so-called improvements that had been added over the years for the benefit of those who preferred the hideously practical over the difficult-and-expensive-to-maintain historically accurate. The house underneath the updating was a typical coastal-plains cottage common in this part of the state, and he put it back to its late-eighteenth-century original condition. It is a charming place, with its low-browed porch and nine paned windows and green louvered shutters. A cedar picket fence, left unstained to gray in the elements, encloses a flower-cutting garden on one side of the house and an authentic kitchen garden on the other, so accurate to the period that for several years in a row, Jerry was cited by the state historical society for the restoration.

I was telling this young woman about all of it over my back fence the other day. She and her husband moved into the house directly behind me, one street over from Central Avenue. She is very pretty in what I call a shiny way. She, her husband and their two little children came to Branch Creek from Ohio. The man drives all the way to Raleigh every day, where he works doing something or other with a company that makes computers. I have trouble remembering their name, and when I do remember it, I have trouble pronouncing it. I like the people fine. They don't seem to know the first thing about the South, however, and it's been fun showing them Southern things, our food and customs and so forth. They call me Myrtle. Never bother with calling me Mrs. Lamm, and I'm old enough to be rotten.

There are quite a few new people in town, most of them are young and came to Branch Creek because of the nice old houses, which they buy and maintain as near to how they found them—except that they like to put a hot tub in the backyard and they always tear out the kitchens and put in stoves that look like television sets and refrigerators that cost three and four thousand dollars. One couple named Barbini put a crystal chandelier in their kitchen, but took it out when they heard that someone in town who'd heard about it pronounced it not quite fine.

Wonder who.

Though none of them really know him, it is because of Jerry that they are attracted to Branch Creek. My sister tried to put a trailer park on some land she bought behind the school, but Jerry got up a petition and stopped her. She had to buy more land out in the country. He single-handedly saved the old train station. It's a shining example of railroad gothic, but there were some who wanted to tear it down to make way for some sort of business that would have been conducted in one of those awful aluminum buildings. Jobs, jobs, jobs is all some people talk about. There never were any jobs to speak of here. Why bother with that now?

He helped to ram through a strict zoning law that keeps any chain outfits from setting up business in the town, and he got a law passed saying that no structure, except the water tower, could be higher than the tallest tree.

He sits out there on that porch in good weather, reading, and watching life go by in Branch Creek. Every so often, a car will slow and you can see the people looking and talking and pointing, and you know they're telling about Jerry.

Maggie's grand centerpiece sits on the dining-room table all the time now. You can see it through the window at night when the dining room is lit up. Once in a while some men will come from Raleigh. Nice-looking men in beautiful suits and driving new cars—foreign models, I don't know what they are—and he'll give a party and you can see them in there, and it is like pressing your nose up against the window of a palace.

But no one in town associates with him, and he keeps to himself. The garden is spectacular and he tends it, only occasionally hiring a man to do heavy pruning or clean out the beds in the fall. It's the most beautiful garden in town. I have seen people stop and look, but he never invites them in, simply waves, and maybe he'll smile.

But the other day I did see something. A little boy was on his way uptown. He was from that trailer park outside the town limits that my sister put up and none of us could do anything about. That's what the child looked like anyway. A little ragged and not so clean, and the fact that you don't see these new town children walking anywhere these days placed this little boy. He was going uptown to buy something, I imagine, and he stopped dead in his tracks when he saw that garden and house and just stood there with his arms dropped down by his sides like he had given up on something that he had tried hard about.

Jerry came off the porch and opened the iron gate and

invited him in. I stood at my front door and watched Jerry take that boy through his garden as thoroughly as if the child had been the judge at a horticultural show. Then he invited the boy into the house, and I could see them through the windows, moving from room to room—see Jerry pointing to things, gesturing to the plasterwork and moldings and such. When the little boy came out, he had a red shopping bag from a nice store. I don't know what was in that bag. The little boy looked as though he had gotten something he'd always wanted. He went on uptown, grinning, satisfied.

But the town children of the new people have been told to stay away from that house, and even on Halloween they go flopping by like fish on a dock to get to the next one quick.

In good weather, most days after he's puttered in his garden a while, you'll see him on the porch reared back in that big old green wicker rocking chair, looking grandly out over Central Avenue toward Dr. Anderson's house, those blue eyes of his clear and confident, bold almost.

Like he knows who he is.

For their guidance and generosity, I thank these people: Sarah I. Ferrell, Jeannine Fencl, Reginald Barton, the Honorable Coy E. Brewer, Jeffrey C. Carter, Esq. and Jacqueline Weld.

I am grateful to the Mrs. Giles Whiting Foundation for its support.

A NOTE ON THE AUTHOR

Anderson Ferrell's first novel, *Where She Was,* was
published by Knopf in 1983 and received a National
Endowment for the Arts grant for literature. His
second novel, *Home for the Day,* was published
by Knopf in 1994. It was selected as one of the
year's best by *New York* magazine and
received a Whiting Award for fiction.

A NOTE ON THE TYPE

The text of this book is set in Linotype Sabon, named after the type founder, Jacques Sabon. It was designed by Jan Tschichold and jointly developed by Linotype, Monotype, and Stempel, in response to a need for a typeface to be available in identical form for mechanical hot metal composition and hand composition using foundry type. Tschichold based his design for Sabon roman on a font engraved by Garamond, and Sabon italic on a font by Granjon. It was first used in 1966 and has proved an enduring modern classic.